The Pleasures of JessicaLynn

The Pleasures of JessicaLynn

Joan Elizabeth Lloyd

Carroll & Graf Publishers, Inc.
New York

Carroll & Graf Publishers, Inc.
260 Fifth Avenue
New York, NY 10001

ISBN 0-7867-0327-X

Manufactured in the United States of America

This book is dedicated to Ed, my editor, my conscience, my partner, my friend.

And my thanks to Angela Preston for her short story entitled "Assimilation" which I use with her permission. A talented writer, Angela has a bright future.

The Pleasures of JessicaLynn

ONE

"Steph, it's Jessie." Thirty-six-year-old JessicaLynn Hanley kicked off her high heels and stretched out against the mountain of pillows on her king-sized bed. She crossed her stocking-clad ankles on the paisley bedspread and, holding the cordless phone between the pillows and her ear, unfastened the thin gold bracelet she had just bought.

"I thought about you a lot today," Jessie's best friend Stephanie Carlton said from a thousand miles away, "and I was hoping you'd call. Is it done?"

"Done," Jessie said, glancing at her watch. "According to my lawyer, for three hours and seventeen minutes I've been a legally separated woman. All the papers neatly signed by the judge. It's over." Through surprisingly misty eyes, she glanced around the tastefully decorated room in which she had slept for the last nine years of her marriage and the fourteen months since Rob moved out.

"You knew this day would come," Steph's soft voice said. "Weren't you prepared?"

"Oh, I guess I was," Jessie said, taking a large swallow from the can of diet Pepsi she had grabbed on her way upstairs, "but, I guess I wasn't quite as ready as I thought I was."

"How do you feel about everything now?" Steph's voice was filled with concern.

Jessie let out a long breath. "Mixed emotions. I thought about Rob a lot this afternoon and, hell, he's still the person I spent all those years with, thinking we were happy. Part of me is sad, like something died." She shook her head. "Of course, most of me still wants to shoot the bastard." She closed her eyes and the moment that changed her life played behind her lids like a movie.

It had been more than a year since she had arrived at her husband's dental office late one afternoon with swatches of fabric for new chairs for the waiting room. His receptionist had left for the day, so Jessie had wandered back toward his private office where he often worked late getting his paperwork in order. As she glanced into the main operatory, she had been greeted by the vision of her husband's bare ass, muscles clenching, back arching as he crouched over the contour dental chair and drove his cock into his recently hired twenty-two-year-old dental assistant. "Harder Robby baby, harder," the girl had been screaming. "Fuck me good. Fill me up."

Snapping back to the present, Jessie said, "You know, Steph, all I could think of when I walked in on the two of them fucking was the old joke about the voluptuous woman who goes into the dentist's office. After a brief exam, he tells her that she needs quite a bit of very expensive dental work. 'Oh fuck,' she says. 'Okay,' says the dentist, 'just tell me which cavity you want me to fill and I'll adjust the chair.' "

Jessie enjoyed her friend's deep husky laugh. During their senior year at Ottawa High in Ottawa, Illinois, Steph, her steady boyfriend and now husband Brian, Jessie and Rob had hung out together. They had gone to the drive-in in LaSalle in Rob's father's Pontiac and pretended to watch the latest movie, shared burgers

2

and fries at Bianchi's or the Root Beer Stand, and planned their futures.

"Wall Street," Brian had said, over and over. "I'm going to make millions and then Steph and I will get married and have a dozen kids."

Immediately after graduation Brian, true to his dreams, had moved to New York and had made a great deal of money as a commodities trader. He had sent for Steph and they had married and moved to Westchester County. Unfortunately, their only child, Theresa, had been killed at the age of nine. She had been riding her bicycle near the elementary school when a drunken driver ran his car onto the sidewalk and struck the child.

"I'm going to be a doctor or dentist and make scads of money," Rob had said from the driver's seat of the Pontiac. "I'll join the country club and play tennis every Thursday afternoon." And Rob had done just that; gone to college and dental school while Jessie had worked to support both of them. Insisting that he wouldn't make a good father, Rob had also decided that the couple would have no children.

Through the years, though a thousand miles apart, Steph and Jessie had kept in touch and had remained close. Jessie had even visited the Carltons' home in Harrison occasionally.

"It's good to hear that you haven't lost your sense of humor," Steph said.

Jessie sat on the edge of the bed and began to pull the pins from her carefully arranged titian French knot. An attractive, green-eyed redhead, she had freckleless ivory skin and a slender figure with ample curves in all the right places. "My funny bone is still intact. Actually, I feel a little sorry for the jerk. I get weekly reports from some of our old supposedly well-meaning friends who think I need blow-by-blow accounts of their comings and goings, pardon the pun. I understand that he's going to marry the bimbo. She has the brains of a thumbtack and giggles all the time, but you know all the stories about the seven-year itch. Rob always was a bit slow. It took him thirteen years to feel it. I hope they'll be very happy, snarl. I'll retract my claws now." Jessie's voice dropped. "Anyway, maybe she's good in bed, better than I ever was." Jessie was amazed at the knot of bitterness that was lodged in the pit of her stomach. She and Rob hadn't had a volcanic sex life but she had been content. Content. What a horrible word to describe a sex life.

"Do I hear a note of self-pity?" Steph asked. When her comment was followed by a long pause, she continued, "Cut that out, Jessie."

"I know. It's just that I thought we were happy. I feel duped, somehow." She stood up and walked to the window, overlooking the backyard. She raised the sash and inhaled the fragrance of freshly cut grass. "And suddenly I feel very lonely, very foreign here."

Steph changed the subject quickly. "Are you changing your name back?"

"No. I thought about it, but so much of my business life is under the name Hanley that I'm going to keep the name. And, after all, it's so much easier to pronounce and spell than Florcyk."

"Lord knows you're right about that," Steph said. "Remember, in school, how we always waited for the teacher to get to your name the first day. No one could ever say it right."

Jessie smiled. "Remember Mr. Honeywell? He never did learn to pronounce it. He got as far as Fler-cuck and called me that all year." Jessie pictured their senior English teacher. He had held all the girls spellbound with his sensual reading of eighteenth-century English poetry.

"God, he was something," Steph said with a small sigh. "I still get the hots just thinking about him. He had the greatest buns in those tight jeans he wore."

"A tight, flat rear and that fantastic bulge in the front. We speculated for hours about whether he wore padding in his shorts." Jessie smiled. She hadn't thought sexy, outrageous things like that in years, and, she suddenly realized, she missed it.

"And what about men in your life?" Steph asked. "Are you dating yet?"

"Yes and no. There's a guy I've known for a few months. We've been to dinner a few times in the past few months and I think he's interested."

"And you? How do you feel?"

"I don't know. Maybe I'm not ready yet. Steve, that's his name, Steve's sweet and kind and thoughtful. But I feel, I can't explain it, sort of closed in."

"So come back here and stay with Brian and me for a few weeks or longer." Steph had been trying to convince Jessie to visit for months. "You're selling the house so you have to move anyway. Let someone in your office handle the arrangements and get the hell out of town for a while."

"Oh, Steph, I wish I could."

"Why can't you?"

"I have responsibilities here."

"Like what?"

"Like the office." Jessie owned Ferncrest Realty, a small but successful real estate agency specializing in newly built town houses. "And selling the house. Packing, organizing, you know."

"You've told me over and over that the office runs like clock-work. I'm sure you hate to admit that it can get along without you, but it can and it will. And how will it feel showing strangers through your house, knowing that they're criticizing your land-scaping and your wallpaper? You don't need that right now."

Jessie looked down at the backyard. She remembered planting most of the red, white, and pink azaleas that blazed in full bloom along the foundation. "I know that, but I don't mind selling the house. It was always too ostentatious for my taste. Rob was the one who wanted a big, showy house in which to entertain. His lawyer told me that he wanted to keep it, buy me out but I told him no. I won't have Rob and bimbette living here." Her eyes misted as she stared into the master bath and took in the new fixtures she and Rob had had installed just a month before 'the event.' "I just can't bear that."

"I understand, Jessie. If, God forbid, anything like that ever happened to Brian and me, I wouldn't want him to live here either."

"Everything has two sides, you know, and sometimes my feelings change from minute to minute. There's a big part of me that still feels the history in here. So much entertaining: the bridge games, the country club crowd that Rob wanted so much to be a part of, barbecues on the deck." Jessie tucked the phone between her ear and shoulder and, with all the pins now removed from her long, red hair, combed her slender fingers through the strands and rubbed her scalp. "That's all over now."

"So, why stay there? Come to Harrison and stay with us. You know this huge old place has plenty of room. You could have the entire end of the house you had when you were here two years ago. All the privacy you could want, and all of my company you can stand."

"Oh Steph, it sounds so tempting."

"I wish you'd come. Harrison has so much to offer you, especially at this point in your life. It will be like old times. Girl talk, movies. We can lounge by the pool and talk about life, love and good sex, not necessarily in that order."

"What about my life here? I've got to find a place to live."

"Do it later. You don't want to make any long-term decisions right now anyway and you can certainly afford to dump most of your stuff. Put things you really want to keep in storage and split." Jessie paused, so Steph continued, "It would be so great. You and me, on our own near the big city. Nobody gleefully keeping you up to date on Rob's escapades. Just Broadway plays, expensive restaurants, museums, Bergdorfs, Bloomingdales, Saks, Lord & Taylor's, the works."

"Not too many restaurants," Jessie said, running her palm down her flat stomach. "My figure couldn't stand the calories."

"Calories are overrated." Steph stopped suddenly. "Whoa. Wait a minute. Was that a yes I heard?"

6

Jessie flopped back onto a stack of pillows. "Why the hell not? For a couple of weeks anyway."

Steph squealed like the girls had when they were kids. "Wonderful. I never believed you'd actually agree."

"Are you sure you're not regretting your offer now that I've said yes?"

"Of course not. It will be great. I don't mean to push my luck but how soon can you get here?"

Jessie giggled and pulled her datebook from her bedside table. She flipped the pages. "Okay. It's May seventeenth." She planned out loud. "Give me a month to get a few arrangements made. Make it six weeks. I'm selling most of the furniture anyway, so all I have to do is sort out some personal stuff. God, the amount of crap one collects in nine years."

"Just pull out what you want and let Rob sort out the rest. Since you're there, you get first dibs."

"It's all in that long-discussed separation agreement anyway. Now let's see." She planned out loud, her pencil tapping the dates on the calendar in her book. "The house goes on the market July first. I'll put a few things in storage, pack a couple of bags. . . . How about I fly out June twenty-fifth. That's a Sunday. I'll plan to stay for. . . ."

"Leave your return open. Maybe I'll be able to convince you to stay for the whole summer."

"Okay. No return just yet." Jessie wrote 'Go to Harrison' across the space for June twenty-fifth, then slammed her datebook shut and dropped it onto the bed. "Oh Steph, thanks. Now that I've made the decision, I feel so relieved. I guess I didn't realize how much this divorce has taken out of me."

"Well I did, and I'm delighted that you've finally made the right decision."

The two women talked for another half an hour, and, after she hung up, Jessie pulled off her clothes and soaked in a hot bath. Then, after a dinner of pasta, salad, and a glass of Beck's Dark, she collapsed into bed and slept through the night for the first time in weeks.

*   *   *

Later that evening, in her bedroom in Harrison, Stephanie stretched out beside her husband Brian. "I can't believe I actually talked her into coming out here. It will be so good for her."

Steph was Jessie's physical opposite, tall and angular with long legs and a slender, tight figure. She had recently had her almost-black hair styled into a shoulder-length bob that framed her conventionally pretty face. She needed almost no makeup to highlight her doelike deep brown eyes, cute turned-up nose, and full, sensuous lips.

Brian rubbed his palm over his wife's naked hip. "What about us? You know. How much does Jessie know about the way we live?"

"Not much yet, love," Steph said, sliding her fingers through the heavy black hair on Brian's chest and gazing into his unusually pale, blue eyes. "But she will, soon enough. It will be an enlightening experience for her."

"I've always had the feeling that there was so much more to her than Rob ever saw. The jerk. While we were making out in the backseat, I used to listen to them in the front."

"You're kidding," Steph said, caressing her husband's flat stomach with the tips of her fingers. "I was always too busy trying to control your hands, or pretending to, to pay attention to anything else."

"Oh, I just heard bits and pieces, before and after. He always satisfied himself but I had the feeling that he didn't pay much attention to whether Jessie was satisfied or not."

"Tell me the truth," Steph said. "You always had the hots for her, didn't you?"

Brian's breathing quickened. "She was a sexy little number. I know there's animal sensuality hidden beneath the surface, fighting to get out through all that carefully orchestrated facade. I'd love to be the one to let it out."

"You and she never made it?"

"Unfortunately, no."

Steph wrapped her long fingers around Brian's hard cock. "There's still hope, you know."

"I know, babe," he said, sliding his index finger over her wet inner lips. "I know." Brian rolled his wife onto her back and slammed into her until they both came, screaming.

After a long and delightfully uneventful flight from Chicago, Jessie walked down the long corridor at Newark Airport and grinned as she saw Steph waving. Just outside the security gate, Jessie dropped her carry-on bag and the two women hugged. Jostled from all sides, they moved out of the line of deplaning passengers. "You look tremendous," Steph said.

"You like?" Jessie said, turning so Steph could appreciate her new navy linen pantsuit and pale pink tailored blouse. "I went shopping yesterday. I'm new from the skin out." She lifted one foot and waggled it to show off her new navy low-heeled opera pumps. "And from the top down."

"You look fabulous," Steph said, "but I'm disappointed. I wanted to take you shopping myself. You need jeans, shorts, T-shirts, things like that. And, although I lead a denim kind of life most of the time, you'll need a dress or two."

"We will shop until we drop, to coin a phrase," Jessie said, settling the strap of her suitcase on her shoulder. "I only bought a few things and I brought my checkbook and my credit cards."

"You're doing okay, financially, I gather."

"I'm doing just fine. The business is thriving despite the economy and Rob, under mild duress, was very generous, bless his pointed little head."

"Are you getting alimony?"

"We hassled for a while. His practice nets him in the low six figures but I just wanted payment for the years I spent putting him through dental school so he could drill his bimbo."

"Bitter, darling?" Steph asked, raising one eyebrow.

Jessie sighed. "I have my moments. But on to better topics. What do we have planned for the next week or so?"

"I thought you might want to relax for a few days. Become a vegetable. So I arranged my schedule so that I'm at the gift shop at the hospital Monday and Thursday, but for the rest of the week, I'm yours." Steph had been working at the shop at the hospital for several years and, since her arrival, it had become a profitable business for the small local institution.

"You like working at the hospital. I wish I had something like that, something that made me feel good about myself."

"So do it. When you get back. . . . No, I won't talk about you going back to Illinois. It'll spoil my good mood."

"And how's Brian?"

"He's great, working hard and playing hard. He's got a tennis game this afternoon, but he said to give you a kiss and tell you he'd see you at dinner."

"God, I'm so glad to see you," Jessie said, hugging her friend again.

The two women walked toward the baggage claim area stopping occasionally to hug again. "How much luggage did you bring?" Steph asked, matching her stride to her friend's.

"Only one large suitcase with some essentials and enough clothes to hold me for a few days. I didn't want any leftovers." She heaved a great sigh. "The house is ready to go. And I do mean go. It's well priced and should sell quickly. And the office is better organized than I'd like to admit."

In the baggage claim area, they spotted the illuminated sign for the flight from Chicago and reached the edge of the carousel just as it started to move. "We're looking for a beige tapestry suitcase with brown trim," Jessie said.

As they watched, the first bag over the top of the chute and onto the turning plates was Jessie's. "That's never happened to me before," Jessie said, her mouth hanging open. "My suitcase is usually so far down the line that almost everyone has already left."

"Well," Steph said, "it's an omen." She hefted the bag from the moving platform. "Good luck and good things are coming."

"Oh, I hope so." Jessie fumbled in her purse for her baggage stub. "Sometimes I'm so up, excited about starting a new phase in my life." She looked her best friend in the eyes. "Then, at other times, I'm so down. Rob and I were comfortable and good together. I knew what he was thinking and he knew. . . ." Her eyes began to fill. "It's so final."

"None of that," Steph said, linking her free arm with her friend's. "Only good thoughts will be permitted."

Jessie shook her head and a wisp of hair fell from her French knot. Impatiently she stuffed it into one of the bobby pins that pulled her hair tight against her head. "Right. Only good thoughts."

They arrived in Harrison and had just pulled Jessie's suitcase from the trunk of Steph's BMW when Brian drove up the long driveway, honking the horn of his Lexus and grinning through the windshield. He pulled to a stop, jumped out of the car, and enveloped Jessie in a giant bearhug. "Oh, JJ," he said, reverting to Jessie's nickname from their days in high school. "I'm so glad to see you."

"Me too," she said, hugging him back. "I'd almost forgotten the days of being called JJ. You're the only one who calls me that anymore. It takes me back."

"If you hadn't been so hooked on Rob, I would have jumped you back then and Steph would have had to find someone else."

"You are so full of it, Brian," Jessie said, laughing, swatting him on the ass. "You should have been born Irish."

"Okay, okay, so I exaggerate a bit. But I am glad to see you."

Jessie pushed Brian to arm's length and looked him over. Although he was not particularly tall, Brian was a big man, with large hands and feet and an open, ingenuous smile that lit up his ordinary-looking face. His tennis whites accentuated his oversized arms and legs, all covered with heavy black hair. His skin was heavily tanned, making his eyes look even paler than she remembered. She hugged him again, enjoying the feel of a virile man after so many months alone. "You look fantastic, sir," she said, a bit embarrassed by the erotic thoughts his tight shorts aroused. "And happy."

Brian reached out and draped his arm around his wife's shoulders. "Happy doesn't describe it." He pecked Steph on the cheek, then said, "When's dinner? I'm starved."

"Everything's in the fridge and ready to go. You get the fire started and I'll show Jessie to her room."

"Will do. I'll start the grill, then take a quick shower. Dinner should be ready in less than an hour."

Just over an hour later, the three friends were filling their plates with rare steak, a rice pilaf that Steph had just removed from the microwave, and a crisp green salad with tiny shrimp and bacon bits. "I hope you're not watching your calories," Steph said. "At least not for today. I decided that in honor of your arrival I would make all the things I don't ordinarily eat. To hell with cholesterol."

Brian uncorked a bottle of California Cabernet and poured some into each glass. Jessie looked at the label on the bottle. "Stag's Leap. 1984. Very nice wine."

Brian lifted his glass. "For a very nice lady and her new life. To JJ." His eyes locked with Jessie's and, after a moment, she looked away.

This is silly, Jessie told herself. It feels like he's flirting with me. It only goes to show that I've been celibate too long. He's my best friend's husband, for heaven's sake. She shook it off and spent the rest of the evening chatting amiably with Steph and Brian.

The following day Jessie unwound. Between Brian's job and Steph's stint at the hospital, Jessie saw nothing of either of them. Content to be alone she sat beside the pool until her skin turned a luscious shade of soft apricot, read a romance novel, soaked in a bubble bath for an hour in the oversized jacuzzi-tub in her bathroom, and generally exorcised Rob from her consciousness.

She saw Steph briefly late that afternoon. Jessie had grabbed a container of yogurt from the fridge and was sitting at the table in the kitchen, eating with one hand and holding her book open with the other.

"Hi, Steph," she said, looking up from her book. "What's up? How was your day?"

"The day was great, but I now have a delightful idea. Brian got two tickets for a concert tonight from some client and we can easily get a third. Very last minute. It's the Julliard String Quartet. Brian and I love them and we don't get to hear them very often. How about us both joining him in the city? Dinner, the concert? It would do you a world of good."

"I'm not a concert kind of person, Steph. All that music, particularly after a good dinner, just puts me to sleep. You go, and have a great time."

"But we haven't spent any time together. You've been alone all day."

"And I've enjoyed every minute of it. Go and enjoy your concert. I want to get to bed early anyway. All this relaxing is making me tired." To emphasize her drowsiness, she yawned. "I don't want you to feel you have to entertain me. I do just fine on my own."

"I feel so guilty. But we're best friends and I'll trust you to be honest. So if you're sure you don't mind I'd really like to see this. And the next two days, and Friday as well, are ours. Shopping. Bloomies maybe?"

"Done. See you in the morning."

The next morning, dressed in jeans and a white tank top, Jessie sat in a long white lounge chair in her favorite room in the Carltons' house. Jessie knew that, when Steph and Brian had bought the house a dozen years before, the room had been an open flagstone patio overlooking the pool, shaded at each end by a huge red maple. The couple had immediately seen its potential and had enclosed it with louvered windows and white wood. They had furnished it in white wicker and cluttered it with dozens of pillows in primary colors.

Once the room was constructed, Steph had worked with a florist, learning everything she could about houseplants. She decorated the room with carefully selected specimens, and then tended them with loving care. One end contained cactuses, many blooming with either flowers or colored globes. The other end was all greenery, with ivys, ferns, and a six-foot-high fig tree. In the center, where there was sun most of the day, Steph had put florals with several plants in bloom at all times—African violets in exotic shades, orchids and lilies, anything that caught her fancy. One section was her hospital. The owner of the florist shop frequently gave Steph plants that weren't doing well, for her to nurse back to health. She spent time almost every day misting, watering, pruning, and removing dead blooms.

Jessie had gotten up early that morning and, although it was only eight-thirty, she was sitting and reading, a cup of fresh coffee at her elbow. As she read, she suddenly became aware of sounds from the pool. She shifted her position and peered through the leaves of a deep orange hibiscus. She couldn't believe what she saw.

Not twenty feet away, beside the pool, Steph lay, stretched out on a lounge chair, dressed in only the top of a tiny black bikini. The bottom of the suit lay on the concrete beside her chair. Her legs straddled the cushions and a man lay between her thighs, his head buried in her pussy. "Ummm," Jessie heard Steph mumble. "That's wonderful." As Jessie watched she became aware of a smooth, tanned back and a tight, tiny ass. She realized that the head that bobbed in Steph's lap was blond. It was not Brian.

Jessie could hear slurping sounds and moans. Wanting to turn away yet fascinated, Jessie watched through the leaves and blossoms.

"Oh Tony," Steph moaned. "Do that more." Her legs trembled and her fists clenched and unclenched. "Yes, just like that." She reached behind her back and untied the top of her bathing suit to free her breasts. As the young man lapped, she pinched her nipples and squirmed. Jessie saw Tony hold Steph's hips still as

14

his mouth worked its magic. Jessie's body throbbed and she could almost feel Tony's tongue as it brought Steph closer and closer to orgasm.

"Oh baby," Steph yelled, "don't stop!"

Jessie wiggled her hips to scratch the itch that grew between her legs. She clenched her vaginal muscles as Steph yelled, "Now, baby. Stick me now!"

Tony plunged two fingers into Steph's body. His arm worked like a piston as Steph's hips thrashed. "Yes," she screamed. "Yes!" As she clutched the arms of the lounge chair and arched her back, the man could barely keep his face against her cunt and his fingers pistoning.

Jessie could almost feel her friend's orgasm and, as she heard Steph's heavy breathing slow, Jessie snuck back into the house and up to her room.

What the hell was that all about? she wondered as she closed the door to her room and dropped onto the bed. She took a few deep breaths to calm her excited body, then propped her head on the pillows. Steph had been a bit wild as a kid, she remembered. She had dated several boys before she met Brian and had told Jessie in great detail about one particular gymnast who finally convinced her to go 'all the way' in the backseat of his father's Oldsmobile. "Boy," Steph had told her, "his gymnastics aren't limited to the gymnasium."

Jessie shook her head. I never thought she'd cheat on Brian like this, she thought, her eyes filling. What is it about sex that makes good people like Steph and Rob do such impossible things, lie and cheat? What is it about sex?

It was after ten when Jessie heard a light knock on her bedroom door. "You up?" a voice whispered.

Jessie wiped her eyes, composed her face and, trying not to look as upset as she felt, said, "Sure. Come on in."

"Well, good morning sleepyhead," Steph said. She had changed into a pair of tight-fitting jeans and a short-sleeved, navy-blue shirt.

"Good morning yourself," Jessie answered, not totally successful at keeping the edge from her voice.

"What's wrong, Jessie?" Steph said. "You sound upset."

"Nothing's wrong," Jessie said. "Just a bit cranky this morning."

"Don't kid me, babe," Steph said, plopping onto the edge of the bed. "Something's up." When Jessie was silent, Steph dropped the novel Jessie had been reading onto the bed beside her. "I found this in the plant room. Does this have anything to do with your mood this morning?"

Jessie picked up the book and put it on the bedside table. "I must have left it there last evening."

"Don't, babe. You never were a very good liar. You saw Tony and me earlier, didn't you."

Jessie blushed, but remained silent.

"You're embarrassed. I can understand that, but what Tony and I did was just clean, honest fun. He comes to tend to the pool and, occasionally, he tends to me as well. It's really nothing."

"Nothing?" Jessie spat. "What about Brian? I'm sure he wouldn't think it was nothing if he knew."

"Of course he knows," Steph said softly. "Come on downstairs. Let's get some coffee and I'll explain everything. I was going to tell you about things before this, but I haven't gotten a chance."

"What things?"

"Coffee first. I need some right about now. I promise I'll tell you everything."

Fifteen minutes later, the two women sat in the plant room, each with a fresh cup of coffee and a toasted english muffin. The coffeepot sat on a warmer near Steph. As she munched on her muffin Jessie's lay untouched on the plate beside her. They had not spoken a word.

"Okay, Jessie," Steph said with a long sigh, "let me try to explain." She sipped her coffee. "About three years ago, Brian was infatuated with a single woman in his office. He told me about it and, for a while, telling about what it might be like if they ever got together made for wild times in bed. Finally, I asked him if he'd like to actually be with her. You know, make love. He said yes."

"He told you that he wanted to go to bed with another woman?" Jessie was horrified.

"There isn't a man on this earth who hasn't thought about doing that at one time or another. Brian was just honest enough to admit it. He would never lie to me and I knew that he wouldn't do anything without telling me."

"And you allowed him to be with someone else?"

"Allowed is an interesting word. I hate to think that I'm in charge of his sex life. I gave it a lot of thought and I decided that I wanted him to be happy. I guess I'm very strong because I didn't feel threatened. It wasn't that kind of thing. He wasn't in love with her, just in lust."

Jessie laughed and started to relax. "In lust. That's an interesting way to put it."

"Well, that's really what it was. Haven't you ever felt that pull, that almost irresistible urge to jump into some man's pants?" When her friend was silent, Steph continued, "You, my love, haven't lived. It's a great feeling, even if you never get to do anything about it."

"I guess I've got no sex drive," Jessie said softly. "And no sex appeal either."

"Bullshit," Steph said. "You just haven't discovered them yet. Anyway, getting back to Valerie. That was her name, Valerie. I never saw her, but Brian described her to me. Tall and shapely, with big, soft tits and great, long legs. But it wasn't her body that turned Brian on. It was her obvious attraction to him. Her eye contact, smiles, movements."

"He told you all that?"

"He described everything in detail afterward, in bed. And the telling got him so hot that we fucked like bunnies."

Jessie shook her head. "I don't believe it. You lay in bed discussing another woman fucking your husband."

17

Steph nodded, silently letting Jessie absorb what she had heard.

Jessie picked up her muffin and took a bite. "Amazing. How long did it last?"

"He was only with her for about two months, then it all wore off for both of them. So much of being in lust is the expectation, not the actuality. Reality is frequently a letdown."

Despite her amazement, Jessie was fascinated. "You still haven't told me about this morning."

"Give me time," Steph said. "It's a long story. It was several months after that and Brian and I had spent an evening playing Boggle with Lara and Hank Cortez, friends of ours from Scarsdale. Have you ever played Boggle? It's a word game and it's lots of fun. Your score is based on the number of words you can make that no one else wrote down. Well, everyone had had quite a bit to drink and, toward the end of the evening, we had gotten very silly."

TWO

———◆◆◆———

"I have only one word left," Hank said. "Pussy." He grinned at Lara and licked his lips. "Anyone else have pussy?"

"Not me," Brian said. "I haven't had any good pussy in quite a while. Except Steph's, of course, but a wife's pussy doesn't count."

Hank refilled the wine glasses and then threw the letter-dice again. "Cunt," Hank said, triumphantly pointing out the word among the letters before anyone had had time to write anything. "And look. You can make *suck* and *fuck*."

Lara giggled and squeezed Brian's arm. "Such nice words, don't you think?" She looked up at Brian and blinked.

Brian looked at Steph, then stroked Lara's face. "Very nice words."

"I've got an idea," Hank said. "Let's play strip-Boggle. The winner is the one with the most dirty words and everyone else has to take off one article of clothing." He looked at Brian and Steph. "Game?"

Hank was not a particularly good-looking man but the twinkle in his eye and his delightful sense of humor made him attractive. Steph had always been interested in him, but had never before thought about doing anything about it. "Want to?" Brian whispered into Steph's ear.

Steph thought a minute. Yes, she really did. She gave a tiny nod. "Okay, let's do it," Brian said.

After six rounds of the game, the men were down to their socks and shorts, and Lara, who had won three of the rounds, was still wearing her blouse and underwear. Steph had a particular love of delicate undies, and was glad she had worn a black, demi-cup bra with matching lace panties, which, by now, was all she was wearing. "You are one gorgeous woman," Hank said, admiring the way Steph's small, yet soft breasts filled the tiny cups. "I knew you'd be sensational without clothes."

"Not without clothes yet," Steph said. "I'm not wearing any less than I'd be in a bikini."

"I know, but it's knowing that it's not a bikini that's such a turn-on," Hank said.

Brian was gazing silently at Lara's legs and the dark shadow he could make out through the crotch of her white nylon panties. She also still wore her short-sleeved, flowered blouse. "I feel I've been gypped," he said to Lara. "You're still decent."

Lara lowered her head and looked up at him through her lashes. "I'm afraid you won't have the same thrill. I haven't nearly the body that your wife has. As a matter of fact, I'm so flat-chested I don't usually wear a bra. And I've certainly got my share of stretch marks from the babies."

Brian reached over and brushed his hand down the front of Lara's blouse, feeling her erect nipple rub his palm. "I bet you're beautiful under there," Brian said. "Will you take the blouse off, just for me?"

Lara looked at her husband and raised one eyebrow.

"Does everyone understand where this is going?" Hank asked. When everyone nodded, he said, "Then why don't we separate this party. Lara, you and Brian can have the bedroom and Steph

20

and I will take the guest room." He rubbed his knuckles down Steph's cheek. "I want this lady all alone."

As Brian stood up and took Lara's hand, Steph swallowed hard. She was suddenly terrified.

"Baby," Brian said softly, looking at his wife and immediately sensing her discomfort, "this isn't a command performance. It's supposed to be fun. You look like a deer caught in the headlights. Talk to me."

"Did you and Hank set this up? I don't think it's as spur of the moment as it might appear."

"We talked about it," Brian admitted. "Hank has had the hots for you for a long time, and I know he turns you on. It's kind of like me and Valerie. I think we will all get pleasure from this evening, but if you don't want to we can leave right now."

Steph looked at Lara. "What about you? Did you know about this?" Although the question sounded accusatory, her voice was soft and gentle.

"Hank and I have done this sort of thing a few times. It's a game, fun and harmless. We have our rules, of course. Things only happen if everyone's willing and anyone can call things off at any time. And, of course, condoms at all times."

Steph giggled nervously. "Where have I been while all this has been going on?" she asked. "I always thought you two were so conservative."

"Shows how much you know," Lara said. She smiled and squeezed Hank's hand. "We have a few friends who like to play the same games we enjoy."

Steph took a swallow of her wine and looked at Brian. "You want to do this, don't you?"

"Only if you do."

Hank took Steph's hand and placed it gently on the crotch of his shorts. "I want you very much, and I'd love to show you how good it can be with someone new."

Steph sighed, torn between the indignation she ought to feel and the excitement that was making her pulse pound. Deciding that she did indeed want this, she relaxed her arm and let Hank use her hand to stroke his cock. She smiled and looked from Lara to Brian. "Why don't you two go upstairs. I need a few minutes to get comfortable with this and I think Hank is just the one to help me do that."

Arm in arm, Lara and Brian went upstairs and Hank, clad only in his shorts and socks, sat on the tweed sofa. "Why don't you come and sit beside me?" Steph moved to the couch and sat with a few inches of space between her and Hank. "Baby, I've wanted you for a very long time, but I can wait until you're ready. I want to touch you and hold you. I want to make you wet and hot."

Steph sighed and leaned her head on the back of the sofa. Without touching her, Hank rested his head beside hers and spoke softly. "You know what I'd like to do? I'd like to take off that bra and watch your nipples get hard. I'd like to lick them and then blow on the wet skin. Your nipples will get as hard as tiny pebbles."

Hank watched Steph's body relax, then warm to the sound of his voice. "Then I'll take one nipple between my thumb and index finger and pinch it, hard. You'll think it should hurt, but it won't. It will make your pussy twitch and you'll have a hard time keeping your legs together. While I'm pinching one, I'll take the other in my mouth and bite it gently."

Steph's eyes closed as Hank continued. "I'll alternate, pinching one nipple and sucking and biting the other. Can you feel it, Steph? Can you feel my fingers and my teeth on your breasts? Tell me. Can you?"

"Yes," Steph said, squirming, unsuccessfully trying to keep her body still.

Hank moved his mouth closer to Steph's ear, his hot breath adding fuel to her fire. "Oh yes, I know how you feel." He grasped the snap between the cups of Steph's bra and unclipped the fastener. As he separated the sides, freeing her breasts, her hard, erect nipples reached for Hank's mouth. "Like this," he purred, pinching

Steph's left nipple. "And this." He pinched the right. "And this." He leaned over and nipped at her pebbled breast. "So delicious."

When Steph reached out to touch Hank's arm, he gently pressed her hand back onto the back of the sofa. "This is entirely for you. I want you to lie there and just enjoy. I've wanted to do this for so long."

Her voice hoarse and breathless, Steph asked, "What exactly did you imagine?"

He leaned close to her face, his breath hot on the side of her neck. "I imagined breathing into your ear and watching you shiver with pleasure." He caressed the skin on her cheeks and forehead with the pad of his index finger. "I imagined stroking your face and touching your lips with the tip of my tongue." He licked the sensitive skin around the edges of her lips until it was almost torture for Steph not to rub the ticklish spot. He brushed his tongue along the joining of her lips until her mouth opened. "And I dreamed of tasting you." He pressed his mouth against Steph's until their tongues found each other and played deep inside the sensual depths.

"Oh, baby," Hank purred when they separated. "I knew it would be this good."

Steph opened her eyes and gazed at Hank. She should be ashamed of what was happening, but she wasn't. She was revelling in the sensations and in the knowledge that this wasn't her husband. This was a sensual man who wanted to make love with her. In the small part of her brain that was still capable of coherent thought, she realized that it was okay. No, she corrected herself. It was wonderful. She smiled.

"Oh yes, baby," Hank said, almost able to read her mind. "Let me make love to you. Shall we go upstairs to where we can be more comfortable?"

Steph stood and, barefoot, wearing only her tiny, lace panties, she followed Hank upstairs to the guest room. While he ripped the spread off the bed and heaped the covers on the floor, she stood in the center of the room now eager to let Hank make love to her.

Hank turned and allowed his gaze to roam over Steph's almost-naked body. "I can't believe this is really happening," he whispered.

"It is happening," she purred, feeling sexual power and strength flow through her.

When she started to pull the tiny wisp of lace down over her hips, Hank knelt and took her hands. "Let me do this the way I've fantasized." Then he pressed his mouth against her flat belly, flicking his tongue into her navel. He slowly lowered her undies and inhaled her fragrance. He helped Steph step out of her undies, then nudged her legs apart to make it easier for him to touch and taste and smell her.

He reached his tongue between her legs and pressed it against her swollen clit. He felt her legs tremble. "So excited," he whispered, standing and scooping her into his arms and gently laying her on the cool sheets. He crawled between her spread legs and lowered his face to her cunt. He blew hot air through her pussy hair, further inflaming her, then brushed his chin lightly against her fur, just barely touching it, watching her hips buck and reach for him. "Tell me now, baby. Tell me how hot you are."

"Oh God, Hank, I need you so much. I want you."

"And I want you. My cock is so hard that most of me wants to climb onto you and fuck you until we both come. But I'm going to wait. I'm going to give you more pleasure than you think you can stand." He brushed her pussy with his finger, then slid the length of her slit, parting her lips but not entering.

"That's torture," Steph moaned. She raised her hips but Hank kept his fingers just touching her.

Hank's laugh was deep and sexy. "Yes. It certainly is." He pressed just a tiny bit harder so his finger penetrated only a small way.

"Oh God," she moaned. "Oh God."

Hank tightened his tongue and flicked the tip over Steph's hard, swollen clit.

With his breath on her skin, his tongue stroking her nub, and his finger rubbing her pussy lips, Steph could hold out no longer. "I'm going to come," she cried.

As he felt her body begin to spasm, Hank forced three fingers deep into her body and sucked her swollen clit into his mouth.

Waves of liquid heat pulsed through Steph's body, filling her belly and cunt. He seemed to know just how to rub and lick, when to make it hard and when to stroke. Her orgasm continued for what seemed like hours.

"Hold on to it and don't let it down," Hank said as he climbed over her quivering body.

Steph wasn't sure what he meant, but she concentrated on not relaxing, on reaching for more of the glorious sensations and not letting them ebb. When Hank plunged his fully erect cock into her soaking passage, it triggered more spasms of erotic pleasure. He thrust into her over and over until he climaxed and she came again.

"Lord," Hank said as his breathing returned to normal. "It was even better than I dreamed."

"It was fantastic," Steph said.

Back in the kitchen in Harrison, Jessie listened to her friend's story with increasing amazement. When Steph sat back on the kitchen chair, Jessie was silent for a long while. "I'm flabbergasted," she said finally. "I'm . . . I'm . . . I don't know what I am."

Steph stared into her empty coffee cup. "Horrified? Disgusted?"

"No, of course not." She got up and poured a fresh cup of coffee for herself and her friend. On the way back to her chair, she give Steph a quick hug. "Not horrified or disgusted. Surprised and, I guess, a bit curious. Can I ask you a few questions?"

"Of course. This wasn't intended as a monologue. I wanted you to know. For lots of reasons."

Jessie remembered the picture of Steph, draped over the lawn chair. "This obviously wasn't the only time."

"Actually, Brian and I are now what you would probably call swingers. We have a wonderful life together, but we also have other relationships." When she saw Jessie's eyebrow go up, she said quickly, "None serious. Just playtimes."

"You have people you go to bed with and Brian does too? Like a lover? It's not just the occasional couples swapping partners?"

"That's exactly what I mean." Steph wasn't sure how much Jessie was ready for so she decided just to react to questions for a while. "Right now I have two men with whom I get together from time to time, and Brian is currently seeing a wonderful woman, a systems designer in the computer department at his office."

"The mind boggles," Jessie said, then giggled. "That's how it all started. Boggle, I mean."

Steph let out a deep breath. She hadn't been sure of Jessie's reaction but she had wanted very badly for her best friend to understand. "You're okay with this?"

Jessie reached across the table and took Steph's hand. "I'm fine with this, as long as it works for you and Brian. It was the lying that upset me so much before. But you don't lie to each other. This is all very new to me, but I love you both and you seem very happy." She pulled back and grew thoughtful. "I guess I never thought about women who make love to other people's husbands."

"Hold it," Steph said. "I never make love to anyone who is married, unless the wife knows what's going on. No lying. That's my first and most important rule. No lying. To Brian, to the man involved, or to wives. Period."

"No lying," Jessie said softly.

"In my mind, that's the cardinal sin, the commandment, if you will, that Rob broke with his bimbo, as you call her. He lied to you and he probably lied to himself. It's the dishonesty that makes me want to wring his scrawny neck."

"I guess I never looked at it that way, exactly. For me it was two things. The dishonesty, of course, but it was also the fact that

I obviously wasn't good enough for him in bed." Jessie's eyes filled and she looked down.

"Bullshit!" Steph put a finger under Jessie's chin and gently raised her head so the women were looking into each other's eyes. "Listen to me good, JessicaLynn Hanley, you're not good or bad in bed alone. If you and scrawny-neck didn't make it together, it was a mutual failing. Individuals aren't good or bad at making love. Only couples are."

"Yeah, but . . ."

"No 'yeah but.' You're a warm, caring person and you're as good in bed, or as bad, as the chemistry and communication between you and the man you're with." As she looked into her friend's face, she continued, "Don't look at me like I just told you that the earth was flat. It's true."

"But Rob told me. . . ."

"Rob isn't the sexpert of all times, you know. Besides, was he ever with anyone else beside you?"

"He says that bimbette was the first," Jessie said, snuffing.

"What about before you two got married. Was there ever anyone else?"

"No. The first time for both of us was in the front seat of his father's Pontiac." Her face softened. "He almost came on my jeans trying to get them open."

"So what makes him the ultimate judge of sexuality? Certainly not experience."

"I don't know. If I were being brutally honest, I'd have to admit that it wasn't very good. He used to give me a shot of alcohol to 'loosen me up.' He said I was uptight and needed to relax." Her voice dropped and she wiped a tear from her cheek with the back of her hand. "He said I was frigid."

"He can say anything he wants, Jessie, but he can't make you believe it. And I don't believe it."

"But I don't think I've ever had an orgasm."

"And whose fault is that?"

Jessie's head jerked up and she was silent for a minute. "I never thought about it that way. You mean there might not be anything wrong with me?"

"Probably not. You're healthy. No physical problems. No drug abuse. You probably weren't excited enough to come. I read something a while ago that has stuck in my mind. Someone wrote that a man flames like a match and a woman heats like an iron. That timing requires some coordination. It takes a woman twenty or thirty minutes from a cold start."

"A cold start." She laughed. "That's an unusual way to put it. It makes me sound like an auto engine on a winter morning."

"Is that such a bad analogy?"

"Maybe not. I was always a cold start. I came to dread sex."

"Make that forty-five minutes to warm up," Steph said. "Jessie, relax. You're fine. It's scrawny-neck I want to kill."

"Thanks for that, Steph. You always were a good friend."

"And I still am. Let's table this topic for the moment, get dressed up and do some outrageous damage to your credit card at Bloomingdales."

Jessie took a deep, shuddering breath. "Good idea. You've given me lots to think about, and I'd like to continue this discussion another time."

"Any time, babe. I love to talk about sex."

Steph and Jessie spent the afternoon shopping. At first, Jessie selected outfits that were conservative and concealing. At one point, however, Steph convinced Jessie to try on a low-cut, Indian-silk sundress with a very full, soft skirt. When her friend came out of the dressing room, Steph grinned. "You look wonderful." The dress, in shades of soft peach and rose, complemented Jessie's red hair and sun-warmed complexion.

"I do? Isn't it a bit much?" She yanked upward on the neckline, trying to minimize her deep cleavage. "I mean isn't it a bit young for me?"

"Young? Come on. You're thirty-six years old. That's young

enough for almost anything, except maybe being proofed at a bar. I think you look terrific, and with a little makeup. . . ."

"Don't get carried away." She swung back and forth in front of the mirror watching the skirt move with her body. As she watched herself, her smile broadened. "But although it's not my usual, I do like this dress."

"Now you need shoes to go with it," Steph said to Jessie's back as she disappeared back into the fitting room. "And a new bathing suit and a few other things I can think of."

When they arrived home, the two women dumped their purchases on the sofa and adjourned to the plant room with two glasses and a bottle of California chardonnay. When they had settled into long chairs side by side, and sipped some wine, Jessie reopened the earlier topic. "I guess I've digested some of our conversation of before. Now I'm curious. How did Brian react to your first encounter with Hank?"

"He was pretty quiet for a day or so, then, in bed a few nights later, he asked me all about it."

"He wanted the gory details?"

"Not specifically, but he wanted to know whether I enjoyed it and whether I came."

"Did you tell him? I mean, weren't you worried that he'd be jealous or something."

"Jessie," Steph said, turning to fully face her friend. "I will never lie to Brian. That's the bottom line. If he doesn't like something that happens we can change the rules but I will never lie. I told him it was wonderful. To me, lovemaking isn't a contest. It's not who's better than whom at this or that. It's pleasure for the sake of pleasure and that's all it is. And, of course, there's never a substitute for first times in bed together. It's the greatest kick in the world."

"Wow. That's quite an attitude."

"I guess, but it's one that Brian and I share completely. We have a deal that if something makes one of us uncomfortable, either about what we are doing ourself or what the other is doing, we talk about it and decide how to rearrange things, if necessary."

"Has he ever been jealous? Have you?"

"Once in a while one of us becomes obsessed with someone for a short time. But it's always hottest at the beginning and eventually it all cools."

Jessie hesitated. "Am I cramping your style?"

"Of course not. There are a few couples in the neighborhood who get together for fun from time to time and we will, either with you or without, in the near future."

"Me?"

"Yes, you. We've found quite a few honest, open kindred spirits." She smiled. "You know, some people who claim to be open-minded have said to me, 'Just don't tell my wife the details. I don't want her to know about. . . .' Honest my foot. They have more secrets than the FBI. We don't find that type of person very congenial."

"Hey, girls, your lord and master is home," a voice yelled from the front hall.

"Hi lord and master," Steph yelled back. "Bring a wineglass. We're killing a bottle of chardonnay and need an accomplice."

"Let me change and I'll be right in."

"You really found the best one," Jessie said wistfully.

"I know I did. But he didn't make out badly in the deal."

Jessie's head snapped up. "I didn't mean. . . ."

Steph laughed. "Of course you didn't. You know you could talk to Brian about all this too."

"Talk to Brian? I'd be too embarrassed."

"Nonsense. He can tell you better than I can how he feels about it all."

"I don't think I'm up to discussing this with him just yet."

"Do you mind if I tell him that we talked?"

"I guess not. It's just so, I don't know, so intimate."

"That it is. And try not to treat him differently because you know what's going on."

"That will be a tall order. I never dreamed there was a tiger under that teddy bear."

At that moment, Brian walked in, wearing a pair of form-fitting swim trunks and carrying a wineglass. The two women burst out laughing. "Okay," Brian said, filling his glass, "what's the joke?"

"We were just talking about what could be hiding under your teddy bear exterior." Steph took a minute to control her laughter. "Then you walk in in those tight little nothings you're wearing and we know you can't hide a thing."

Brian looked down at his body with its heavy black hair. "Okay, ladies, now I'm insulted. Teddy bear indeed. I've always wanted to be a centerfold." He posed with his arms flexed. "A sex symbol. Like Burt Reynolds."

"You're my sex symbol darling," Steph giggled.

Brian walked over and gave his wife a kiss on the top of her head then started toward the pool. "Thanks," he said over his shoulder. "I'll just take this teddy bear body and go for a swim. Join me?"

"Sure." The two women followed Brian to the pool and while he swam laps, Jessie and Steph talked about gardening.

As he swam, Jessie watched Brian's shoulders. He always did have great shoulders, she thought. He fools around. With other women. She watched his huge hands cut through the water. Now stop that, she told herself as a warm flush spread through her body. That's Stephanie's husband you're leering at. But, she said to herself, he fools around with Steph's permission. Interesting.

The following day was Wednesday, matinee day in Manhattan. Steph knocked on Jessie's door and Jessie called, "Come on in." She stood in her bra and panties, rummaging in the dresser drawers for a clean polo shirt.

"Good," Steph said, one hand buried in the pocket of her flowered terrycloth robe. "I caught you before you got dressed. Put on your best city duds, I've got a treasure." She raised her hand and waved a small white envelope. "*Phantom of the Opera*. This very afternoon. Two tickets, row eight."

"Oh Steph. I've wanted to see that show for ages." She slammed the dresser drawer and opened the closet door. "City duds. How's the outfit I arrived in?"

"Just fine," Steph said, looking at her watch. "I'd like to make the ten o'clock train. We can lunch someplace nice, then go to the theater. I'll give Brian a call and he can meet us for an outrageous dinner."

"Sounds terrific."

The day was perfect. The weather was unusually temperate for New York in late June, temperatures in the high seventies and low humidity. The two women window-shopped, ate a quick lunch at Twenty-One, and enjoyed the theater. Brian met them at Le Cirque and the three spent hours gorging themselves on fine food and memorable wine. After dinner, Jessie snuck out to the maitre d' and secretly gave him her credit card. When Brian asked for the check, the waiter nodded toward Jessie. "The madam has already taken care of it."

"Jessie, you shouldn't have."

"That's to say thank you for everything. You're the best friends anyone could ever have and I'm grateful."

Brian stood up, walked around to Jessie's chair and gave her a soft kiss on the cheek. "You're our best friend and we love you." He slid the tip of his finger up the nape of Jessie's neck, ending just below her tight French knot. A shiver slithered down Jessie's spine.

Thursday, Steph spent the day at the hospital and, since Brian had a business dinner, the two women ate in the kitchen, dressed in shorts and T-shirts. "Oh lord, Steph," Jessie said as her friend pulled a casserole dish out of the oven. "Franks and beans. I haven't had franks and beans in . . . gosh, since we were in high school. Rob always said that beans gave him gas and he always watched his fat intake so franks were out."

"So? You never made some just for you?"

Ruefully, Jessie shook her head. "You don't have any of that brown spiced bread we used to have, do you?"

Steph pulled the cylinder of deep brown, spicy bread from the microwave. "Only ze best for ze madam," she said in a bad, mock French accent.

Over coffee, Steph said, "Jessie, I'd like to invite some friends over to meet you on Tuesday night. That's the Fourth of July. Just a few couples we know and particularly like. I think you'll like them too."

"Couples you and Brian fool around with?" As soon as the words were out of her mouth, Jessie regretted them. "I'm sorry."

"That's okay. And the answer is yes and no. I'd like to invite three couples, nice normal everyday folks, one of whom we've swapped with, two we haven't. I challenge you to figure out which couple we've swapped with. I had intended to invite two single men so you wouldn't find the evening so couples-oriented but one of them, a wonderful man named Gary, is out of town. You will get to meet him too, eventually. He's a very long story, but suffice it to say that he gives the best parties. You'll have to attend one with us some evening. I know you'll like the other man I've invited. Eric Langden's a doll, divorced and gorgeous. And no, I've never been with either Gary or Eric. Exactly."

Jessie let that final remark pass, for the moment. "Are you trying to fix me up?"

"Frankly, yes. But not fix you up with someone specific. It's just that you should have some fun now. It's been over a year and Rob's past history. It's time for the next phase of Jessie's life."

"I don't think I'm ready for that yet, Steph."

"For what? All I'm planning is a nice evening with nice people. Period. No sex, nothing kinky. No future plans unless you want some. No awkward foursomes. Just people. And no Jessie and Rob. Just Jessie."

"Just Jessie." She nodded. "Okay. Sounds wonderful."

The long holiday weekend sped by. Tuesday afternoon, Steph and Jessie sat chatting in the plant room. "By the way, Jessie," Steph asked, "what are you wearing this evening?"

"I thought I'd wear that same navy linen suit. Why? Is it too dressy?"

"Well. . . ." Steph hesitated. "May I make a suggestion? I'd love to see you wear that print dress we bought last week."

"Oh no, Steph. Not for tonight. It's so, I don't know, so flamboyant."

"But it's a party and that light, pretty party dress will make you feel like a party. And anyway, what's wrong with a little flamboyance? Let's look at this as a coming-out party for a new Jessie, a JessicaLynn party."

"That's silly."

"It is not silly. Let's look at it this way. If you decide to leave sometime soon—and I'm not for one moment suggesting that you should—you'll never see any of these people again. If you stay, they'll have met the new you and I'm sure they'll love you as much as I do. Let's create a new look for you to match your new life."

"Oh Steph, I don't know."

"I know you very well, JessicaLynn Hanley, and somewhere inside you a little JessicaLynn-voice is saying, 'Do it. Have some fun for a change.' Another, louder Jessie-voice is saying, 'That's ridiculous. Be yourself, conservative and proper.' Tell that Jessie-voice to stuff it and let JessicaLynn out."

Jessie laughed. "You do know me well, don't you. That's exactly what's going through my brain. I would really like to be Jessica-Lynn, fun-loving party-girl, but on the inside I'm still Jessie, proper and restrained." When Steph didn't respond, Jessie raised an eyebrow. "The flowered dress?"

"The flowered dress."

"The strappy sandals we bought to go with it?"

Steph nodded, then added, "And no tightly organized French twist. Wear your hair softer, maybe even loose."

"But that's not me," Jessie protested softly.

"It's JessicaLynn."

"It's JessicaLynn," she whispered. "Okay. I'll wear the dress and the shoes, but I don't know about the hair."

"Yippee. JessicaLynn gets to come out and play."

The party was scheduled for eight o'clock so the three friends had a bite to eat around six. Then Jessie went to her room, took a long shower, and scrubbed her long red hair until it squeaked. She wrapped herself in a towel, then wandered into the bedroom, opened the closet door and stood before the full-length mirror. Her fine, soft hair was already drying and flowing softly around her shoulders. The summer sun had turned the ivory skin on her face, arms, and legs a soft peachy color.

She hadn't really looked at herself in years, so Jessie took a deep breath and dropped the towel. Her figure was softer and more rounded than it had been in high school. Her breasts were high and full, her nipples deep smoky-pink. Her hips were wide enough to accentuate her small waist. Her legs were long and shapely. She smiled. I should be thinking about my thick thighs and my not-too-flat stomach, she thought. But JessicaLynn wouldn't do that.

She put on a white lace bra and panties, added a short half-slip, and then she was ready for the dress. Jessie took the hanger from the closet and, without looking in the mirror, pulled it over her head and zipped it up. She looked down and all she could see was the deep shadowed valley between her breasts. She wiggled her hips and pulled up at the neckline. "I can't do this," she said. Then she glanced up and looked at her reflection. "Wow," she said.

The dress was perfect. It hugged her upper body and cascaded in soft flowing lines over her hips and thighs. The skirt fell to just below her knees and below her short slip it was slightly translucent. She looked five years younger than she had looked a half an hour before and, she admitted to herself, she felt ten years younger.

She struggled with the tiny straps on her sandals and finally got them adjusted to her satisfaction. Again she looked at herself and grinned. "Okay, JessicaLynn, what about this hair?" Part of her wanted to put it into her traditional French twist but she stopped herself. She brushed it until it was soft and dry and pulled it back from her face. She tried a ponytail at the back of her head, then one at the nape of her neck, and finally one on top of her head. None of them were right. She pulled it one way, then another. Nothing looked the way she wanted.

She almost surrendered and put her hair up in her usual style when she remembered a long silver-colored comb she had once pushed into the fold of her twist. She found the comb in the bottom of her cosmetic bag and used it to pull one side of her hair back behind her ear. "Oh my God," she muttered as she saw the sexy woman in the mirror. "Is that me?"

It is if you want it to be, JessicaLynn said in her mind.

But is this the conservative midwesterner you've always been? Jessie asked.

No. And so what? JessicaLynn answered.

But what would Rob think?

Out loud, JessicaLynn said, "Who gives a fuck!" She dusted her cheeks with blush, pencilled on a line of eyeliner, and colored her lips with a coral lipstick. "Well, JessicaLynn, here goes."

THREE

———◆◆◆———

Jessica walked into the kitchen where Steph and Brian were doing a few last-minute things for the party. They had bought several party platters at the local gourmet food store and, while Steph filled a bowl with mixed nuts, Brian was dropping fresh fruit into the blender. Steph was wearing a white cotton halter-top dress with a navy belt and sandals. Brian wore identical colors, a white short-sleeved shirt, white duck slacks with a navy belt, and navy deck shoes.

"Did you two dress to match on purpose?" Jessica asked.

At the sound of her voice, Brian and Steph turned. "Holy cow," Steph said while Brian just whistled long and low. "You look fabulous."

"Now I see what I've always known," Brian said, staring. "You are not only a lovely looking woman, you're sexy as hell."

"JessicaLynn," Steph said, "you're amazing."

"JessicaLynn?" Brian said.

"We decided that the person you've seen for the past week is

37

Jessie, but it's time to let her sensual alter ego out." Steph waved her arm at the gorgeous woman standing in the doorway. "This is JessicaLynn."

"Actually, I'd prefer to be Jessica for the moment. I'm not yet ready to become JessicaLynn but this," she swirled her skirt, "isn't Jessie either."

"Okay, what's this name thing you two have got going?" Brian asked.

Jessica motioned for Steph to explain. "Jessie lives in the midwest. She's a bit conservative and sexually repressed."

"Steph!"

"Well, she is," Steph said.

As Brian laughed, he asked, "And JessicaLynn?"

"She's a swinger. She loves sex and games and fun." Steph gave her husband a peck on the cheek. "Like us, darling."

Brian looked at Jessica and, after a moment, said, "You're telling me that you're halfway there."

"Not yet. I am telling you that I'm trying to open my mind to everything. But it's a slow process."

"Okay, Jessica it is," Steph said.

"Well, lovely lady," Brian said, crossing the kitchen and wrapping one bearlike arm around Jessica's waist, "I like your new name and your new attitude. Will you dance with me?" He swept her into his arms and they twirled around the kitchen.

"You know, Brian," Jessica said, laughing, "I never knew you were such a good dancer."

Brian pivoted, raised his arm, and let Jessica twirl underneath it. "You never gave me a chance." They danced into the living room and, gazing into her eyes, he bent her over his arm in a deep dip.

"You're flirting with me," she said, moving from his embrace.

"And why not?"

"Your wife, my best friend, is in the kitchen. Remember her?"

"Of course. But I know she told you about our unusual relationship and I've wanted to hold you for a very long time." As he watched the confusion flash over Jessica's face, Brian said, "Haven't you ever thought about how it might feel to be in my arms?"

At that moment, the doorbell rang, signalling the arrival of the first guests. "Saved by the bell," Jessica said.

"One last thing. I would never make you uncomfortable, JJ, I mean Jessica. You know that. I'll back off any time you say. But you're sexy and attractive and I enjoy playing with you, wherever it leads."

Jessica smiled as she heard Steph's footsteps in the hallway. "I understand, but it does make me a little uncomfortable." When Brian looked crestfallen, Jessica added, "But it's a nice discomfort."

As they separated, Brian ran his fingertip up Jessica's spine, then walked toward the hallway to greet their guests.

As the first couple walked into the living room, followed almost immediately by two more, Jessica remembered Steph's words. *I challenge you to figure out which couple we've swapped with.* As she was introduced to each, Jessica had to admit that she had no idea who Brian and Steph had slept with. All six people were delightful, bright, interesting, and interested.

Chuck O'Malley worked at the same brokerage firm as Brian and his wife Marcy was the vice president of an international bank. They had a married daughter who was expecting their first grandchild in two months. "Of course," Marcy said as she settled in the living room, "I'm only going to be a grandmother because I had Betsy when I was six years old."

"I know," Chuck said, "and Betsy's only nine now."

"Right!" Marcy said, giggling. "That makes me. . . ."

Chuck snatched the drink Brian offered before Marcy could take it. "That makes you only fifteen and too young to drink."

Pete Cross worked at General Foods as a research chemist and his wife Gloria was deeply involved in local politics. They had five children, ranging in age from seven to eighteen, and regaled the group with tales of their adventures in parenthood.

Steve Albright was the biggest, blackest man Jessica had ever seen. At six foot six, with skin that was almost blue, he was an imposing figure. In contrast his wife Nan was five foot one with cafe au lait skin that was stretched to its limit by her eight and a half months of pregnancy. Steve was a junior partner in a prestigious Wall Street law firm and would be a full partner before he was thirty-five. "Our first," Steve said, lovingly rubbing his wife's belly.

"And, if this pregnancy is any indication," Nan said, easing her body into a soft chair, "my last. I waddle like a duck, I sleep sitting up and I haven't seen my feet in six weeks. I've finally had to stop working, too." Jessica's ears had perked up when she learned that Nan had worked for a local real estate agency and would go back to work part-time after the birth of the baby.

"I've been wondering," Steve added, "why they call it morning sickness. Nan's been nauseated since day one, all day."

"I think they call it morning sickness because it starts in the morning," Nan said, sipping the glass of club soda Steve handed her and nibbling on the saltine crackers she always kept at hand. "But only a couple of weeks to go. The doctor says that little Stevie's right on schedule."

"You know it's a boy?" Jessica said, her envy obvious to Steph.

When Jessie and Rob had married, she had wanted several children. Over the months and years, Rob had talked her out of it. 'We want so many things. Travel, freedom. Kids would just get in the way,' Rob had said. Jessica gazed wistfully at Nan's enlarged belly.

"It's a boy. Steven James Albright Junior." She beamed at her husband. "But the doctor also said that he's already over seven pounds. Another two weeks and he'll never be able to get out the old-fashioned way."

Steve winked. "He got in there the old-fashioned way."

Over the laughter, Nan cocked her head to one side, paused, then said, "Oooohhh, yes. I remember. That sex thing. It used to be very nice, back when such a thing was possible."

"Don't give us that," Steve said. "We've found ways. Oral sex has never been as pleasant."

"Oral sex is always pleasant," Gloria said.

"And we found the most delicious goo in a sex catalog," Pete added. "I hate the ones that taste like fruit juice. This one's cinnamon. Very spicy."

Gloria winked. "Just like me."

Jessica was amazed with the openness of the talk about sex. Rob had always found the subject distasteful, so it never came up in conversation with their friends.

As the group chatted in the large living room, the doorbell rang again. That must be Eric, Jessica thought, her palms damp. Not a date, Jessica told herself. Just a man coming to a party.

Eric Langden was about six feet tall with iron-gray hair and a well-trimmed, iron-gray moustache and beard. An architect, he had been divorced for five years. The group was obviously comfortable together and they all made an effort to draw Jessica into the conversation.

Over rum and fruit drinks that Brian whipped up in a constantly whirring blender, they talked for several hours about everything from world tensions to real-estate prices, from television shows and movies to crabgrass. When she stopped to think about it, Jessica realized that she hadn't had such a light, tensionless evening in a long time.

"By the way, did anyone see Sally Jessie this afternoon?" Nan asked, sipping her club soda.

"Most of us have to work," Marcy said. "And anyway, since when have you been interested in the adventures of dysfunctional families airing their dirty little secrets in public?"

"I'm practicing to stay home for a few months at least. You have to watch at least two hours of talk shows and an hour of soaps each afternoon to keep your daytime TV certification. Actually, there's not much else on."

"So which dirty little secret did Sally Jessie reveal today?" Steph asked. "Transvestite lesbian cannibals?"

"People who've had plastic surgery on their penises," Chuck said.

"Women who've been fucked by Elvis's ghost."

"Couples who've been abducted by alien polar bears."

"A family of seven who've lived at the bottom of a well for three years."

"All right," Nan said, holding up her hands. "Take pity on the pregnant lady, will you? The show was about sexual fantasies and it got me thinking. They had couples dressed up as their favorite fantasy. One was a pirate and his captive, one was an Arabian guy with his harem girl, you know. The nice thing was no one had a Barbie and Ken shape or anything. They were just regular people and very free with their conversation."

"Sounds kinky," Chuck said with a leer. "Like Gary's party. Remember?"

"Who could forget that night?" Marcy said. "But that was before you guys moved here," she said to the Albrights.

"We've heard about Gary's parties," Steve said, patting his wife's belly. "We're not up to that yet."

When Jessica looked particularly puzzled, Steph winked at her and said, "It's a long story. I'll tell you at length sometime."

"Actually, Sally Jessie was interesting. God I hate to hear me saying that. Talk shows and interesting in the same sentence. Ugh. But anyway, some of the people discussed how difficult it had been in the beginning to tell their wife or husband about their fantasy."

"It must be for some people," Steph said seriously.

"These days I fantasize a lot," Nan continued. "I think it's lack of good sex that does it. And I know it would be hard for me to share the details with Steve. I was just wondering whether any of you have fantasies and whether you tell each other."

"You know," Marcy said, "now that you've admitted to having fantasies that you haven't shared, Steve will force all that sexy information out of you." She twirled a nonexistent moustache. "Force you to tell all the yummy details, all those sexy four-letter words."

Steve and Nan looked at each other, their look saying, 'We'll talk later.' "I guess he will," Nan said. "But now I'm curious. Do you have fantasies and have you shared them?"

As Brian poured another round of fruity drinks, he said, "I've shared most of mine with Steph, but I've kept one or two secret."

Steph jumped in, "You have?"

"Yes. Telling a fantasy and acting it out, as we have, is delicious. And yes, we've acted a few out so you guys can all eat your hearts out. But it also takes the erotic edge off of it somehow."

"What's your favorite fantasy?" Nan asked Steph and Brian.

Steph answered, "He likes to pretend that he's kidnapped me and taken me to a cabin deep in the woods. That way he can have his way with me in private."

"Oooo, yummy," Gloria said, winking at her husband.

"Would you like me to abduct you?" Pete asked. "I could have my way with you and you couldn't object."

"Why do you suppose so many fantasies revolve around being made love to forcibly?" Nan asked. "I've always thought it was evil somehow."

"Rape fantasies aren't about rape," Brian said. "They're about power. I love to have Steph under my control. That way I feel free to do some of the things I might not otherwise. I can demand. But I also know that Steph will let me know if I've gone too far."

"And I enjoy being under Brian's control," Steph said, sipping her drink and enjoying the buzz she had developed. "I don't have to worry about my reactions, what I'm supposed to be doing. I can lay back and enjoy things."

Jessica sat there enthralled. She had never heard people admit to having sexual fantasies before, much less discuss the plot. "You sure do speak your minds," she said softly.

"I'm so sorry, Jessica. Are we embarrassing you?" Nan said quickly. "You fit in so well with us that I forgot that you're new to this little group. We're pretty open-minded."

"And openmouthed," Steve added.

"I'm not really embarrassed." Jessica paused then added, "Yes I am, but it's a fun embarrassment. And I'm fascinated by the way you all talk about this stuff so freely."

"Didn't you and your ex talk about sex?"

"Rob? Not a chance. I think his only fantasy was to have a larger dental office. Sex for him was a routine. Releasing his precious bodily fluids. He wasn't the creative type."

"That's sad," Eric said. "How can you understand what you like and don't like unless you try different things?"

His look lingered on Jessica's face a bit longer than was necessary. She could feel the tingle deep in her body. "I never really thought about it. I guess we were pretty 'missionary position' and totally noncreative."

"My ex and I had a dynamite life in bed," Eric said. "It was out of bed that we fought like cats and dogs."

"How about you guys," Nan asked, turning to Chuck and Marcy. "Any sexual fun and games you'd like to share?"

"Actually," Marcy said, "Chuck has the greatest hands. He gives the most interesting massages." Chuck blushed and silently munched on a cracker and brie. "I guess," Marcy continued, "that we'd show up on Sally with me dressed in a towel and Chuck in a white uniform."

"Pete and I have a fantasy too," Gloria admitted. "We haven't acted it out, but we like to turn out all the lights and. . . ."

"Hey, babe," Pete said. "Aren't we going to have any secrets left?"

"Not a one. We're among friends. We tell a story in the dark. He's a doctor and I'm his unsuspecting patient."

"Babe . . ." Pete warned.

"Okay, okay. I'll say no more."

"Have you ever actually acted it out?" Nan asked.

"So far, no," Gloria said. "But now that you mention it. . . ."

"This conversation is making me very hot," Pete said. "Anyone for a swim?"

"Not me," Nan said, rubbing her belly, "but I'll sit by the pool."

"I turned the heater on just before you folks got here," Brian said. He turned to Jessica. "Suits are optional. Some wear them, some don't. Dealer's choice."

"I think I'll put a suit on," Jessica said, "if that's okay. I'm not that liberated yet."

"You won't be upset if I don't, will you?" Brian asked.

"I don't think so. If I am, I'll look the other way."

In her room, Jessica pulled her three bathing suits from the drawer. The one she had brought from Ottawa, a one-piece floral print, held her in in all the right places. Too conservative and definitely Jessie. She held up the bikini that she and Steph had bought on their recent shopping trip. It barely covered any of her. She dropped it back into the drawer and compromised on a one-piece black suit that mock-laced up the front and left a panel of barely concealed flesh from waist to cleavage. As she wiggled into the suit, she realized that she was slightly drunk, totally relaxed, and very aroused. Her nipples were hard and showed prominently through the tight black fabric.

This sexual tension was a revelation. Poor old Rob, she thought. He would never do anything like this. He missed a lot, and so have I. Well, she told herself, maybe he experiments with bimbette. You know, I really hope he can. She shook her head. I must be mellowing, but I do hope he's getting some good sex. I know I will get mine, eventually. Maybe sooner, rather than later. She fluffed her hair and, barefoot, she ran down the stairs.

When she arrived at the pool, all the patio lights were out with just the underwater lights to illuminate the soft mist rising from the water. Nan was stretched out in a lounge chair with Gloria and Pete sitting in chairs on either side of her. Everyone else was in the water and through the choppy surface it was impossible to tell who had clothes on and who didn't. Steph and Steve were involved in a splash fight at the shallow end, with Chuck egging them on. Brian, Eric, and Marcy were hanging onto the ladder at the deep end, talking. Jessica found herself looking at Brian's muscular shoulders and wondering what he looked like without a bathing suit.

Jessica walked to the deep end and dove cleanly into the eight-foot-deep water. She came up beside Brian, facing the side of the pool, holding on to the edge. "The water's perfect," she said, pushing her sopping red hair out of her face.

"So are you in that bathing suit. I could rape you right here," he whispered, pressing his obviously naked body with its ridge of hard male flesh against her side. "You look so sexy." He released the pressure of his body. "But I won't rush you. I just want you to know that our time will come, eventually, if I have my way." He let go, pushed Marcy under the water and together they swam to the other side, leaving Jessica with Eric.

"That suit looks terrific," Eric said, moving nearer. "It's actually more sensual than being nude." When she was silent, Eric continued, "I'm sorry if I come on too heavy. You're new to this crazy life we have here. But we're just free spirits and we do what feels good and doesn't hurt anyone else. I won't embarrass you, but I would be less than honest if I denied that you turn me on."

Remembering that Eric had been divorced for several years, she asked, "Were you and your wife swingers?"

"We had occasional flings, with each other's knowledge, of course. We were very creative in the bedroom."

"If you'll pardon me for asking, what caused your breakup?"

"Money, mostly." He pulled himself from the water and sat on the edge of the pool while Jessica remained in the water next to his ankles. As water sluiced from his torso she admired his body, substantial in his brief red trunks. "I made some, she spent more. She always wanted me to do things that made more money, I wanted to do things that made me happy. When I was offered a new job with a large architectural firm in the city at an unseemly increase in salary, she begged me to take it."

"You didn't want to?"

"Not really. Commuting was not my idea of how to spend three hours a day. And that job would have also meant weeks, even months travelling. I had commuted and travelled before and it took too much out of me. That's why I took the job in Scarsdale in the first place. It was a small firm but we created some wonderful buildings.

"So we argued about the job. She whined about all the things she wanted out of life. I tried to explain that all I wanted was to stay in Scarsdale, enjoy my ten-minute drive to work, and have enough money to do the things that were important to me. And that wasn't a big house, a maid five days a week, and trips to Europe several times a year."

"What is important to you?"

"I love my kids. They're boys, twins, and they were fourteen then. I liked being able to get to their soccer games and parent conferences. She wanted them in a private school. I like tennis and golf. And I like my friends." He looked around the group. "I wanted to have something left at the end of the day, not get up at the crack of dawn, work, come home, eat, fall into bed so I can get up with the roosters and do it all again."

"And your wife wanted you to take the city job?"

"She demanded. She gave me the 'If you loved me' bit and I thought about it and discovered that I didn't love her. At least not enough to do everything the way she wanted. So we split. We still see each other occasionally, though not as much now that the boys are in college. I miss them, especially since they're spending their summer together in Colorado. Anyway, Marilyn lives in Hartsdale, in a large condo I bought her, and I think she's happy. But her happiness isn't my responsibility anymore. It took me a long time to realize that nothing I did was going to make her happy anyway."

"That's a very grown-up attitude," Jessica said.

"How about your divorce. Was it very difficult?"

Jessica told him about Rob and bimbette. "I find I'm becoming less bitter day by day. Being here has opened my eyes a lot."

"And, if you'll pardon my asking, was your sex life really as boring as you alluded to before?"

Jessica sighed and sipped the drink Brian had set on the edge of the pool for her. "I guess so. I'm not sure how much was his fault and how much was mine."

"Why does it have to be anyone's fault?"

"Not fault, exactly, but I'm just not responsive enough." Why in the world had she admitted that? Now he won't be interested. She looked at the glass in her hand and put it down. And she realized that she wanted Eric to be interested.

"Did he tell you that?" When she nodded, he said, "A sensual woman like you? He has to be a jerk."

Jessica laughed and, bobbing in the warm water, moved slightly away from the side of the pool and kicked her legs. "Thanks for that. But why do you say I'm sensual? What do you know about me?"

"I know that your nipples are hard and it's getting difficult for you to hold still." When her cheeks pinked, he said, "And you're blushing. I love that." He grinned. "I know this is sudden, but could we get together one evening soon?"

"Is this a proposition, sir?" Jessica said, flirtatiousness coming easily from somewhere deep inside her.

"Maybe. I have to admit that I'd love to teach you how sexy you really are, but let's start with dinner. It can progress as quickly or as slowly as we like from there. Or not at all, if that's what we decide."

Jessica smiled. This man was making a pass at her and she was revelling in it. "I'd love to have dinner with you."

"Friday? I can pick you up here at about six?"

"Friday it is."

"Did you have a nice evening?" Steph asked as she and Jessica tidied up the kitchen. They could see Brian, a towel around his waist, wandering around the pool area, stuffing plastic plates and glasses into a large black garbage bag.

"I had an amazing evening," Jessica said. "Your friends are terrific people. I like them all so much."

"I knew you would. They're the greatest."

"Okay. I think I'm ready for the big revelation. Which of them have you slept with?"

Steph laughed. "Couldn't tell, could you."

"Not a clue. Everyone's so open and sexy. I'd sleep with any one of the guys."

"So, my dear, would I. However. . . ." She stuffed a large platter into the dishwasher. "Okay, okay," she said, catching Jessica's look. "Steve and Nan only moved here about a year ago and they were trying desperately to get pregnant. We discussed our lifestyle with them, and they were tempted. Isn't he the most gorgeous thing? Makes me sweat just to think about those arms around me. Anyway, they didn't want to confuse things. I hope, after the baby's born. . . ."

"You're right about him. He's got the greatest body."

"That's my Jessica talking. I think Jessie's long buried."

Jessica sighed. "You may be right. What about the others? Who did and who didn't?"

"Pete and Gloria discussed it and decided that they didn't want to risk the jealousy that they were both afraid would surface. They tried swapping once, many years ago, and Pete particularly found it very hard to deal with the thought of someone else making love to his wife. They go to most of the parties but they stay together."

"So you've been with Chuck and Marcy."

Steph just grinned as Brian walked up behind her and wrapped his arms around her waist. "The four of us," Brian said, "spent a weekend in the Adirondacks together last January. Get Steph to tell you about it sometime. It was incredible." He nibbled his wife's neck. "Just incredible."

"Certainly was," Steph agreed. "And, by the way, I also spent a creative evening with Gary about six months ago. I was sorry he couldn't come tonight. He's the sexiest man I know, with the exception of Brian, of course."

"Is he very handsome?"

Steph thought about it. "Actually, not at all. He sort of reminds me of Ichabod Crane. He's about six foot two or three and probably doesn't weigh one fifty. Long legs, long arms, sort of like a stork. He wears mismatched clothes that hang on him. He always looks like he's just lost fifty pounds and his wardrobe hasn't caught up."

"But you said. . . ."

"I said sexy and attractive, not handsome. There's a big difference."

"Like . . . ?"

"He listens when you talk and concentrates like you're the only one in the world who matters at that moment. He touches you, accidentally on purpose, if you know what I mean. A hand on your shoulder as you sit down, or a palm in the small of your back to guide you through a doorway. And he looks at you like he wants to make long slow love to you all the time."

"Where was Brian all this time, while you were out with Gary?"

"I was here," Brian said, walking through the large sliding glass door. "It doesn't have to be a couples thing with us. I've had my . . . adventures too. Solo. It's really okay with us."

"And what did you think of Eric?" When Jessica blushed, Steph continued, "Did he ask you out?"

"We're having dinner on Friday," Jessica said softly.

"That's great," Brian said. "He's one of the nicest people I know and you two should get along well."

"I liked him a lot. He's bright and so open about things."

"Well," Steph said, "I'm beat." She closed the dishwasher and turned it on.

Jessica glanced at the clock on the microwave. "Holy cow. Is it really after one?"

"Yup," Steph said. "Time sure rushes by when you're having fun."

Brian grabbed Steph by the arm and dragged her toward the sliding glass door. "Let's go out by the pool so I can ravish you before bed."

Steph giggled. "Weallll suh," she laid on a thick southern accent. "What kahnd of a girl do you tahke me foah?"

"I know what kind of girl you are," Brian said, still tugging. "That's why I want to take you out to the pool."

"Nighty night, Jessica," Steph said as Brian dragged her out the door.

"Good night, folks," Jessica said. "I love you both."

Brian blew her a kiss and he and Steph disappeared into the darkness.

Upstairs, Jessica pulled off her bathing suit, took a quick shower, and collapsed onto her bed. Despite the late hour, she couldn't sleep. Images of the people she'd met that evening and an image of herself so different from anything she could have imagined a few weeks before crowded her brain. Finally, she dropped into an exhausted slumber.

In her dream she rode on a merry-go-round. The calliope played random notes that didn't combine into anything she recognized, but surrounded her and filled her head with erotic music. Multi-colored lights winked and flashed in a primitive rhythm.

She was gloriously naked. The snow-white horse rose and fell between her thighs, cool against her heated flesh. She leaned forward and pressed the cool metal bar against the valley between her breasts, against her flaming forehead.

As the merry-go-round turned, Jessica closed her eyes and let the wind blow her hair until it flew behind her like the tail of the horse she rode. Up and down the horse moved, carrying her with it.

Suddenly, there was a man seated on the horse with her, the fronts of his thighs against the backs of hers. She felt the prickle of the coarse hairs on his legs against her delicate skin. Just ignore him, she told herself. But she couldn't. When she started to turn to look at him, he placed his hands gently on the sides of her head, effectively preventing her from seeing who he was. When he lowered his hands to her waist, she didn't try to turn again. Around and around they rode, his hands on her waist and his thighs against her legs.

Gradually, he leaned forward until the length of his chest pressed against her back. Hands splayed on her belly, he used the tip of his tongue to tickle the hollow just behind her right ear. Holding her against him, he bit the tip of her earlobe, then sucked it into his mouth.

As the erotic power of his mouth held her against him, he slid his hands up to cup her aching breasts. He filled his hands with them, weighed and massaged them. Jessica looked down and admired the contrast between his dark fingers and her white skin. She watched in fascination as the hands kneaded her soft fullness and moved ever closer to her fully erect nipples. Squeeze me, she whispered to herself. Pinch me. Make me feel you.

"I will," the man's voice breathed into her ear. "I will give you everything you want. But at my pace." He caressed her breasts lightly. "Just ride the horse. Feel the wind in your face. Close your eyes. Feel." His fingers reached her nipples and he held the left between his finger and thumb. "Feel." He pinched and pulled, causing a sensation that was almost pain.

Erotic heat knifed through her body, stabbing deep into her secret spaces. Don't stop, she thought. Oh God, don't stop. She wanted to tell him, say it out loud, but she couldn't. The words echoed in her head.

"You don't have to say it," he whispered. "I won't stop." One hand pressed her belly and forced her buttocks to cradle his mammoth erection. The other hand shifted to her right breast, grasping it tightly and twisting.

"You're hurting me," Jessica said, not sure whether it was true.

"No, it doesn't really hurt although you think it should. It gives you pleasure; hot demanding pleasure. It makes you hungry. So hungry that you are being devoured by it. Aren't you?" When she remained silent, he moved his hips so his cock slid more deeply into the crack between her cheeks while his fingers worked on her nipple. "Aren't you?"

"Yes," she sighed. "Oh yes."

He shifted his hips and lifted her body. Suddenly his cock was touching her hot, moist entrance. "You want this," the voice whispered, the heated breath tickling her ear. "But you'll have to take it."

Between Jessica's thighs, the merry-go-round horse continued its unrelenting up and down movement. She supported her weight on the stirrups and held herself above his cock. Her thigh muscles quivered from the effort of holding herself up.

"Take it," he whispered. "Let your body go. Take what you and I both know you want."

Yes, she admitted to herself, she did want this. Slowly, she lowered her body so she filled herself with his cock. The merry-go-round went faster and faster and with each note of the calliope the horse rose, carrying him deeper inside. She rode him, synchronizing her movements with the rhythm of the horse. Her mind splintered, sensations darting from the fingers on her nipples to his mouth on her neck to his cock, filling, caressing. Faster and faster she rode until she was a bubble about to burst.

And burst she did, a million colors surrounding her. The lights of the carousel flashed, penetrating her lowered eyelids. She screamed, but then couldn't get her breath. She flew, then plunged with the horse and the man beneath her, the wind unable to cool her body. On and on they rode, climax after rending climax, until she collapsed.

Jessica awoke in a pool of sweat, the sheets tangled around her naked body. Her breathing was rapid and her heart pounded. She could almost hear the music and see the lights. She lay in the darkness until her body calmed, then took another shower. Afterward, she climbed back into bed and slept dreamlessly until morning.

Thursday evening Eric called and he and Jessica talked for almost an hour. "About tomorrow evening," Eric said. "If you agree, there's a concert at a place I think you'd enjoy called Caramoor. There'll be a small jazz group playing in a part of the estate called the Venetian Gardens. I thought we'd have a little picnic on the lawn before the music."

"That sounds lovely."

"Great. Wear jeans and something long-sleeved. It's supposed to be cool and it does get a bit buggy. I'll bring the dinner and the bug spray and pick you up around six."

"I'll see you then."

Jessica flopped back onto her bed. She was both jittery and excited, looking forward to the following evening with a combination of terror and delight. Okay, she thought, jeans. She mentally flipped through her small collection of clothes and selected a soft buttercup-yellow silk shirt. Should I take a jacket? It's only a picnic. But it might get cool later in the evening. But I might look pretentious. Sneakers? Maybe loafers? Or what about sandals?

That night and most of the next day while Steph was at the hospital, Jessica selected, discarded, and reselected. She sat in the garden room and tried to read, only to get up and pace around the pool. "This is ridiculous," she said aloud. "I'm acting like a kid on her first date." Then she grinned. "I am a kid on her first date."

At about four o'clock, she soaked in a tub and managed to relax for a short while. Then she put on the clothes she had selected, changed her shirt, then changed back. At six o'clock, Jessica was dressed in the outfit she had first selected, yellow shirt, soft, well-washed jeans she had had for many years, tennis shoes, and socks. Then, at the last minute, she added a fitted denim vest.

She put her hair up, then held a pair of earrings near her ears. She discarded them and picked another pair, which she also dropped back into the drawer. Something bigger, she thought. But it's only a picnic. Maybe no earrings. She settled on a pair of medium-sized wooden hoops. She gazed into the mirror, smiled, added blush and lipstick and hurried downstairs, glad the house was empty.

As she heard Eric's car in the driveway, Jessica stood inside the front door debating whether to open it and walk outside or wait for him to ring the bell. You're jumpy as a cat, she said to herself, turning the knob in her right hand and pulling the door open. Eric stood with his hand poised above the doorbell.

God, he's sexy, she thought as he stood, openly appraising her. He was dressed in tight jeans and a white tennis sweater with the sleeves pushed up to the elbows, showing off well-muscled forearms. He wasn't gorgeous and she doubted that anyone would stop in their tracks and stare at him. But there was a gleam in his eyes as he looked her over that created a small flutter deep in her belly. His eyes lingered on her breasts as they pressed against the silky fabric of her shirt, then wandered lower to her narrow waist and full hips.

"Very nice," he said. "Although I've seen you in a bathing suit, I still enjoyed speculating about the way you'd fill out your jeans." As she colored, he continued, "You're blushing again." He used the knuckle of his index finger to raise her face, then he dropped a light kiss on her lips. "It's sort of virginal. I love it." Then he took her elbow and guided her out the door.

Together they walked toward the driveway where Eric's vintage BMW 2002 was parked. Bright red with slick black leather upholstery, it was in mint condition. "That's some car," Jessica commented.

"I love old BMWs. I found this one about a year ago and I had it restored. It cost more than buying a new one and it's silly of me, but I get a kick out of it. Drivers of these old cars flick their lights at each other in recognition and I like that kind of camaraderie."

Jessica stroked the supple leather seat beneath her, silently wondering how he could afford to 'restore' a classic car like this one. Did architects make that kind of money?

Eric and Jessica passed the next twenty minutes in comfortable conversation, driving along the tree-lined roadways of Westchester County. They arrived at Caramoor, passed through the big iron gates and drove to a grassy parking area. He helped her out of the car and, arm in arm, they walked along the dirt pathways toward a small picnic area. Before they arrived at the tables, however, Eric turned into a small area of lawn surrounded by a low hedge. In the middle was an old fountain, now filled with flowering plants.

"By the way," Jessica said, her stomach reminding her that she hadn't eaten since breakfast, "you're not carrying any basket. I thought you mentioned dinner."

"I did."

They approached a large plaid wool blanket spread on the lawn under a large maple tree, set with fine china plates, full settings of silverware, and crystal champagne flutes. Each place setting was accompanied by a white linen napkin and a red leather seat cushion.

But it was the man who stood beside the blanket who caught Jessica's attention. He was immense, probably over two hundred and fifty pounds, but well muscled with a long golden ponytail and a heavy gold hoop in one ear. He looked like he might have been a football player or a prize fighter, with gigantic hands and a face that looked like it had taken a punch of two in its time. Beautifully groomed, the man wore tan slacks and a forest-green polo shirt. He was obviously waiting for the lady he would share his feast with.

"Isn't that lovely," she said to Eric. "What an elegant presentation."

"Why thank you," he said, approaching the blanket. "I'll tell Timmy you're impressed."

As Jessica turned to Eric, puzzled, the man near the blanket said, "There you are, sir. I was afraid the food would get warm."

"Not to worry, Timmy," Eric said. "I know better than to keep one of your sumptuous meals waiting." He turned to Jessica. "Jessica, this is Timmy Whitmore. He's my right-hand man and my chauffeur when I want one. He's in charge of my house and he's the best damn cook in the county."

Timmy inclined his head slightly. "It's nice to meet you Ms. . . ."

Totally nonplussed, Jessica answered automatically. "Hanley. It's

Jessica Hanley." She turned to Eric who looked sheepish. "Didn't you say you were a modestly well-off suburban architect who used to argue with your wife about money?"

"I did, didn't I. I know that I owe you an explanation but can it wait until after dinner? Timmy's meals are always works of art and he gets very huffy if his food isn't presented just so."

"Of course it can wait," Jessica said. "But you'll have to give me a moment to adjust." Eric held her arm as she settled onto one of the leather cushions.

With a flourish Timmy pulled two plates from a hamper a few feet away and set one in front of each of them. Artfully arranged on fresh lettuce and watercress were half a dozen of the largest shrimp Jessica had ever seen, with a dollop of dill sauce and a few small toast-rounds on the side. "Good grief, Timmy," Eric said. "These shrimp look like they should have saddles."

"I know," Timmy said, looking downcast and a bit irritated. "I tried to get U12s but all they had were U5s. They're really too large to be as tender as I'd like, but the man in the fish store swore that they were superb. If they're not. . . ."

Eric tasted one. "Well, Timmy, your man was right. They are delicate and crisp, cooked exactly right. Not chewy at all."

Timmy beamed, the smile giving his singularly unattractive face an appealing glow. "Thank you sir."

Feeling like she was in the middle of a James Bond movie, Jessica speared a shrimp with a slender shrimp fork and tasted, then dipped the shrimp into the sauce and took another bite. "These are delicious," she said and watched Timmy's smile grow still wider. "I make cold shrimp often, but with cocktail sauce with extra horseradish, or a cold mayonnaise. I've never made anything like this sauce. It's wonderful."

"Thank you. I've met only a few people who appreciate shrimp with mayonnaise," Timmy said.

While they ate in silence, she watched Timmy deftly open a bottle of Dom Perignon and fill two flutes, each half full. "This meal is delightful," Jessica said as she lifted her glass.

"And the company is a perfect complement," Eric whispered, holding her gaze until her hand shook. He lifted his glass and touched the rim to hers, enjoying the single clear note it produced. "To an enjoyable evening, the first of many I hope."

"To an enjoyable evening." She sipped the wine, knowing she was already intoxicated.

When they had finished their shrimp, Timmy whisked the plates away and replaced them with larger, prearranged dinner plates. "I made cold smoked breast of duck with a chilled pasta primavera." Moving with surprising grace for such a large man he placed a sauceboat on the blanket. "There's a light vinaigrette for the duck." He placed small bread plates, each with two tiny hot rolls, beside Eric and Jessica. Jessica was amazed that the surface of each butter pat was covered with a tiny staff and notes of music. "These are beautiful, Timmy," she said.

"I enjoy doing that. You might call it a hobby of mine."

"That's along with cake decorating and baking the most delicious breads you've ever tasted."

"Actually, I once worked as a food stylist on photos for a cookbook," Timmy boasted, removing the champagne glasses and replacing them with white wine glasses. "I have a sauvignon blanc from Chili, 1992. It will go perfectly with the duck and was very reasonable."

"Timmy haunts the local wine stores."

"I found this one at Zachy's actually. It was so well priced that I bought us a case," Timmy said.

"Jessica?" Eric asked.

"If Timmy recommends it, how can I argue?"

Timmy beamed as he uncorked the wine and poured a small amount into Eric's glass.

"Anyone can find a good fifty-dollar bottle of wine," Timmy said. "I can find a good bottle of wine at under ten dollars. What do you think?"

Eric tasted and nodded. "Right as usual."

Beaming, Timmy handed Eric the cork and half-filled each glass.

"Keep the cork," Eric said, handing it back to Timmy, "and you can recork the bottle before you leave. If we finish even half of this wine, I'll never be able to drive home."

As they ate, they made small talk. "Do you know why the host breaks the wine cork?" he asked.

Jessica took a sip of wine to moisten her dry mouth and tucked her legs underneath her. "I always wondered why the waiter hands it over, but I didn't want to sound as unsophisticated as I felt so I never asked."

"Most of these rituals are left over from the dim past when there was a real need for precautions. Now it's mostly just snobbery and uptight people who like to make a simple glass of wine into a Japanese tea ceremony." He reached out and Timmy handed Eric the cork which he in turn handed to Jessica, his fingers lingering on hers. "You'll notice that the imprint of the winery is on the cork, with the year." He laid the cork in Jessica's palm, rubbing the rough surface along her skin. "In the olden days unscrupulous people used to fill an empty bottle with jug wine, then recork it and sell it as the expensive stuff. So, rather than break the expensive bottle so that wouldn't happen, they broke the inexpensive cork."

"Oh. That makes sense." She held the cork under her nose. "Why do they smell the cork?"

"Before wine was sterilized, pasteurized, and otherwise purified, occasionally bad yeasts would get into the vats and, instead of fine wine, you'd get fine vinegar. Actually the word vinegar is from the French, *vin* meaning wine and *agre* meaning sour. And if the wine was sour, you could smell it in the cork." Eric smiled. "These days, wine is never sour and there's no need to smell the cork. The only ones who sniff it are those who want everyone to think they know something." He reached over and wrapped his long fingers around Jessica's then slowly drew the cork from her hand.

As his fingers slid from her hand, Jessica's breath caught. She gazed at the attractive man who sat across from her, then looked at her plate. She lifted a small forkful of the duck to her mouth and tasted it, unsure of whether she'd be able to swallow. To break the tension she was feeling, she said, "This is very unusual, Timmy. I really like it."

"I'm so glad. I didn't know anything about you or your taste in food, so it was difficult to plan the meal."

"Well, Timmy, I'm easy. I enjoy tasting new things and I can't imagine anything that you created that I wouldn't like."

Eric gazed into her eyes. "I'm glad you enjoy trying new things, Jessica."

The food turned to cardboard in her mouth and she sipped her wine to moisten her lips. Although it was difficult for her to eat with Eric's hot gaze on her, she couldn't insult Timmy so she finished every bite along with two glasses of wine.

"I'm so glad the meal pleased you, Ms. Hanley," Timmy said as he removed the plates and the wine glasses. "I have a triple-crème blue cheese and fruit for dessert. There's coffee and I've taken the liberty of opening a 1971 Chateau D'Yquem. It will go superbly with the cheese and fruit. The pears are especially good." Leaving the platter with the fruit and cheese, china mugs for coffee beside the filled carafe, the decanter, and new glasses for the sauterne, Timmy efficiently packed everything else in a hamper. "I'll be leaving, now. I've left a small basket over there," he pointed, then lifted the heavy hamper as though it weighed nothing. "Everything should fit quite nicely."

"Timmy," Eric said, stretching out on the blanket as people wandered through the gardens around them, "you've done a wonderful job, as usual."

"Thank you, sir," he said, "and it was so nice meeting you Ms. Hanley."

"Thank you for the wonderful meal, Timmy," Jessica said. "I don't think I've ever had better."

"Good night," Timmy said and walked toward the exit with a surprisingly light step for such a big man.

FOUR

———◆━◆◆◆━◆———

"Try the cheese with the sauterne," Eric said. He cut off a bit of pear, spread a small amount of cheese on the morsel and held it in front of Jessica's mouth. She ate from his fingers and he quickly handed her the wine. "Close your eyes and drink this so the tastes are in your mouth at the same time."

When she had sipped the thick, deep yellow liquid, he asked, "What do you taste?"

"Cream and pear and . . . pineapples." She opened her eyes, amazed.

He took a bite of pear and cheese, then sipped his own wine. "Pineapples. Wonderful. A few years ago, someone introduced me to the combination of sauterne and blue-veined cheese. There's a strange synergy. The whole taste is so much more than the sum of its parts." He spread another bit of cheese on another piece of fruit and offered it to Jessica.

She took it from him, placed it on her tongue, and sipped the sauterne. "It is wonderful, but if I have much more to drink,

I'll be incoherent." She dropped onto her back on the soft blanket.

Eric took the glass from her hand. "I certainly don't want you incoherent. I want you to be fully aware of everything that happens."

"And what is going to happen?" Jessica asked, the words out of her mouth before she could stop them.

Eric grinned and licked a tiny crumb of cheese from her lower lip. "Everything and nothing."

"What does that mean?"

"Everything means that I'm going to spend the rest of the evening seducing you with wine and food, music and evening breezes and me."

"And nothing?"

"Nothing means that as much as I want to, and, I hope, as much as you will want me to, I'm not going to make love to you tonight."

"Why not?"

"Because I want you to anticipate how wonderful it will be with us when I undress you and touch you and lick every inch of your skin. I want you to wonder how it will feel when I slide, ever so slowly, into your body and feel your hips reaching for me, unable to wait any longer.

"Then I want you to think about it in the cold, sober light of day. Sex for the sake of sex. Not love, just desire. Then you can decide whether that is truly what you want."

Jessica sighed and closed her eyes. Her thighs were trembling and her heart was pounding. She did want him. Badly. She felt a tickling on her neck and reached up to brush it away. As her hand dropped she felt the tickling again. She slowly opened her eyes and saw Eric, his face close to hers, a blade of grass in his hand. "I know what I want right now," she whispered, unable to stop the words.

"Maybe you do. But I know what we're not going to do. It's important to me that we don't make love because of too much wine or too long since the last time." He saw the disappointment on Jessica's face. "Oh lord," he said, smiling. "This is going to be a long and singularly frustrating evening." He tossed the grass aside and sat up. "I owe you an explanation. About Timmy and all."

Jessica sighed and partially shook off the cloud of desire that surrounded her. She sat up and poured herself a cup of steaming coffee. She looked at him and lifted a cup. When he shook his head, she put the decanter down and added milk to her coffee. "Okay. Tell me."

"Marilyn, my ex-wife, must be, in some ways, the unluckiest woman in the world. When we split, I was, as you put it, a humble architect. I made eighty thousand a year, a nice salary but not enough for her, so she went looking for greener pastures. Maybe there was a deeper reason. But money seemed to be all she thought about."

"Don't tell me you won the lottery or something."

"Let me give you a little background," He sipped his sauterne and watched the people wandering past them. In the far distance he could hear the sensual sound of a clarinet tuning up. "My father took off when I was seven. I think my mother was glad to see him go although it meant that she had to work. He was a heavy drinker, a gambler, a womanizer, and a general pain in the ass. He was never abusive, or anything like that. It was just that he was totally unpredictable. Rich and expansive one minute, poor and depressive the next. He wouldn't come home for days, even weeks at a time. Then he'd arrive home like the prodigal son, frequently reeking of perfume. Of course, at the time, I idolized him, thought he was the greatest, especially when he arrived with his arms full of presents."

"It must have been a tough life for you."

"My mom was a very sane, down-to-earth woman and I was a very happy child in spite of my on-again, off-again father."

Jessica smiled. "You were lucky."

"I guess I was. One evening, my dad arrived home after almost two weeks, and told my mom that he was leaving for good. He packed his things in an old black-and-white suitcase and disappeared. My mom cried for about a week, then pulled herself together and made a good life for herself. She had worked in a local nursing home as an aide and discovered that she enjoyed helping older people. So she put herself through nursing school, then made enough to put me through college. She died the year after I graduated."

"She sounds like a nice woman."

Eric's face softened. "She was the best. Anyway, about a year after Marilyn and I split, I received a visit from a lawyer. My father, it turns out, had done okay for himself. He'd ended up in Vegas and amassed a small fortune. Before he died, he had a will drawn up leaving everything to me. There was a letter from him for me, too. He tried to explain that although he didn't consider himself a bad man, he had been a terrible husband and a worse father and that we had been better off without him. He said that he had spent a lot of years broke and then started a run of luck and had gotten some money together. He hired an investigator who learned that my mom had died and that I was doing very well on my own." Eric ran his long slender fingers through his iron-gray hair.

"Personally, I think he didn't contact me then because we had almost nothing in common except some genetic material. I don't remember him as a bad father, but that's the way he thought about things. I'm just sorry that my mother didn't live to know that he still thought about us. Anyway, I inherited everything. Including Timmy."

"Including Timmy?"

"He was my father's bodyguard, and, I gather, he needed one. He was in some pretty ugly businesses with some pretty nasty people. My father won Timmy, who had spent a few years as a professional wrestler, in a poker game almost ten years before he died. His old manager put up his contract in lieu of five thousand dollars. Fortunately for both my father and Timmy, the manager's full boat, aces over sixes, wasn't as good as my father's four deuces.

"Timmy's a gem and a thoroughly nice man. He was unquestionably loyal and able to take care of himself and my father, particularly in my dad's final months which, I gather, were lousy. Timmy won't talk about those years and the things my father was into. He says it's a closed book now that he's dead. And I guess it is."

"How could he leave Timmy to you?" Jessica asked. "It sounds like some kind of indentured servitude."

"Not at all. My father got to know Timmy very well. Although he left him a generous amount of cash in his will, my father left Timmy something more important. One section of the will guarantees him a job with me for as long as he wants. And that's all he wants. I guess he's like my mom. He wants to take care of someone the way he took care of my father, and he stays because he wants to. He keeps the money my dad left him in the bank. 'For his old age,' he says."

"Your dad sound like a very perceptive man."

"He was."

"And Timmy's cooking?"

"That had been a hobby of his for many years. He used to cook for my father, who taught Timmy to enjoy fine food and good wine. After my father's death, Timmy told me that he had always wanted to study seriously so I encouraged him to take a year to study at the Culinary Institute. Now, as you've gathered, it's more than just a hobby—it's a passion."

"That's quite a story."

Distant strains of jazz filtered through the evening air. "The music's starting," Eric said, stretching out on the blanket. "They discourage listening from here rather than going to the terrace, but I bought six tickets and made a special plea to the staff so they'll leave us alone."

Jessica stretched out beside Eric, her head buzzing with the wine and the music and the feel of Eric's fingers entwined with hers. Together they watched the sky darken and the stars appear while they listened to an erotic baritone saxophone. From time to time, Eric would lift Jessica's hand to his lips and kiss her knuckles, or nip one fingertip. As the first half of the concert ended, he sucked her index finger into his hot mouth and swirled his tongue around the tip.

To calm her fluttering stomach, she said, "With this inheritance of yours, do you still design buildings?"

He chuckled. "Getting too hot for you?" He sucked her finger again, then answered, "Sure. I like to be productive and I don't know what else I'd do. I do one or two projects each year, overall design, not the bathroom fixtures or landscaping. I keep my job within strict limits. I never take on a project that will occupy more time than I want to give, leaving the rest of my time for the parts of my life that give me joy." He bit the tip of Jessica's finger, then swirled his tongue around the palm. "How about you? What was your family life like as a kid?"

Jessica struggled to concentrate enough to answer his question. "Dull. I was born and brought up in Ottawa, Illinois, a small town near Chicago. Steph and I went to high school together and that's where she met Brian and I met Rob, my ex-husband."

Jessica tried to gently withdraw her hand from Eric's but he held her fast. "Tell me about him. He must be some kind of idiot to let something as gorgeous and sexy as you get away."

"I don't mean to make him sound like a total jerk," Jessica said, finally pulling her hand away from Eric. "We met in high school and he knew precisely what he wanted out of life, so it happened. Dental school and a very busy practice in Ottawa."

When Eric took her hand again she sighed and didn't try to pull away. "I gathered from your conversation Saturday night that you and he weren't setting the world on fire in the bedroom."

Jessica laughed softly. "No, we weren't. Most of our problems in bed were probably due to inexperience. We were both virgins or close enough for government work when we met and there never was anyone else for either of us. Not until bimbo."

"He found a sweet young thing?"

Jessica told him about finding Rob in his office that afternoon so many months before. When he laughed at her version of the story, he apologized. "Don't apologize." she said. "Now, looking back on it, it was pretty funny. At the time, however, it seemed my life had ended."

Eric propped himself up on one elbow and slid the tip of his tongue across Jessica's lips. "And how does it seem now?"

Jessica reached up, cupped the back of Eric's head and smiled as she touched her lips to his. "It seems like it might have been the best thing that ever happened to me." When she felt his mouth on hers, it was soft and warm and incredibly exciting. They kissed for a long time, savoring the taste and feel of each other's lips and tongue. Eric stroked Jessica's side until she longed for the feel of his hands on her breasts.

As the second half of the concert began, Jessica lay on her back on the blanket with Eric, who propped himself on his elbow, gazing down at her. "Even though you can barely see me in the dark, you make me self-conscious when you look at me like that," she said.

"Uncomfortable?"

"A little."

"Good. You make me uncomfortable too. All I can think of is how much I want you."

Jessica closed her eyes as Eric continued, "Do you know how it will be with us? It will begin with a glow, soft and warm and gentle. Slowly it will build until it will blaze with fire too hot to touch but too sweet to resist." His hand lay on her flat belly, fingers widely spread. "I can feel your muscles tighten when you're excited. Like now." He placed his mouth beside her ear, his breath tickling her. "I can tell you some of the things we're going to do. Would you like that?"

She groaned. "Tell me."

"First, I'll unbutton your blouse. Wear a blouse next time so I can open each button and lick your skin as I expose what's beneath the material." He ran his finger down her breastbone to the first button of her blouse, then up to the hollow of her neck, feeling her shiver.

"Then I'll open your bra so I can admire your beautiful breasts. I've seen them in my dreams, full and white with hard, dusky brown nipples. They'll be so hard and hungry that I won't be able to resist taking one in my mouth. They will taste of your skin, spicy, tight little nubs. I'll use my teeth and you'll try to pull away from the slight pain, until it turns to hot pleasure flowing through your body." He slid his hand lower, until his fingers rested between Jessica's thighs.

"Then I'll slide your bra and your slacks off until you're wearing only your panties. Have you ever been stroked through the silk of your panties? It slightly muffles the sensation, making it softer, and more delicate." He felt the heat of her body through the crotch of her jeans and slowly rubbed. "I'll rub you there, slowly, back and forth, back and forth until you're filled with such heat that it's hard for you to breathe." He rested his head on his upper arm and used his now-free hand to draw her hair from the comb that held it. "I'll run my fingers through your deep red hair, both here on your head and between your legs."

Jessica tried to draw air into her lungs, but she could only tremble and respond to Eric's touch. The rhythmic pressure of his hand between her legs was becoming almost torture. She wanted him inside of her, to fill her and satisfy the unending hunger he was creating. "Oh Eric," she whispered.

"You'll be so wet and slippery that I'll want to slide my fingers into your body. Maybe one finger, deep inside, maybe two or even three, filling you completely. And you'll be moving your hips, trying to capture my fingers, pull them in deeper."

As he rubbed her body through her jeans, Jessica felt the pressure build somewhere deep inside and flow through her groin and thighs. It grew hotter and hotter, like a fire consuming, yet not satisfying. "So good," she moaned.

Eric placed Jessica's hand over his between her legs. "Feel me rubbing you."

She rested her hand against his and felt the movement of his fingers. "Oh God."

"I'll keep stroking you until you want me more than you've ever wanted anything in your life. My cock will be so hard that it will hurt, but I'll wait until I feel your muscles tense and your back arch like it is now. Yes, baby, let it go. Come for me, baby. Do it."

The fire inside of Jessica's belly smoldered into life. She ignited hot and white, flames roaring in her ears. As she started to moan, Eric covered her mouth with his own, filling himself with her climax. Despite her writhing, Eric managed to keep his fingers between her legs, draining her of the remnants of her orgasm, drawing the final notes from her now-quieting body.

"Oh my God," Jessica breathed, shaking her head in amazement. "Never. . . ."

Eric grinned. "Never what?"

"Never before like that." She tried to catch her breath.

His eyes widened. "You mean no one's ever touched you like that. Your husband never. . . ."

Jessica reached up and pressed her fingers over Eric's lips. "I've never climaxed like that before." As he started to ask more questions, she kept his lips still with her finger. "Give me a sip of coffee and I'll try to explain. Let me catch my breath."

Eric poured Jessica another cup of coffee, then cooled and diluted it with lots of milk. She took the cup in a still-trembling hand and drank the contents. Then she dropped back onto the blanket. "Rob and I were into very simple sex. He loved my breasts. He said they got him hot just thinking about them. When he wanted to make love, which was two or three times a week, although much less frequently toward the end, he'd take off my pajama tops, suckle until he was excited and hard, then we'd do it. You know, missionary position."

"Nothing creative?"

Jessica chuckled. "Being creative wasn't Rob's strong suit. And I didn't know any better. Until now."

A grin split Eric's face. He'd done it for her. "Oh, Jessica. Making love to you is so good."

"It will be."

"It was. What do you think we just did? That was making love just as surely as fucking is. Making love is sharing all the sexual pleasures we can. And there are so many."

Eric became aware that the air was silent. No music. He sat up and looked around. Clusters of people were ambling toward the parking lot. He glanced at his watch. "Good grief, it's almost midnight. Time to get Cinderella back to her castle."

Together they packed the remains of the fruit, wine, and coffee in the hamper, folded the blanket, and placed it on top of the lid. Eric and Jessica each took a handle and they walked back to the car in silence, through the soft summer evening.

When Eric dropped her off at Steph's house, Jessica said, "I don't know what to say, Eric."

"I'd like to invite you to my house, but you need to make a decision before then. In the light of day and with a clear understanding of what it means."

"And what does it mean?"

"It means that I want to share some wonderful pleasures with you. I want to make love to you for several hours, then relax and make love again. It doesn't necessarily mean that I want to spend the rest of my life with you or that I want to be with you and you alone. That's very important. I like you and I want to fuck you until we're both exhausted."

"It's hard for me to grasp. Sex for the fun of it. Like tonight."

"Sex for the fun of it." He thought about it. "That's exactly right. Sex for the fun of it. Think about it, Jessica. I'll call you in a few days."

"I won't be able to think of much else."

Eric leaned across the gearshift lever and placed a soft kiss on Jessica's mouth. "Good night, sexy lady."

"Good night, Eric."

* * *

In her room, Jessica stripped off her clothes and climbed into bed. Sleep, however, was impossible. She lectured herself all night.

Sport fucking, she told herself. That's all it is. Fucking because it feels good seems so . . . sinful. But yet so wonderful. For once, my sexual world is filled with light and pleasure.

Am I in love with Eric? No, she argued, I'm not. Would it make it easier if I believed that I were? Yes. And no. I'm infatuated. That's what it is, and it feels good. And I want more of his love-making. It's like I have a new toy and I want to play with it.

And what's wrong with that.

By morning, she had debated, argued, vacillated, and finally arrived at the conclusion that she wanted to make love with Eric just because it would feel good. And, for once in her life she was going to do something for herself, just because she wanted to.

Steph and Brian were out for the day and Jessica needed an outlet for her new feelings of freedom. She called a rental car company that specialized in sports cars and asked them to deliver a tiny red Alfa Romeo convertible. When the rental agent asked how long she'd be keeping the car, she told them that she had no idea. "Just give me the weekly rate for two weeks and I'll call a few days before the end of the second week and let you know." She gave them her credit card number and hung up.

Two hours later, when the man arrived with her car, she drove him back to the agency, then put the convertible top down, pulled the rubber band from her hair and spent the rest of the morning driving around Westchester County. With the radio turned up loud and the wind in her hair, she felt fifteen years younger than her thirty-six years.

She drove to the Bronx Botanical Gardens and wandered the grounds, stopping to smell the flowers. She ate a hot dog at the Old Snuff Mill, then, realizing she was starving, ordered and ate another, this one smothered in sauerkraut and pickle relish. She drove up to the Bear Mountain Bridge, found a place to park at the Westchester end and walked across and back.

On her way home late that afternoon, she stopped at a delicatessen and picked up a pastrami sandwich with cole slaw and Russian dressing and a sour pickle. Back at Steph's she sat in the kitchen and devoured every bite, washing it all down with three Samuel Adams Dark Beers.

Then she dialed Eric's number. When she heard his voice, she said, "It's Jessica."

"Well, hello," Eric said, his voice tentative. "I didn't expect to hear from you."

"I didn't expect to call, but I wanted to thank you for last evening." She told him about the car she'd rented and the day she had spent. "I feel so good, I just had to thank you. It's like my life is just beginning."

"I'm so glad to be part of that."

"I feel a bit awkward, but I wanted to ask when we can get together again."

"You're sure you understand everything?" Eric said.

When Eric spoke, Jessica could hear the smile in his voice. "I know that what we did last evening felt wonderful and I want to explore," she said. "I'll probably chicken out several times before I see you again, but in my heart of hearts, I know that this is what I want. And, of course, I've had three beers and I'm smashed."

Eric laughed. "I don't want to take advantage. Are you really drunk?"

"No," Jessica admitted. "But it's a good excuse to let go and do what I want."

"Can I pick you up in half an hour?"

She glanced at the clock. It was 7:30. "I'd like that," Jessica said, smiling.

"I'll see you at eight o'clock."

Jessica hung up the phone and giggled. "I've got a date and I know what I'm going to be doing." Her body sang and her mound throbbed. "Jessica," she told herself aloud, "you're a piece of work."

She took a two-minute shower, then put on a short-sleeved red blouse, a pair of white slacks and white flats. She brushed on a bit of blush, lipstick and left her hair loose. She had just left a note on the kitchen table, telling Steph and Brian that she was out and she didn't know when she'd be back when she heard Eric ring the doorbell.

Jessica opened the door and Eric filled the opening. He was wearing the same soft jeans he had worn the evening before, this time with a tailored, navy-blue polo shirt.

"Oh Lord," he said, staring at her, "I feel like a starving man gazing at a gourmet feast."

"You're looking at me like I'm the blue-plate special," she said, squirming.

"Am I embarrassing you?"

"A bit. But I like the way you look at me." She grabbed her purse and closed the door behind her.

"Can we take your car?" Eric asked. "It's warm and I'd love to drive with the top down."

Jessica fumbled in her purse and found the keys. She tossed them to Eric who opened the passenger door for her. Then he climbed into the driver's seat and started the engine. "Do something for me," he said. "Take off your bra."

Jessica paused for a moment, then turned away from him. She unbuttoned her blouse, unhooked her bra, and wriggled it off. She rebuttoned the blouse, feeling the fabric brush across her erect nipples. She stuffed the bra in her purse, snapped her seat belt, and lay her head back against the headrest.

"Nice," Eric said. "That belt falls just in the right spot, right between your luscious breasts." He reached over and traced the belt with his fingers. "Unbutton the blouse so you can feel the wind on your skin."

Jessica gave him a questioning look. Then she opened the buttons and spread the sides so the red fabric just covered her areolas. The canvas of the seat belt was cold against her bare chest.

"Oh yes," Eric said. "We're going to have everything." He tuned the radio and, as they drove out of the driveway, Frank Sinatra's voice filled the warm night.

During the five-minute drive to Eric's house, Jessica closed her eyes and let the sensuality carry her. The wind was cool on her naked skin, the radio mellow. The air smelled sweet, of summer flowers. She was almost disappointed when they drove up the driveway of Eric's house. As the car stopped, Jessica couldn't believe the building in front of her. "You designed this?"

"Yes." The building seemed to be made of rock and glass, lean and low to the ground, almost growing out of the earth. Although the rooms appeared square, each one was at an angle to its neighbor, gently slanting roofs complementing each other. It was a strange harmony of unusual shapes, softened by lots of hundred-year-old maples. "It was an idea of mine that I adapted to this piece of land. You can't see much from here but there's a rocky pool with a little waterfall on this side," he pointed, "and woods in the back. Real woods. We cut down only one tree."

"I want to see it during the daytime. It must be magnificent."

His laughter was deep in his throat. "Some say yes and some think it's ugly. I like it and I'm all that counts." He ushered Jessica inside, through the darkened living room, up the stairs, through the master bedroom, and into the master bath. He lit a small oil lamp in the corner and began to light candles.

"Oh my," she said. The room was dominated by a huge two-person tub that nestled in an alcove surrounded by a redwood-and-tile ledge covered with pots of ferns, interspersed with dozens of glass containers of clear oil with wicks floating inside. Eric poured bath oil into the tub and turned on the tap. Then he lit each candle and they both watched as shadows danced and flickered on the walls and ceiling. The scent of greenery with a hint of flowers filled the room. "Lavender," Jessica whispered.

"Just a wisp, one candle. And, from now on, every time I smell it, I'll think of you." He lit the last candle, turned to a wine bucket he had placed beside the tub and picked out the bottle. He lifted Jessica's right hand, turned it palm up and cupped it in his large hand. Then he poured a tablespoon of cold wine into her palm, leaned down and licked it up with his rough tongue.

Then he filled his palm and held it out to Jessica. She held his hand in hers and slowly licked the wine from his skin. She slid the tip of her tongue down his index finger, then nipped at the tip. She was wanton. She was brazen. She was free.

"Oh, baby," he groaned as she nibbled on the end of his finger. "I thought you were new at this."

"I am," she whispered. "I'm just learning."

"You learn too well," Eric said, pulling his hand away. "I want to take it slowly. Very slowly. I want us to savor every step, every pleasure."

Jessica wanted to take it all slowly, but her body ached for what she knew would happen. She was excited, her body and soul reaching for something she knew she could have at last. She took a deep breath and stepped back. She looked behind Eric and saw the mountain of bubbles threatening to overflow the huge tub. "Eric," she whispered, "we're about to have a minor flood."

Eric turned around and grabbed for the taps, turning them off just before the water sloshed over the edge. "A long time ago I covered the overflow drain with tape so I could fill this beast as high as I liked. I've never lost track of time before." He released the drain to allow a little water to empty from the tub.

"Thank you. I take that as a compliment."

"Oh, believe me, it is." He filled two wine glasses and handed one to Jessica. "Sorry about the plastic, but I won't have glass in here."

"I like the cups we used a moment ago better," she said, raising the glass to her lips and looking up at Eric through lowered lids. She was flirting. She was playing. She tried to control her grin, but didn't succeed. "Oh God," she said, "I'm so happy."

"And a bit drunk?"

"Just enough."

Once a few inches of water had drained from the tub Eric replaced the stopper. "Our bath awaits." He pulled off his shirt, pants and shorts, kicked off his shoes and stepped into the bubbles.

Jessica saw only his back, smooth and firm with tight buttocks and well-muscled legs. He had just a little extra weight, enough to make him look soft and inviting. He kept his back to her, fussing with a few more candles.

Now she had to undress. Can I do this? Can I take off my clothes in front of a man I've known for less than a week? Quickly, while his back was turned, she pulled off her clothes, stepped into the water and sat down, covering herself with bubbles. This makes no sense, she thought. I've made a decision, I've licked wine from his palm and nibbled on his fingers. Why now am I afraid of his seeing me naked?

"Can I turn around now?" Eric asked.

"You knew?"

"Jessica, my sweet, your mixed emotions are written all over your lovely face." He turned, settled into the warm water, took her hand and held it. "I want this to be your decision all the way. I want you to want me and want my lovemaking. And I want you to explore all the things that give you pleasure. I will never knowingly embarrass you, although it might happen without my realizing it, I'm afraid."

"Thank you for understanding my confusion."

"I want you to promise me something. Some things we do will make you want to laugh. Silly stuff. And if you want to laugh, do it. I want this to be fun. Some things we might try will make you a bit uncomfortable and some discomfort is very exciting. But if we ever do anything that makes you want to stop, you must say so. Immediately. Just say 'Eric, stop' and I will. Promise me."

"I promise."

Eric placed a palm on each side of Jessica's face and gazed into her eyes. "If I can be sure that you will tell me to stop, I can do so many things we might enjoy."

"I do promise, Eric."

They were facing each other in the giant tub of warm, bubbly water. Holding her face in his palms, he caressed her with his gaze, softly sweeping from her sea-green eyes to her lips to the sensual line of her throat. "So lovely," he whispered, stroking her cheeks with his thumbs. "Half of me wants to grab you by that gorgeous red hair of yours, throw you down on the floor, and fuck you until we're both exhausted, the other half wants to savor this and make our loving last all night."

She remained silent, enjoying the warm, sensual web he was spinning around her. Slowly all worries about how briefly she'd known Eric ebbed. She wanted him to make love to her. It was that simple. She picked up a cake of soap and lathered her hands. She placed her palms on his shoulders and made lathery circles on his biceps. She felt him lower his hands into the water as she spread lather onto his upper chest. Smooth, tight skin covered his well-developed muscles.

As she slid her slippery hands up the sides of Eric's neck, she watched his head fall slowly backward, exposing his throat to her caress. There was something so intimate about the motion that she smiled and rubbed her thumbs along the line of his jaw. She closed her eyes and her hands returned to his chest, swirling through the soapy lather. "Mmmm. You feel so hard and smooth." Rob has curly chest hair, she thought, then pushed the thought aside.

She opened her eyes and found Eric looking at her. "I told you before that your face tells all. Were you thinking about your ex-husband?"

Without stilling her hands, she said, "Yes. But he's gone now."

"No he's not," Eric said, "and that's okay. He's the only man you've ever been with and it's natural that you should think of him right now. I don't mind."

"He's a fool."

"That may be true, but he's your only measuring device." Eric reached under the bubbles and cupped her breasts in his hands. "I, on the other hand, have had enough experience to know that you will be a sensual delight." He rubbed his thumbs over her nipples and felt them contract until they were tight under his fingers. "We will learn to share so many pleasures." He leaned forward and placed a soft kiss on Jessica's lips. Then he soaped his hands and rubbed the lightly scented lavender soap over her shoulders and upper arms. "Your skin is so soft." He increased the size of the soapy circles until his hands slipped under the water and caressed her breasts.

Jessica let her head fall back, soaking in Eric's touches as she soaked in the water. Her ribs, her underarms, her neck and arms, she felt Eric stroke them all. Then he lifted one of her hands out of the water and carefully soaped each finger, sliding his fingers between hers. Then he dipped the hand into the water and sucked the tip. "You taste soapy," he said. He picked up his wine glass and poured a bit of the cold, clear liquid over her fingers, then drew each, in turn, into his mouth. "Delicious," he whispered. He repeated the ablutions with her other hand.

"I'd like to make love to you right here," he said, "but we need to shower off first."

Puzzled, Jessica looked at him. "They always do it in hot tubs in movies."

"In movies, the actors aren't really covered with soap, that might irritate your tender body. In addition, let me show you something about hot water." He stood up, water and bubbles pouring from his slight belly.

Jessica couldn't help gazing at his penis, small and flaccid. I am a failure, she told herself. Rob was right. I am frigid.

Laughing, Eric said, "Hot water and too much wine. Not you, my love." He lifted her into a standing position and sluiced water and soap from her body with the flats of his hands. "Definitely not you." He caught the drop of soapy water at the tip of one breast with the tip of his tongue.

Jessica shuddered, not sure whether Eric was lying to save her from embarrassment. She watched Eric pull a shower curtain across the open side of the alcove, release the tub's drain, and reach for the shower controls. Suddenly the alcove was filled with soft, warm spray, coming from shower heads in each corner at once. "It's like a soft summer rain," she said.

"There are several settings, but this one is designed for moments like this." As water drained from the tub, warm water poured over their bodies and Jessica turned her face to the spray, rinsing off all traces of soap. "Done?" Eric asked.

"Ummm," she purred.

Eric turned off the water, opened the curtain and wrapped Jessica in a thick, thirsty bath sheet. As she rubbed her hair, Eric, a towel around his waist, walked out through the connecting door. Slowly, as she watched, candlelight began to dance on the walls of the bedroom.

Without giving Jessica time to think, Eric returned, swept her into his arms, and carried her to the bed. He spread a dry towel on the satin spread, laid her on it and stepped back, feasting on her naked body. "God, you're lovely." He nipped her toes and kissed his way up her shin.

Jessica looked at the wavy gray hair on the man who was quite purposefully making love to her. It wasn't Rob. It was Eric. Then she felt Eric's hot breath on the hair between her legs and she couldn't think anymore. Reflexively, she pulled her knees together.

"Oh, baby," Eric whispered. "You're so sweet." He pulled her legs open and blew a cool stream of air on the hot flesh between her thighs.

"But. . . ." She willed her muscles to relax, but they wouldn't.

"Rob never kissed you here?" he asked.

"No." Her voice was barely audible.

"Does it feel bad?"

"I don't think so. Just odd."

He lightly rubbed his index finger over her clitoris. "And this?"

Her mind was filled with colors, swirling reds and purples, oranges and bright sulfurous yellows. "God no. It feels . . . indescribable."

"How about this?" He surrounded her clit with his lips, swirled his tongue across it, then sucked it into his mouth. As he felt her body tighten, he slid two fingers into her drenched pussy.

The sensations were too much for Jessica. The colors exploded, pinwheels and kaleidoscopes, angles and shards of color and light. "Eric," she screamed, arching her back and clenching her fists. "Eric."

"There's so much more I want with you," Eric said, "but I can't wait right now." He unwrapped a condom, unrolled the latex over his engorged penis, crouched between Jessica's legs and pressed his cock against her opening. "Feel that?" he said. "Feel how hard for you?" He slid it into her passage, a bit at a time. "Feel how it fills you, stretches you? Feel how I want you." When he had filled her completely, he held still above her, balanced on the heels of his hands. "Open your eyes, Jessica. Look at the man who wants you beyond everything right now."

Jessica opened her eyes and looked at Eric, his face tight as he held his body in check for one last moment. She watched the control in his passion-clouded eyes. *That passion and control is for me,* she thought. A small smile curled the corners of her mouth. He was holding back. He was controlling his excitement. She clenched her vaginal muscles and squeezed the cock that filled her.

"Oh baby," he groaned, pulling back, then plunging deeper inside, giving in to the needs of his body.

Jessica's last coherent thought was that she had caused him to lose control. She, Jessica. One-time frigid wife of Rob the asshole. *Oh lord, I've missed so much. But not anymore.* Then waves of an incredibly intense orgasm overtook her.

FIVE

They lay together on the bed, and dozed for almost an hour. When she opened her eyes Jessica found Eric gazing at her. "You're staring," she said, a grin spreading across her face.

"I guess I am. I knew you'd be wonderful, but I didn't expect to be overwhelmed."

Jessica giggled. "I'm overwhelming, am I?"

"Jessica, you're priceless and wonderful. Not only do I get the joy of making love with you, but I get the delight of watching you discover yourself. What more is there?"

Jessica turned and propped herself on her elbow. "This takes a bit of getting used to," she admitted. "I guess I've been told that there was something lacking in me for so long that it's hard to grok that it wasn't true."

"Grok?"

"My word, actually Heinlein's, for something that's even deeper than just understanding. It's like someone telling you that the world really is flat and that round was just propaganda."

"You've got an unusually honest way of looking at things."

"Maybe I do. It's just that here and now, I find it necessary to put some things into words for which there aren't really words."

"Ummm." Eric took her hand. "Can I tell you something very personal, Jessica?"

Was he going to reject her? Tell her she really was frigid? Fearing the worst, Jessica tightened her abdominal muscles, closed her eyes, and nodded.

Eric barked a single laugh. "Oh baby, don't look so stricken." He kissed her fingers. "I just want to say that I'm starved. I was so excited when you called that I never ate dinner."

Jessica let out a long breath, then cocked her head to one side. "Me too." She rolled over on her back and grinned, sliding her arms and legs over the sheets like she used to as a child when she and her friends made snow angels. Life was fun.

Eric got them each a fluffy, terrycloth bathrobe and, laughing like schoolchildren, they ran down to the kitchen. Jessica walked into the white Formica room and gasped. It was larger than her living room in Ottawa.

"I know," Eric said. "It's ridiculous. But it's Timmy's playground and I let him design it when I built the house."

"I can see that," Jessica said, gazing at the wide counters, hanging baker's racks, and masses of cabinets and closets. There was a six-burner stove, a microwave, a conventional oven, and a convection one. Eric crossed to the industrial-size refrigerator that dominated one end of the room and opened the double doors. "You know," he said, reaching for a slice of strawberry cheesecake, "one should really eat healthy stuff, especially after good sex."

"One certainly should," Jessica said, looking over his shoulder at the second shelf, which held a plastic container of something that appeared to be chocolate pudding.

Eric put the cheesecake on the counter, then grabbed a jar of peanut butter and a loaf of bread from the refrigerator. "Good choice," Jessica said, grabbing the pudding, then shutting the door with her hip. "Got a toaster?"

"You're kidding. Toast and peanut butter was always my favorite. I haven't had it since Timmy arrived."

"And where is he tonight?" Jessica asked, inserting two slices of white bread into the toaster.

"I gave him a quarter and sent him to the movies." When Jessica laughed, he admitted, "Actually, Timmy lives in the guest house on the far side of the garage and I saw him earlier, just getting back from a day with friends in Jersey. When you called I asked him to stay away from the house for the evening." He winked. "Timmy said to say hello to you."

Blushing slightly, Jessica said, "He knows? About us? About this?"

"He knows that I find you exciting and that I intended to do something to scratch the itch, yes."

The toast popped up and Jessica put the two slices on a plate and put two more into the toaster. She handed the plate to Eric who slathered chunky peanut butter on each piece. "You know what goes with toast and peanut butter?" he asked.

"What?"

"V8."

"We must be long-lost twins," Jessica said, smiling. "When I was in high school on my way home I would stop at the store and get a loaf of bread, a jar of Skippy, and the oversized can of V8."

"Actually," Eric said, getting glasses from an upper cabinet, "you were much healthier than I was. I'd usually get a bag of potato chips, a container of sour cream, and a box of onion soup mix. That and a bottle of Pepsi and I was set for the afternoon. Peanut butter and V8 were for bedtime."

"Were you into sports or after-school activities?"

"I went to elementary and junior high school in Manhattan." Eric pulled out a large can of juice and filled two glasses with thick, red liquid. "There wasn't much of that sort of stuff to do. Then I went to Bronx Science High School, mostly eggheads with a calculator in their pocket. I guess I was a bit of a nerd."

"I was the artsy type back then," Jessica said. "Before I met Rob, I was into writing, both short stories and, of all things, poetry."

"Why do you say 'of all things' like that? What's wrong with writing poetry?"

"Nothing, really. I just wasn't the type."

"And why not? What type writes poetry?"

"People with things worth saying. Important things about life and love."

"Nonsense. People write poetry because they want to write poetry. Even I wrote some at one time. Did you write good poetry?"

"Oh lord. It was very free-form, sophomoric stuff filled with suppressed desire. You know, now that I think back, it was probably sexual frustration, pure and simple. In most of my images, two lovers raced toward each other across a flower-filled meadow. That sort of thing." The toaster popped and Jessica put a piece of toast on top of each peanut-buttered one.

"Ummm, suppressed sexual desire. I like that. But now that it's not suppressed anymore, you'll just have to write some erotic poetry and attend one of our evening readings."

"Readings?"

"You know there are several people, including a few whom you met at Steph's party, who make up a very enlightened group. We sometimes get together and read erotic literature out loud, and sometimes Gary tells a story."

"I've heard about Gary. Steph told me he gives great parties. She didn't elaborate."

"He does, and he has the money to indulge in all his hitherto suppressed sexual desires. He has the most wonderful imagination and has no reticence about using it to plan outrageous gatherings."

"Erotic readings?" Jessica smiled.

"Don't laugh. At one of his parties, Gary turned out the lights and we all lay around on the floor while he told erotic fantasy tales. There was a lot of suppressed desire when he was done, I'll tell you, although it didn't remain suppressed for long."

Jessica took a bite of her sandwich and chewed for a minute.

This was still all so new to her. "Ummm," she said. "Good peanut butter." Her words came out muffled through the mouthful.

"You make a hell of a sandwich," said Eric. Sensing her need to digest more than the peanut butter, Eric let the conversation veer off in a different direction. They shared their companionable meal, then pigged out on chocolate pudding and Timmy's best strawberry cheesecake. When they had put the dishes in the dishwasher, Eric said abruptly, "I think it's time for me to drive you home."

Nodding, Jessica said, "I think I understand." Eric had made the rules and they both were keeping their new-found intimacy within tight boundaries.

When Eric grinned, Jessica continued, "But we'll see each other soon, I hope."

"That's the difficult part. I'm sorry to say that I have an assignment that requires my presence in San Francisco. My job only demands that I be on site occasionally, but this is one of those occasions. I found out today that I have to leave first thing tomorrow so I can be ready for Monday morning. Then I'll work all week and red-eye back Friday night. The timing stinks."

"Yeah. It does," Jessica said, disappointed that they weren't going to see each other for a week. Sexual freedom felt like her new toy and she wanted to play with it. "We can talk on the phone, though."

"Of course." He told her the name of his hotel and they arranged for her to call. Then he hugged her and they went back upstairs, located their clothes and dressed in silence. As they climbed into Jessica's car, Eric said, "We need to be totally honest from the outset. Sex can be good with anyone who has an open mind and a desire to please."

"I know. But I have just come to terms with extracurricular activities with you."

"Extracurricular activities. That's one way to put it. Just remember, however, that you have no curriculum any more. Play. Have fun. Rob is history and good riddance."

"To bad rubbish."

It was almost one in the morning when they drove into the driveway and parked next to the Carltons' two cars. Eric kissed her hard, then quickly climbed into his own car and drove away.

Jessica gazed after him, then turned. She walked over to Brian's car and stopped, resting her hand on the cold hood. "Extracurricular activities." She slid her hand along the highly waxed surface, then walked into the house.

Stephanie found Jessica the following morning, sitting in the plant room staring into space. "Morning, Jessica," Steph said.

Jessica looked up. "Morning," she said, a strange look on her face.

"We saw Eric's car when we got in last evening," Steph said, "and I got your note. Wanna tell me about it?"

"Eric and I went back to his place."

"And. . . ."

Jessica burst into delighted laughter. "And wow and double wow. It was sensational. Lights, colors, bells, whistles, candlelight, and peanut butter."

"Peanut butter?" Steph settled into the chair next to her best friend.

"Oh, Steph, I'm so glad I came to Harrison."

"So am I. Are you and Eric an item? He's a really nice man and Brian and I are very fond of him."

"Not exactly an item. Not that way. We understand each other. We make love like rockets and supernovas, but it doesn't mean anything more than that."

"Sounds like you're a different person than you were when you left Illinois."

"Well," Jessica giggled, "I know I'm not in Kansas anymore. God, who's been hiding orgasms all these years. I think mine registered on the Richter scale at one point."

Steph leaned over and hugged Jessica. "I'm so happy for you.

Maybe we should send scrawny-neck and bimbette a blow by blow. Pardon the expression."

"I don't even want to think about Rob. You know, though, I feel kinda sorry for him. He has no idea what he's missing."

"Are you seeing Eric tonight?"

"That's the sad part. Even as we speak, he's winging his way to the west coast. Some big job he's got to work on."

"Oh, Jessica, that's too bad. How long will he be gone?"

"Til the end of the week, he thinks. We have a date for next Saturday."

"That's great. Eric's a wonderful guy." Steph looked at her watch. "Okay. It's almost nine and Brian's still in bed. What shall we do today?"

"Let's drive around, have a high-calorie lunch, and pick up guys."

"JessicaLynn Hanley, I love you." Her voice dropped. "There's a party a week from Saturday at Gary's. Not just couples but it *is* a swinger's get-together. Fun and games, and I do mean games. Interested?"

"Being with Eric has opened up a whole new world for me. I want to explore. But I'm not ready for an orgy, I'm afraid."

"Not an orgy at all. These swingers' parties are very tightly controlled because not everyone is interested in the same thing."

"Controlled how?"

"Well, for example, the living room and kitchen are off-limits for any hankypanky. They're safe zones where people who don't want to play or haven't decided yet can gather. That way no one will ever be embarrassed by something they don't want to see or do. There are pieces of colored yarn on or beside every door. A black ribbon on the door means off-limits. Like, if we had a party at my house, your room would be off-limits. A red ribbon on a door means the room is occupied, stay out. Like that."

"Sounds like you've thought this through."

"We have. And we've made mistakes and learned. We want to have a good time and not hurt anyone."

87

Jessica thought a moment, then smiled. "I don't know whether I'm ready for something like that yet. Maybe. I assume that, if you guys go, they're all nice people. No weirdos."

"The only new faces will be people personally endorsed but mostly it's the same people. Like the ones you met here last weekend. And then there are very specific rules about safe words."

"Safe words?"

"We use 'cease and desist' for an absolute stop. If anyone says 'cease and desist,' whatever is going on that involves them must stop. Immediately. And you must use that phrase if things get uncomfortable. No martyrs or endurance contests. We use 'time out' for things like, my foot itches or my arm is cramped."

"I don't get it. Why don't you just say stop?"

"If you say stop, no one knows whether you really want to stop or not. It can be fun to say, 'Please no' or 'Don't do that' without worrying that someone will actually stop. Control games can be very exciting."

"Control games?"

"You're just beginning your sexual education. Let's leave control games for a graduate-level course. Suffice it to say that dominant and submissive fantasies have been around for centuries and can be a lot of fun to play out."

"I always thought you were so suburban yuppy, so conservative."

"Shows how much you know."

"You know what I'd like to do today, really? Let's drag Brian to the Bronx Zoo."

"I haven't been to the zoo in years. Great idea. Then seafood for dinner. I know a great spot on City Island." Steph stuck her head out into the hallway and yelled at the top of her voice. "Hey Brian, get dressed, you bum. We've got the day all planned."

The following Tuesday morning, Jessica stretched out on the bedspread in her room at Steph's. The room was cool, with off-white, grass-cloth wallpaper, green and off-white sheets and a dark green flowered comforter. The carpeting was thick and a deep forest green, giving the room the look of a forest glade.

Since she wanted to be free to say anything to Eric she picked up her cellular phone and dialed The Stanford Court, Eric's hotel in San Francisco. The switchboard connected her immediately. After only one ring, a sleepy voice answered. "Hello?"

"Good morning, Eric. You did say I should call you at this ungodly hour." Jessica could hear the rustling of Eric's body as he moved around in bed three thousand miles away.

"Good morning. And yes, this time is fine. I have to get up anyway and what better way is there to be awakened?"

Eric told Jessica that his job was going well. "I should have no problem getting back by the end of the week. How about you? What have you been doing?"

Jessica told Eric about her time with Steph and Brian, trying to put her feelings into words. "It's like someone just lit a lamp in a part of my life that I didn't know existed."

"Well, I'll be sure to have my flashlight with me at all times so I can illuminate more dark corners."

"It's so much more than sex. It's me. I'm free to do and say things I haven't done or said since I was in high school. I didn't realize how much of my life I've lived with the feeling that Rob was looking over my shoulder, judging me."

"It must be wonderful to feel so liberated."

"And, of course, it's all that good lovemaking we did. The only problem now is that my mind seems consumed with thoughts of you and your gorgeous body." As the picture of Eric's naked body flashed across her mind, she realized that he wasn't really well built at all. He was soft and a bit overweight. But he was sexy and attractive and a total turn-on.

"I'm glad you think I'm gorgeous, although it does make one wonder about your eyesight. By the way, what are you wearing?" Eric asked.

"That's a question out of left field. I'm wearing shorts and a polo shirt. Why?"

"Well, I'm not wearing anything, and I want you the same way. Put the phone down and take your clothes off." When there was silence, Eric added, "Please."

"This is silly."

"Come on. Pull the shirt off over your head, take your bra off and get out of those shorts and underpants."

Jessica giggled, then complied. She cradled the phone against her ear and lay back down on the bed. "Okay. I've taken my clothes off. Why?"

"Because we're going to make love."

"Three thousand miles apart?"

"Yes, three thousand miles apart. Stretch out on the bed and close your eyes. I'll close mine. What are you lying on? A bedspread? A quilt?"

"A comforter."

"Okay. Feel the cool, smooth cloth on your back. Feel it on your buttocks and calfs, on your heels. Stroke the comforter with one foot and feel the smoothness against your sole. Can you feel it?"

"Yes."

"Is the window open or do you use the air conditioner? It was pretty cool when I left."

"It is cool and I have the window open."

"Good. Feel the air that is coming in the window. Feel it against your skin, all over. Listen to the birds and the leaves rustling. Smell the green smell of the grass and the trees. Part your lips and breathe in through your mouth. Now run your tongue around your lips and taste the cool air. Feel the coldness as you breathe in again."

Jessica did as Eric asked. She had never been as aware of all the sensations around her.

"Lick your thumb. Taste your own skin."

She did, feeling only a tiny bit silly. "It's tangy, spicy kind of."

"Good. Now put your fingertips on your breast bone, right between your beautiful breasts. Stroke up and down, from your throat to your belly. With my eyes closed I can imagine that I'm watching and touching you."

Still feeling awkward, Jessica placed her fingertips against her chest and stroked her skin the way Eric wanted her to.

"Are you doing it?"

"Yes," she said softly.

"Does it feel good?"

"Yes." It did feel good. Soft and gentle.

"Jessica, have you ever touched yourself, explored your body?"

"I shower every day," she said, laughing nervously.

"That's not what I mean and you know it. When I was a kid, I touched my body, rubbed my cock, discovered the things that felt good. It was hard not to because all the feel-good parts were right out there, aching to be touched. I think every boy knows those places, if not before puberty, then about twenty minutes after. But, somehow, I don't think girls do. Did you ever touch yourself like that?"

"No," she admitted. Jessica could hear more rustling through the phone. Eric was obviously moving around in bed.

"How can you know what will feel good when a man touches you," he said softly, "if you don't know yourself? How can you help him to find the feel-good places if you don't know where they are?"

"I never thought about it."

"Well, you will now. Let's find out together. Swirl your fingers over your right breast. Your fingers feel the soft skin of your tit, and your breast feels the rougher texture of your fingers. Don't touch the areola, just the soft white skin. Are you doing that?"

"Yes," she whispered, torn between the erotic sensations and the feeling that she shouldn't be doing this.

"And it feels good. Don't answer that. Just indulge me for a few minutes. Just do as I ask without thinking. Now, slide your fingers up your side, to your underarm. Are you ticklish?"

"Not really."

"Good. I know that feels good, but we're looking now for places that make you hot. Slide your fingers over your neck and behind your ears, then across your face. Touch yourself."

Jessica was doing exactly what Eric was asking of her and it did feel good. Her skin tingled and she felt more alive, somehow.

"Now slide your fingers back to your breast. I know how sensitive your nipples are. If I close my eyes I can see them getting hard and tight. Fondle them and make them hard. Squeeze and pull. Make it feel good."

Jessica sighed, and touched her right nipple. She felt it contract and become more erect under her fingers. She dropped her hand and took a breath, about to tell Eric that this was ridiculous. Then she stopped herself and put her fingers back on her nipple. "It does feel good. It does."

"I know it does. And it makes other parts of your body feel good too. You are becoming aware of the heat between your legs. You don't really want to think about it, but you can't help it. Your mind keeps travelling to the tightness low in your abdomen and you can feel the area between your legs swell and get hot and wet. Slide your fingers down your belly and make large, swirling circles. Use your palm."

Jessica could hear him chuckle and she smiled. "What are you laughing at?"

"I know what's going on in your brain right now. Part of you wants to explore, wants to find out what mysteries are hiding between your legs, waiting to have the light shone on them like the lights we turned on a few nights ago. But part of you is still, wondering whether nice people do things like this. You're brain is yelling words like 'masturbation' and remembering all the things your mother told you would happen if you touched yourself."

Jessica nodded. "She said I'd spoil it for lovemaking with my husband. She told me that if I touched myself, then I would always need that kind of stimulation in order to become excited. It would become a habit. Therefore I would never get any pleasure from relations with my husband. It sounds so uptight when I say it out loud now."

"Lots of people believe it. But, if you never know your own body and what gives you pleasure, then how can you ever help a man to know how to please you?"

Jessica was still sliding her palm over her belly. "Men were just supposed to know."

"Yeah. Right. That's been the bane of men's existence since we lived in caves. Don't help us, just expect us to know. No wonder sex becomes tedious."

"I guess that's not really fair."

"No, it's not. But it's a very common attitude. I enjoy making love and I've made love to lots of women. It's a unique experience when I find someone like you and I can introduce you to all kinds of exciting new activities, but I also like it when a woman knows her body and what she enjoys." His voice dropped and softened. "What do you enjoy, Jessica?" Without giving her time to answer, he continued, "Do you like it when the ends of your fingers brush the springy hair between your legs? Do that. Just brush your bright red bush very lightly."

Jessica did as Eric asked. She had washed herself every day in the shower, but this was different. She never thought about her body in the shower. Now she could think of little else.

"Part your knees. Let your legs open wide. Feel the cool air on the hot, wet skin that's probably never felt cool air on it before."

"That feels strange," Jessica said, "forbidden somehow."

"I can hear your mother now. Keep your knees together. It's not ladylike to allow anyone to even think about what's between your legs." As if sensing her feelings, Eric said, "No, no. Don't slide them closed. Keep them spread wide apart. Reach between your legs and touch the hair there."

"How do you know what I'm thinking?"

"You're a sensuous woman who's never had any opportunity to revel in her sexuality, in her body. This is all new, exciting, and a little scary. Am I on the right track?"

"Actually, it's very exciting and very scary."

"Good. Scary is exciting, too. Are you touching yourself?"

Jessica's fingers just grazed the hair between her legs. She knew she got wet, but she'd never actually felt it before. God, it felt good, both on her fingers and on her swollen lips. "Yes," she whispered.

"Touch yourself more. Let yourself explore. Feel. Your body is slick, and rubbing it makes you want things you've never allowed yourself to want before. Are you touching all the crevices and folds? Tell me, Jessica, are you?"

Jessica was sliding her fingers into places she'd never touched for pleasure before. And it felt so good. Her outer lips were open, giving her access to the areas within. Her inner lips were covered with slippery wetness. She found that some places felt better than others. "Yes," she answered.

"This will be more difficult for you, Jessica, but I want you to touch your clit. You've been avoiding touching that part, but your clitoris can give you intense pleasure. Slide two fingers into the fold between your outer lips and find that hard, swollen little nub of nerve endings. Slip one finger on either side and stroke back and forth. And shut off your mind, except for the parts that feel and hear. Just rub. And if you find a spot that feels particularly good, rub more. Find the places that make your toes curl and your back arch. Find the places that seem darkest and most erotic. Stroke yourself, baby. Do it for me."

Jessica touched her swollen clit. Torn between the intense pleasure and the feelings left over from her past life, she did as Eric's voice told her to. She rubbed. And she rose higher and higher. It became easier and easier to touch the places that gave her the most pleasure. She closed her eyes.

Eric's voice was husky as he continued. "Let me tell you what I'm doing while you're touching yourself. I've got my hand on my hard cock and I'm squeezing and stroking it. I'm caressing my balls, then holding my cock."

Knowing that Eric was touching himself made what she was doing seem less dirty somehow. This was part of a mutual experience.

"Remember how it felt when I touched you? Reach for those

feelings. Do things that bring you closer to those swirling colors you told me about. Touch just the right places. Pretend that those are my fingers, if you need to, but feel the erotic intensity growing."

"Oh yes, Eric. It feels so good."

"Don't stop. Prop the phone against your ear and take the other hand and use your index finger to rub your slick inner lips. Rub the opening of your slit. If you want to, slide one finger into your body. If that doesn't feel good, don't do it."

"It all feels good."

Jessica heard Eric chuckle. "You're magic, baby," he said. "Feel the orgasm coiled inside you, waiting for you to release it. Find the places that tighten that coiled spring. Find them. Use them. Wind it tighter and tighter."

Jessica was burning. She rubbed her body with both hands, and squirmed on top the comforter. She rubbed her feet on the material and arched her back. She found a tiny ball of light and touched the places that made the light grow. Higher and hotter, she didn't want to stop. Her slippery fingers offered her ecstasy and she reached for more. The light changed from soft yellow to white and grew brighter. Suddenly it exploded, enveloping her in heat and brightness. "Oh," she said, her breathing hard and fast. "Eric."

For long moments she was filled with lava, reaching every nerve in her body. She was lost in it, yet aware of every sensation. Never before had anything like this ever happened while she was alone. And somewhere a tiny part of her was sad for all the lost opportunities.

"I came with you," Eric whispered. "God, that was great."

Jessica laughed. "It certainly was." She looked at the clock on her bedside table. They had been on the phone almost forty-five minutes. "Look at the time," she said.

"Time flies when you're having fun. But I do have to get to work. And a shower is most definitely necessary now."

Jessica lay on the bed, limp and smiling. "This is all so incredible," she whispered.

"Unfortunately, I have to get up," Eric said. "But you lay there until you want to move. And don't think. Feel. And when those thoughts about what's right to do and what isn't surface, and they will, tell them to get stuffed."

"Yeah. Get stuffed. I'll do that."

"I'll call you when I know my schedule."

She needed to tell him one last thing. "There's a party at Gary's a week from Saturday. Steph invited me to go."

"Great. Gary called me and I'll be there too. But even if I weren't going to be there, you'd have a wonderful time and get to explore the new you."

"But, you'll be there?"

"Yes. And I want to make love to you in every way possible, in every place possible. I want you to explore your new-found sexual understanding with others, too. Meet new men and make love if they turn you on. Women too, if that gives you pleasure. You're a new person, Jessica."

"I don't think I'm ready to do this alone."

"I'll be back on Friday and, if you're free, we can see each other Saturday night. By then, I'm sure you'll be more comfortable with the new you. Okay?"

"Great." Jessica took a deep breath.

"I'll call you later in the week if I can."

"Okay," she said, disappointed that he didn't say that he'd definitely call tomorrow. "Don't work too hard."

"Jessica, have a terrific week, and don't play too hard." They both hung up.

It was almost eleven when Jessica wandered into the kitchen. Brian was standing at the counter, pouring Cheerios into a bowl. "Good morning, JJ."

"What are you doing here?"

Grinning, Brian said, "I live here."

"That's not what I meant and you know it. Why aren't you at work?"

"Day off. I'm allowed, you know. Even us Wall Street types get time off for good behavior." He leered at her long legs, exposed beneath her brief denim shorts. "Or bad behavior."

Jessica blushed and sat down at the table.

"JJ, I'm sorry," Brian said, sitting across from her. "I don't ever mean to make you uncomfortable. Steph told me about you and Eric and I understand how you're feeling right now. I know Eric well enough to be sure that he's told you that he's a free-spirited guy with a girl in every port."

"He has, of course."

"This is all new and strange. You've suddenly realized that men are attracted to you and, if you wanted, you could enjoy more than dinner and a movie together." He reached across the table and took Jessica's hand. "And, you've never thought of me as anyone but Steph's husband. However, I am attracted to you. I won't deny that. Just understand that I will never knowingly do anything to hurt you. If I tease you a bit, or make a remark, it's because I care about you as a friend and as an attractive woman. Okay?"

Jessica smiled warmly. "Yes, Brian, I do understand."

"And I want to make love to you in seven different positions."

Jessica's laughter filled the sunlit kitchen. She looked at Brian for a moment, then added, "And maybe you'll get your wish, eventually."

Brian stood up and retrieved his bowl of cereal. "You give an old man hope," he said.

"Old, my foot," Jessica said. "You're exactly three months older than I am, if I remember correctly."

"But I'm several decades more experienced."

Jessica shook her head ruefully. "I certainly do have a lot of catching up to do."

Brian raised his hand high in the air. "I'll help," he said, waving the hand around. "Ooooh, oooh, pick me."

"Good morning, everyone," Steph said, interrupting the conversation. "What are you volunteering for so enthusiastically?"

"Never you mind, snoopy," Brian said. "That's between JJ and me."

"Sorry I asked." She grinned and kissed Brian on the cheek, then hugged Jessica good morning. "What should we do today?"

"I'd just like to lounge around the pool," Brian said. "And I've got a few errands to run. And how about some tennis later?"

The threesome spent the remainder of the morning beside the Carltons' pool then made chef salads for lunch. Late that afternoon, Jessica watched as Steph beat Brian in two sets of tennis at their country club. The two opponents were laughing together as they walked back to where Jessica sat beside the court with a diet Coke in her hand. Sweat dripped from their bodies, soaking their tennis whites. "I'd say six-four, six-two is a thorough trouncing," Steph said. "And that doesn't happen often."

"I was distracted looking at JJ's legs in those tiny shorts," Brian said. "She kept crossing and uncrossing them at just the wrong moments." He groaned. "And when you decided you needed more sunblock on your thighs I double-faulted three times in a row."

Jessica stretched her long legs in front of her and ran a finger up the inside of one thigh. "If you can't take the distractions," she said, then winked at Steph, "tough."

Brian whacked his wife on the arm. "Did you plan this?"

"Well . . ." the two women said in unison.

"JessicaLynn Hanley," Brian said, grinning, "you're becoming entirely too frisky."

Jessica grinned. "Thanks," she said. "And I'm not *too* frisky, but I am just right."

"You sure are. Okay, I'll meet you ladies in the bar in fifteen minutes," he said. "Gotta shower and shave." He walked toward the men's locker room.

"I'll meet you there," Steph said, handing Jessica her racket.

While Steph and Brian took showers, Jessica settled at a tiny table in the bar and ordered a Bloody Mary. As she nibbled on a piece of celery, a man of about forty leaned over the table. He was wearing crisp white tennis shorts and a light blue soft-collared shirt with a tiny Donald Duck stitched above the left breast.

"You're Steph and Brian Carlton's friend JJ, aren't you? From the midwest."

"Yes," she said, warily.

"I thought it might be you. Brian described you several times. My name's Cameron Hampstead, but everyone calls me Cam. I work in the city and I ride Metro North with Brian. When I saw him yesterday, he mentioned that he and Steph had a tennis date this afternoon." He held out his right hand and Jessica placed hers in it. His palm was warm and soft, his grip strong.

"Hmmm," Jessica muttered. "And I thought this tennis game was spur of the moment." Aloud Jessica said, "And how did you recognize me?"

"Brian's described you as a gorgeous redhead with green eyes."

"Oh," Jessica said, a bit nonplussed.

He looked at the other chair at the small table. "May I?"

"Sure," Jessica said, not totally comfortable with being picked up in a bar, despite the club's exorbitant annual dues.

He sat down and placed his racquet and tote on the floor beside him. "I guess this is where I'm supposed to ask you what your sign is, or something inane."

Totally puzzled, Jessica's head snapped up. "Excuse me?"

"I'm sorry, but this isn't my usual thing."

"Okay, you've lost me. What isn't?"

"Picking up women in bars. Brian told me yesterday that he and Steph would be here with you today and he suggested that I might meet you. He thought you and I would get along splendidly."

"He set this up?"

Cam smiled ruefully. "He did. He's a big fan of yours and, I suppose, of mine too. I guess he thought we'd hit it off."

"I'm very embarrassed," Jessica snapped. "I really don't need Brian fixing me up."

"I'm so sorry. I know he meant well. I'm the one who botched this." There was a slight trace of an English accent in Cam's voice, which had gotten more pronounced as the conversation progressed. "This was a really bad idea."

As Cam rose to leave, Jessica placed her hand on his, where it rested on the table. "This is dumb and awkward," she said, somehow warming to Cam's openness, "but not an entirely bad idea. Brian's intentions were good and your only fault is one that I suffer from as well. Honesty. Let's start again."

His grin lit Cam's ordinary-looking face. "Thanks." He sat back down.

"Hi." Jessica extended her right hand. "My name's Jessica. Jessica Hanley. Nice to meet you."

Cam's grin widened still further and he took her hand. "Mine's Cameron."

"Cameron. That's an unusual name."

"It's a family name." He deliberately broadened his accent. "Very British and all that. Actually, I hate it. Cam's much better."

"Well, Cam, until recently, people called me Jessie, and only Brian calls me JJ. Right now I prefer Jessica."

"Jessica it is." Cam ordered a glass of cabernet. "What takes you into the city on the train with Brian?"

"I'm in advertising. TV commercials. Lots of pressure, lots of late nights and coffee. Lots of famous people being temperamental and thinking that they know my business better than I do. And lots of sponsors who think they know my business better than I do."

"Sounds awful."

Cam smiled ruefully. "It does, doesn't it. To be truthful, I love it."

Jessica liked Cam's grin and she matched it with one of her own. "Someone has to," she said.

Over the next five minutes, Jessica told Cam briefly about her divorce and her extended visit to Harrison.

"I was married briefly," Cam said, "but my wife was killed in an auto accident." When Jessica looked distressed, he added, "That was almost fifteen years ago. I guess that I've idealized her over the years, and I just haven't found anyone since that I wanted to spend my life with."

Brian arrived at the table dressed in navy shorts and a plaid sport shirt, pulled up a chair and dropped into it. "Well, Cam, fancy meeting you here."

"I told her, Brian," Cam said. "Everything."

"Uh-oh." He looked a bit sheepish. "I got caught. I'm really sorry, JJ."

"You should be," Jessica said, wanting to make him suffer for a few minutes. "You made both Cam and me very uncomfortable."

Brian picked Jessica's hand up from where it lay on the table. He kissed her fingertips, one by one. "Am I forgiven?" He gave her an I'm-too-cute-to-be-mad-at look. "Please?"

Jessica burst out laughing. "Okay. I'll forgive you. But just this once. From now on I'll select my own friends."

"I agree," Steph's voice said from behind Jessica. "When Brian told me about this. . . ."

"She didn't know in advance," Brian said, jumping in to keep his wife in Jessica's good graces. "I told her between our two sets. Honest."

"Hi, Cam," Steph said. "I'm glad to see you, even under these circumstances." She cuffed Brian on the arm. "You're impossible."

Brian grabbed Steph's arm and pulled until she plopped into his lap. "I'm entirely possible," he said. "And you love it. Am I forgiven?"

Steph wriggled into her own chair. "Buy me a club soda and I'll think about it."

"Jessica? Forgive me?"

"Well. . . ."

The four talked for about half an hour, then Brian glanced at his watch and said, "It's almost six-thirty. If I haven't entirely turned you two off about each other, I'd like to suggest that the four of us have dinner together. Cam?"

"I'd love to join you all for dinner. But only if Jessica has forgiven both of us for our subterfuge." He looked at her. "Have you?"

There was a boyish, attractive quality about Cam, Jessica thought. He's charming and good company. She thought briefly about Eric, then said, "I'd like that." She looked down at her bare legs. "I'm obviously not dressed for anything fancy."

"I know a great place for Texas-style barbecued ribs and chicken," Cam suggested. "It's up-county in Yorktown. A place called Rattlesnake's. And they have an appetizer platter with things called rattlers that will cook the fillings in your teeth."

When Steph looked dubious, Cam added, "Not everything is hot, but I happen to like chili peppers."

"Sounds good to me," Jessica said. "And I don't mind having my teeth rattled occasionally."

"Really?" Brian leered, waggling an imaginary cigar, Groucho-style.

"Sounds good to me too," Cam added, holding Jessica's gaze a fraction too long.

"Okay, you two," Steph said, wanting to bail her friend out of a potentially uncomfortable situation. "Enough of the double entendres. You're embarrassing the two refined ladies at this table."

"Where?" Jessica said. "I only see two grown women and two attractive guys, one of whom you're married to."

Both Cam and Brian beamed. "Thank you, Jessica," Cam said.

"Rattlesnake's, it is," Brian said.

After getting directions to the restaurant, they separated. Steph and Brian drove away in Brian's Lexus and Jessica and Cam in Cam's Toyota. After half an hour of good conversation, Jessica and Cam met Steph and Brian in front of the restaurant and they were shown to a table in front of a wide window. They ordered beers and, while the other three looked at the menu, Cam ordered the Rattlesnake PuPu appetizer platter.

When the platter arrived, they ordered a barbecued chicken and a rack of baby back ribs, deciding to share. Cam gave the other three a guided tour of the enormous plate of appetizers. He pointed to a shapeless lump, breaded and fried. "This is a popper, a hot pepper filled with cheese and deep fried, and this is a rattler, a shrimp stuffed with a hot pepper. Warning!"

Jessica picked up a rattler and bit off a small piece. Her mouth flamed almost immediately. "Holy cow," she said, grabbing a taco chip from the pile of nachos and stuffing it into her mouth. "These do smart a bit."

"How about the wings?" Steph asked.

Brian bit one and answered, "Just at the borderline of your heat tolerance. I think you'll like it."

Stephanie did, and the rest of the meal as well. When the check arrived, Cam laid his credit card on the tray. Jessica reached for her purse. "Brian, Steph, and I have agreed," she said. "We split checks." She wondered how Cam would react, and in her mind, it was a test of sorts. Would he be gracious?

"Okay, if that's what makes you comfortable," Cam said. "About twenty each ought to do it."

Jessica pulled a twenty-dollar bill from her wallet and handed it to Cam. Without fanfare, he tucked it into his pocket.

As they left the restaurant, Jessica walked with Cam toward Brian's car. "I'd like to take you to dinner," Cam said. "Would you like that?"

Jessica linked her arm in Cam's. He was charming, and refined, and, she admitted to herself, without any overt effort, very attractive. "I would, very much."

"Would tomorrow night be too soon? I could pick you up about six. I know an Indian place that makes the best shrimp vindaloo. It will sizzle your tail feathers."

"I haven't had my tail feathers sizzled in a while. I love vindaloo."

Again, Cam's smile lit up his face. "Six it is." Jessica nodded as she climbed into the backseat of Brian's car. "See you tomorrow," she said.

Cam leaned in through the open door and kissed Jessica lightly on the mouth, then ran his tongue across her upper lip. "Till then."

As they drove south, Brian said, "Hey, JJ. I hope I'm forgiven. I guess it was a bit sneaky."

Jessica pictured Cam's face. "You're forgiven, but no more. Okay?"

"Okay."

SIX

The following day, Steph joined Jessica at breakfast. After some small talk, Steph asked, "Have you ever considered having your hair done? Maybe getting a body wave?"

"That's out of left field," Jessica responded. She ran her fingers through her long hair and tucked a strand behind her ear. "Actually, I wanted to cut and soften it a few years ago, but Rob thought it was pretentious so I dropped it." She made a face.

"I'd love to see you shorten it, and give it some soft waves."

"What brought this on?" Jessica asked.

"I've got a hairdresser appointment this morning and I was wondering whether you'd like to come along and maybe do something a bit experimental. Something more Jessica and less Jessie."

Jessica thought about her long, straight hair, which she now wore either in a ponytail or just hanging loose down her back. She fluffed out the sides, which fell back against her face. "I don't know. How about if I join you, and consider my options later?"

John's of Harrison was an incredibly opulent salon. Ten full-time operators cut, styled, blow-dried, and colored the hair of Harrison's rich and pampered. When anything new was considered for any of its slightly spoiled patrons, five-foot five-inch John Matucci bustled over and discussed the changes at length. No one, absolutely no one, would make a move without John's specific approval. Several women put off stylings if John wasn't at the salon.

When Stephanie and Jessica arrived, the salon was only half full. A woman in a pink and gray jumpsuit hurried over. "Good morning, Ms. Carlton. We were expecting you. As you can see we're not very crowded so we can do as much as you'd like today."

"As much as you'd like?" Jessica muttered.

"You'll see," Steph said, turning to the perfectly groomed receptionist. "Gina, I'd like to introduce my friend Jessica Hanley. She's from my old hometown, here visiting for the summer."

"Ms. Hanley. How nice to meet you. Will you have time for anything today? You have magnificent skin," Gina said. "Maybe a facial?"

"Jessica, John's does massages, body wraps, waxing, just about anything you could want."

"Sounds delightfully decadent," Jessica said.

"Have you thought about your hair? Maybe a soft wave?" Steph asked.

Gina reached out and took a strand of Jessica's hair and rubbed it between her fingers. "Such wonderful hair. With a light rinse and loose wave, you'd be spectacular." She lifted one of Jessica's hands. "And wonderful long fingers. How about a manicure and an herbal hand-wrap?"

"Gina, down girl," Steph said. "She's just visiting. Don't go overboard."

Gina leaned over so her face was close to the two women. "John's here today and he's even got some time." She leaned even closer to Jessica's ear. "I could fit you in."

Jessica sighed and smiled. "Okay. What the hell. Tell John to do his worst."

"But, he will do his best," the woman said, unused to Jessica's bantering.

"Of course. It will be his best." Jessica and Steph laughed, then got ready to be pampered. While Jessica's hair was rinsed with a gentle highlighter then waved, she had an herbal wrap on her hands, a manicure, a facial, and an hour-long massage. When Steph replaced her on the massage table, she said, "Isn't that the most hedonistic thing you've ever done?"

"God, Steph," Jessica admitted. "I've never had a massage before. That's heaven."

"Imagine how it would feel if a man did it on his bed, with his hands awakening all those feelings in your body, then satisfying all those hungers. God."

Jessica felt the prickling between her legs. "I'll bet it would be unbelievably erotic."

While the manicurist massaged Jessica's feet, filed off the calluses, and applied bright red polish to her toenails, Jessica nibbled on a light tuna salad with melba toast.

When John combed out her hair and blew it dry Jessica was delighted with the subtle difference in her appearance. He had shortened her hair until it fell just at her shoulders, longer in back and waving loosely around her face. He had enhanced her existing style without making any dramatic changes. "What do you think?" the talented, officious salon owner asked.

"It's just lovely," Jessica answered, truly impressed by the improvement. "I look years younger."

"Lovely? Of course not. John does not do lovely." He seemed to refer to himself in the third person frequently. "John does magnificent. John does terrific. But lovely?"

Steph walked over. "John, it's sensational."

Jessica quickly agreed. "Yes, of course John," she said, trying not to laugh. "It's magnificent."

John smiled, and tried to look humble without success. "Thank you Ms. Hanley, Ms. Carlton." He took Jessica's hand and guided her from the chair. "And such soft hands." He kissed her knuckles.

Steph and Jessica settled their exorbitant bills with their credit cards and left the shop, giggling like schoolgirls.

Cam picked her up that evening and commented on how nice she looked in tight beige slacks and a soft off-white silk blouse. She wore her hair loose and it now flowed softly around her face.

"You look different," Cam said. "Softer."

The curry was terrific, hot enough to awaken every nerve in her mouth, but not so hot as to deaden her taste buds. They shared tales of past curries, compared life in England and Ottawa, Illinois, favorite movies, TV shows, and books. As they sat over rasamalai and spiced tea, Cam said, "I'm sorry to say that I've got to end our evening early. I've got an impossible job to finish that will take the rest of the week and all weekend."

"I'm sorry too," Jessica said. "When is it due?"

"Tuesday morning, at eight a.m., come hell or high water."

"Oh Cam, I'm sorry. You should have called and cancelled tonight. I feel so guilty."

Cam covered her hand with his. "Don't. I wanted to see you again and it was worth whatever time it took. I'm just sorry that we can't continue this evening. With final revisions and everything, I should be off the hook by the middle of next week. Could I interest you in a drive out to Connecticut for dinner? The traffic might be awful, but I know a place that has the best steamers and makes flounder that's so fresh. . . ."

"I'd love to, Cam." She was seeing Eric on Saturday, now Cam next week and the party the following Saturday. God, she felt good.

"Great. I'll call you at the beginning of the week and we'll set a definite date."

Cam drove her back to Steph's and helped her out of the car. As she stood up, he took her in his arms and softly pressed his lips against hers. They kissed for a long time, exploring each other, pressing their bodies tightly together, feeling the soft, yet building

THE PLEASURES OF JESSICALYNN

arousal. When he pulled away, Cam said, "If I keep doing that, I'll throw you into the car, take you back to my place, and ravish you in the driveway."

Jessica kept her arms around Cam's neck. "You would, would you?" she said, savoring her slightly aggressive feelings. She wanted him and they were both adult, single and capable of making their own decisions. Then she pressed her mouth against Cam's and kissed him for another long minute. "A bit more of that and I might let you."

Cam flashed her his most charming smile. "You're quite a woman, Jessica."

"And you're quite a guy, Cam. Thanks for dinner."

"Till next week?"

"Till next week. Call me when your job's finished."

Jessica turned and walked into the house, happier than she had been in a long time.

The following morning she called Eric. After a few pleasantries, she said, "I had a date last evening."

"Great. Have fun?"

"Yes. I did. It's a whole new thing, this dating."

"I'm happy for you, Jessica."

When she told him about her day at John's he asked, "Are you gorgeous? More so than when I left?"

"You know, I feel gorgeous and I've never felt like that before. I feel like men might want to look at me, might find me attractive. That's a new thing for me." She laughed. "I also had a massage. What an experience."

"If we're still on for Saturday, I'll give you one of Eric's patented massages, no holds barred."

Jessica felt heat flow through her body. "I'd like that," she said huskily. "Then could I give you one?" She had never explored Rob's body and now she found that she wanted to touch all of Eric's.

"That sounds like an offer I can't refuse." He picked up his watch from the table beside his bed. "It's after nine-thirty there. Are you still in bed?"

"Yes," Jessica said. She stretched, liking the feeling of cool sheets against her naked skin.

"Well, I need to know something. When I give you that massage where would you like me to touch you?"

"Where?"

"Where. Exactly."

"Oh, just everywhere," Jessica said, suddenly shy.

"Your breasts? Touch them and see whether they would like that."

Jessica pressed the palm of her hand against her breast and felt her swollen nipple fill her hand. "Oh yes."

"And you'll want me to rub your thighs and your beautiful ass. Then I'll rib your clit until you come. It won't take long, will it?"

Without thinking, Jessica slipped her hand between her legs and found her swollen, wet clit. She rubbed long and slow, then harder and faster. "No," she whispered. "It won't take long at all." She felt the familiar tight knot in her belly.

"Are you rubbing where it feels so good, baby?"

"Yes," she moaned.

"Don't stop. Stroke and touch. Do exactly what feels best. Reach out for the orgasm and pull it closer. Use your mind to see your fingers as they rub and give you pleasure."

Jessica reached for the climax and drew it closer and closer. As it flowed up her thighs, she tensed her legs and arched her back slightly. "Yes," she groaned and it overtook her. "Yes." It filled her, swirling in hot shards of orange and gold. It came so hard it almost hurt. She gritted her teeth and felt it curl her toes.

After a short silence, Eric said, "You did it, didn't you. You gave yourself pleasure. You were responsible for your own orgasm."

Jessica caught her breath. "I guess I was."

"I hope you've recovered from those feelings that Rob stuffed you full of."

She smiled. "Not entirely, but it's hard to feel frigid when a man can make you come over the phone."

She heard Eric's rich laugh. "True enough. Saturday? My place? Timmy's wonderful dinner, then whatever?"

"Yes. What time?"

"I'll come get you at about six-thirty, if that's okay."

"Great," she said, feeling her languid body sink into the mattress. "See you then."

The rest of the week sped by. As had become a habit, Thursday afternoon she called her office in Ottawa and talked at length to Vivian Whitman, her second-in-command and, next to Steph, her best friend. She made a few necessary business decisions and was gratified to learn that everything was running as smoothly without her as it did when she was there. "Viv," she said, "you make me feel unnecessary."

"Jessie, we all love you and we want you to take this time off. We're deliberately not bothering you with anything but the most important stuff." Viv's voice lowered. "Are you having any fun?"

Jessica could picture the slightly overweight black woman who, right now, had her head bowed with the phone tucked between her shoulder and her ear. One hand would be cupped over her mouth, as she always did when she was being conspiratorial.

"Oh lord, Viv," Jessica said, "I'm having more fun than I could have imagined." Leaving out the more lurid details, she told her friend about Eric and about Cam. "I feel attractive and sexy and free."

"That's great. I'm so happy for you."

Jessica could hear a note of sadness. "What's wrong, Viv?"

"I guess I'm scared you won't come back. I miss you." Viv and Jessie had become friends several years before although Rob had always declined offers to have dinner with Viv and her husband.

"I miss you too, Viv," Jessica said.

"Dates are not coming out of the woodwork here. Nice men are in short supply, as you may remember. I'm just afraid you'll decide to stay in New York."

Jessica felt uncomfortable with Viv's correct assessment of Ottawa, Illinois. It was a bit dull. "Any nibbles on my house?"

"We've gotten several repeat visits, but no offers yet. I'll call you if anything appears promising. Oh, and by the way, your ex seems to have dropped out of sight. Do you know anything?"

Jessica found that she wasn't hurt by the mention of Rob's name. Now, she was angry. "Not a thing, and I really don't want to either."

"Sorry."

"Don't be. And I didn't mean to sound waspish. I hope he's happy. Remember the line from *Fiddler on the Roof*? 'May God bless and keep the tsar . . . far away from us.' That's how I feel right now. They should be happy, and invisible." Jessica could hear Viv's giggle over the phone lines.

"Lord, I do miss you, girl."

"Me too, Viv. Talk to you next week."

"Till then."

Eric picked Jessica up that Saturday evening and they sped to his house. As they drove up the driveway, Jessica was struck by the way the low-slung, strong, rugged, rough-hewn house matched Eric's looks and personality. She glanced at his angular chin and close-cut, granite-gray beard and said, "The house fits you."

"Thank you." He stopped the car and pulled up the emergency brake.

"I didn't really see it the last time I was here. I was a bit distracted, if you remember. I'm awed by how perfectly your house suits you. It's beautiful."

"Thank you. And don't be awed. That's what I do for a living, you know."

"I didn't know you were so good."

"I'll bow modestly and admit that I'm damn good. Actually what I'm good at is finding out what people are and what they want."

He rested his head on the headrest. "I get people to paint me a picture of the way they see themselves, then I design a frame to put that picture into."

"I've been selling real estate for a long time and I'm hard to impress." She waved her arm to take in the house and the subtle landscaping. "This impresses me."

"Thanks." He got out, rounded the car and opened the door for Jessica. "Very non-politically-correct."

Jessica extended her hand and Eric grasped it. "Very," she said as she unfolded herself from the tiny car, "and I like it." Without releasing his hand, she stood very close to Eric's body, looking into his smoky-gray eyes. The day was hot and humid, but it couldn't match the heat radiating from her body and Eric's.

He raised her hand to his lips and, without releasing her gaze, he swirled his tongue around her palm. Then he pulled a length of thick dark-gray yarn from his pocket and tied it around Jessica's wrist. "You may not remember from your last trip here, but my bedroom is decorated in shades of gray, from the palest hue, which looks almost white, to the deepest shade, the color of the ocean in a storm. This," he finished the knot, "is the color of the sheets on my bed. Tonight, you will be there, with your red hair spread on my pillow, your green eyes clouded with passion, your body needing me."

Jessica swallowed hard, around the lump in her throat.

"And you know what you'll be doing?"

"What?" she croaked.

"You'll be begging me to fill you up. And I won't. I'll tease you and drive you crazy."

"Oh."

He grinned. "But we have to have dinner first. Timmy's been expecting you." He aimed her at the front door.

They walked down a short hallway and through a formal dining room dominated by an oak table that could seat twenty. The chairs were upholstered in a soft rose damask and the deep plush carpeting was a richer shade of the same color.

"Ms. Hanley," Timmy said as they entered the kitchen. "I'm so glad to see you again."

"I'm glad to see you, too, Timmy, but could you call me Jessica?"

"Okay, Jessica," Timmy said, opening the refrigerator door. "You spoke about liking cocktail sauce with horseradish so I gambled that you'd also like Bloody Marys. Was I right?"

"Timmy, you're a mind reader. I love Bloody Marys, extra spicy."

Timmy withdrew a pitcher from the refrigerator and filled two glasses. He garnished the drinks with stalks of celery and thin slices of tomato and onion. "Actually," Jessica said, lifting the celery from the drink, "I like Bloody Marys but I love celery." She bit off a chunk and chewed loudly. "Aren't you having one, Timmy?"

"If I drink before I cook, I don't cook."

Eric patted Timmy on the shoulder. "Occasionally Timmy and I share a bottle of wine or something before dinner. First, the rolls don't get made, then the salad bites the dust. By the time dinner arrives, it's meat and pasta."

"Yes," Timmy said, "but I thought you were usually too sloshed to notice."

"Too true," Eric said. "What's for dinner tonight?"

"I've made a cold cucumber and yogurt soup, chilled chicken breasts with white grapes and watercress, and tabbouleh."

"What's tabbouleh, Timmy?" Jessica asked.

"It's a middle eastern salad made from bulgar, tomatoes, parsley, lemon, and olive oil."

"Bulgar's wheat, isn't it?" Jessica felt Eric ease around behind her. While she talked, he pulled the back of her blue-and-white-striped shirt out of the waistband of her white linen slacks.

"It is wheat, but I have no idea exactly what's been done to it."

Jessica felt Eric insinuate his index finger into the back of her pants and stroke the top of the crack between her buttocks. She swallowed then she said, "That sounds delicious."

"Oh," Timmy said, "it's so nice to have an appreciative audience."

As Eric's fingers lightly brushed the skin in the small of her back she sipped her drink, wanting him to stop, yet not moving away. As Timmy turned back to the refrigerator, Eric licked a wide swathe from her collar up to her hairline. She smiled as she remembered her debate about whether to sweep her hair up to the crown of her head with a silver comb and a narrow blue silk scarf.

"I like your hair up," he said, his breath hot on her ear, "but I want to see how it looks with its new styling."

"Would you like to have your soup now?" Timmy asked, oblivious to what was going on.

Eric tucked Jessica's shirt back in loosely and said, "I want to show Jessica the back. Let's say fifteen minutes?"

"Everything's served cold this evening, so take your time. I'll have soup ready whenever you like."

With Eric's warm palm in the small of her now-covered back, Jessica walked through a gigantic living area, cleverly divided into several seating groups. "Oh Eric, this is fantastic," she said, clearly awed. Although each area had a different pattern to the furniture—florals in one area, stripes in another, solids in a third—the areas were held together by the consistent use of southwestern shades of soft rose, sand, and slate blue. "I would have thought you more the chrome and glass type."

"I went to Tucson about five years ago and fell in love with the country, the people, and the ambiance. I had already built the house, so it's very steel, rock, and glass outside and soft and plushy inside."

"I know a lot of people like that," Jessica commented.

Eric smiled. "Now that I have it the way I want it," Eric said, "I don't use the house much, except for an occasional party."

"But you wouldn't sell this," Jessica said. "It's a part of you."

"I don't feel that way about things, I guess," Eric said, "but it would be a shame to leave this. I would, though, as long as I felt that I was leaving it in good hands." He led her through a sliding glass door and into the backyard.

A flagstone patio about fifteen feet wide ran the length of the back of the house. The area was edged with a three-foot-high wall of natural rock with water gurgling out at intervals into small pools and a six-foot-high waterfall at one end. Shrubs and low ground covers grew in crevices in the rocks and half a dozen large trees closed the area in. To Jessica it looked like an oasis out of an Arabian Nights fantasy or a secret cove on a tropical island. It should be tacky, she thought, but it isn't. It's glorious. Jessica looked around, taking in the beauty of the secluded spot. The air was heavy and humid, filled with the sweet aroma of distant flowering plants. "It's beautiful." A soft breeze brushed her face as Eric stood behind her.

"I pictured you here," he whispered, his fingers deftly unbuttoning her top. "I saw you naked, like some kind of jungle creature, wild and wanton." He unfastened the last button and pulled her shirt loose from her slacks. He took the drink from her hand and put it on a small wicker table. Then he removed her shirt, unhooked her bra, and slid it off her arms.

Jessica stood still, letting the warm breeze pucker her nipples and whisper over her skin. She closed her eyes and let her head fall back as Eric pulled the scarf, then the combs from her hair. She felt the soft mass cascade to her shoulders as Eric buried his fingers in the soft red strands. "You smell wonderful."

His hands were all over her body, touching, moving, dancing. He moved around until he was facing her, then he cupped her breasts and buried his face in the curve of her neck. "Just as I dreamed it would be," he purred. He stepped back and let his fingertips trail toward her nipples. "But not yet," he said.

When she felt him pull back, she opened her eyes, a silent question on her face.

"I want this evening to be filled with sensual pleasures. And I want it to last." He handed her her top, keeping her blue lace bra in his hand.

"I understand," she said. She slipped her arms through the openings and buttoned a few buttons. When he handed her her scarf, she tied it in her hair at the nape of her neck.

"Now feel your nipples against the soft fabric of your blouse." He lifted the end of the scarf and brushed it over her cheek. "Feel everything. Smell everything. Taste everything. We are going to make love all night." He kissed her softly, then led her back into the house.

They ate dinner in a small dining area adjacent to the kitchen. The table was oyster-colored Formica and the place mats and napkins followed the southwestern feel of the living room. The soup was cold but it cooled only a bit of her internal heat. The chicken was delicious, and the salad was the perfect complement. Eric poured each of them a glass of cold, crisp chablis, but she drank only a little. She was gently buzzed and didn't want to get any more so.

Throughout the meal, they talked about unimportant things. He amused her with stories of his travels and some of the unusual people he had designed for. She countered with tales of the weird couples for whom she had tried to find houses.

Although they laughed and shared and nothing overtly sexual was mentioned, a soft, sensual haze pervaded everything they did. Occasionally Eric would reach across the table and tug gently on the yarn around her wrist but she needed no reminders. The picture of her on Eric's bed was never out of her mind.

When they were finished with the main course, Timmy removed the plates and brought simple bowls of fruit sherbet for dessert. He placed a plate of chocolate truffles and tiny butter cookies in the center of the table. He poured coffee into their cups and put the pitcher on the table. "Unless there's anything else you want," Timmy said, "I'm going to go watch the Mets game."

"Nothing else," Eric said. "Who are they playing?"

"Los Angeles. Actually, I'm dying to see that Japanese phenom who's pitching for the Dodgers. Nomo."

"I've heard of him," Jessica said. "He's being considered for rookie of the year, but he's hardly a rookie. He's played for a dozen years in Japan."

"I'm impressed," Eric said. "I didn't know you were a baseball fan."

"When you live within spitting distance of Chicago, it's either the Cubs or the White Sox. I'm a Cub fan, myself, although I only watch games on TV."

"Maybe we can watch together some time," Timmy said.

"That would be fine," Jessica said. "Are you a Mets fan? We can watch a Cubs/Mets game and we can scream during alternate innings."

"I'm not a real rooter in that sense. I watch any sport and any team," Timmy said. "I just enjoy good competition."

"Timmy will watch anything from arm wrestling and surfing championships to chess and gymnastics. We watch a lot together on the weekends."

"Good night, Ms. Hanley." He caught himself, and said, "Good night Jessica. It was nice to see you again. And I'd love to watch the Cubs with you sometime."

"Good night, Timmy. Enjoy your game."

As Timmy left, Eric said, "We'll enjoy our games too." He took the spoon from her sherbet. "First game, no spoon."

"No spoon?"

Eric dipped his finger into the sherbet and extended it to her. She smiled, then licked the cold sweetness from his fingers. Then she scooped a dollop of sherbet and put it into the hollow of her hand.

Eric grinned as she held out her hand and he licked it from her skin with long, slow laps. "You taste heavenly."

Licking sticky sherbet from each other's hands, they ate their dessert. Eric poured them each a cognac, then they walked back onto the patio. As Jessica stood in the middle of the patio, Eric removed the scarf from her hair and held it in front of her at eye level. "May I?"

When Jessica looked puzzled, he lay the scarf across her eyes. "I want you to feel, not see. May I?"

Jessica thought only a moment before nodding. Eric tied the scarf across her eyes, then removed all her clothes, leaving only

118

the yarn around her wrist. Jessica felt him lift first one foot and then the other to remove her sandals.

"Feel how cold the stone is on your feet," he said, stroking her insteps. "You're so beautiful," he said, sliding his hands up her legs. "Your legs are long and shapely, your thighs white and soft." He brushed his knuckles over her red pubic hair. "Red, like fire. Do you burn for me, Jessica?"

"Oh yes," she moaned. She felt him take her hand to lead her across the stones. Jessica hesitated. She couldn't see. What if she spoiled the mood by stubbing her toe or doing something equally awkward. She didn't want to ruin this.

"Trust me," he said softly.

"But. . . ."

He placed a finger against her lips. "Just trust me. Nothing will spoil this." He picked her up in his arms and carried her to the edge of the patio and sat her on the cold stones. Then she felt him take one of her hands and dip it into the cold water of one of the pools. "You're all sticky," he said, carefully rubbing the sherbet from each finger. He did the same with her other hand.

Then, when both her hands were cool and wet, he took her palms and placed them on her breasts. Cool water ran down her ribs in tiny rivulets, tickling her sides. She struggled to hold on to the mood but, as Eric dribbled water onto her belly, she started to laugh.

"Ticklish?" Eric said, laughing with her.

"Not usually, but right now, yes," she said, worried that she had ruined the mood.

"Good. Laughter is necessary." He licked the droplets of water from just below her belly button and she giggled again. Then he suckled at her right breast and heat stabbed through her, making her as hot as she had been. He took her nipple in his teeth and bit gently, just hard enough to make her squirm. "Like that," he said. He took one finger and slid it into her, rubbing the sides of her slick, hot channel. "And that." He withdrew, stood and lifted her into his arms. "Oh yes." He moved her body so her hip rubbed against the bulge in his slacks. "Come upstairs with me. I want you in my bed."

Still blindfolded and naked, Jessica felt herself carried through the house and up the stairs. "I've been dreaming of you in my bedroom all week." Eric set her down on the floor and said, "Sit down, love."

He placed her hand on the edge of his bed and she sat on the smooth slithery sheets. She felt the bed sway just a bit as she settled onto it.

"If you were as excited as I was last weekend, you were too excited to notice that this is a water bed and particularly delightful to make love on. And the sheets are satin, cold and slippery. Lie back."

She stretched out on the cool fabric and spread her arms and legs, moving to intensify the feel of the satin. "Ummm," she purred.

"Now I want to play."

Jessica felt something soft and velvety rub lightly up and down her arm. "That's a rose," Eric said. He brushed the flower across her face and she could smell its light fragrance. She felt the flower caress her breasts then her shins. "Don't move," Eric said when her hips began to move. "Just hold completely still." The flower was gone. "This is a piece of fur from the collar of an old coat." He rubbed the fur over her skin, touching her underarms, the insides of her thighs and the backs of her knees. When her hips moved, he said, "No, no. Don't move."

"But I want to move. It's very hard to keep still."

"That's part of this lesson," Eric said. "You must keep your body completely still. You can't see, you can't move, just feel. Nothing more. Concentrate."

Jessica held still despite the increasing difficulty of controlling her body. Now that she knew what she craved, the heat and orgasmic excitement, she wanted it. She needed it. She reached for it, but Eric skillfully kept it just out of reach.

"You're getting so aroused," he purred. "Your pussy is an open and hungry mouth. But I'm not ready to fill it just yet."

"Yeeooow," Jessica yelled as she felt something icy pressed on the hot, swollen flesh between her legs.

"That's an ice cube." Eric laughed deep and warm. "Hold still."

"I can't," she said as she squirmed to get away from the freezing cube. When she felt the ice being removed from her clit, she took a deep breath and willed her body to relax.

"You know that this is a game we're playing. I'm going to tease and play and you're going to hold perfectly still while I do."

"If it's a game, then what do I get if I win?" Jessica asked, giggling at the sheer joy of it all.

"If you win, you get the best fucking you've ever had."

"And if I lose?"

"Then I get to fuck your brains out."

Jessica laughed. "Then I guess it's important that I win."

She felt Eric press the ice against her right breast and take her left nipple in his mouth. The contrast between the cold and the heat drove her crazy. After about a minute, he switched, placing the ice against her warm breast and his hot mouth on her cold one. It's strange, she thought with the small, coherent part of her brain. The pleasure is the now, the feelings, the eroticism, not the anticipation of the fucking that will come later. It was a revelation for her. It's the journey, not the destination.

Eric took a deep breath and removed Jessica's blindfold, as though he sensed the change in her attitude. She looked at him and grinned.

"You understand what I'm trying to teach you now, don't you?"

"Yes. I always thought foreplay was just to get ready for fucking. But foreplay is fun just for itself."

"You get an 'A' plus. Okay, next lesson. What gives your body pleasure?" When Jessica hesitated, Eric continued, "I've touched you, caressed you, kissed you, made love to you. And I've taught you to do the same. What, exactly, gives you pleasure?"

"That's really hard to talk about."

"I know, but I want you to tell me."

"I like it all."

He made a rude noise. "Cop-out."

"I like it when you kiss me."

Eric leaned over and licked Jessica's lower lip. He slowly inserted his tongue into her mouth and played with the tip of her tongue. He nipped at her lips and sucked her tongue into his mouth.

Heat flowed through her body. A moment before she had been relaxed but now she was tense and wanting. She reached up and held his head against her mouth.

He pulled back, took her wrist, and pressed it back against the sheets. "No hands. You're still under my orders not to move."

"Orders?" she said, the word causing heat to knife through her belly.

"Yes, orders. Now, that last answer was also a cop-out, but I enjoy kissing you too so I'll let it pass. Tell me where you like to be touched, where you want me to kiss you." She remained silent, so Eric said, "Is it difficult to say the words? Do you like it when I suck your tits?"

The crude word again sent waves of heat through her. "Yes," she whispered.

He licked her erect nipple, then said, "Tell me." A smile spread across Eric's face. "Makes you hot, doesn't it. Those words. Okay, first show me with your hands. Hold your tit for my mouth." He placed her hand on the underside of her breast and lifted, holding it upward for his mouth. He drew the hard tip into his mouth and sucked. "Say *tit*," he said as he blew cool air on her hot dusty-rose areola. "Say it."

"Oh baby," she moaned. "Please."

He couldn't resist her and he took her flesh in his mouth, laving and sucking it. "Where now?" he said.

Jessica took his hand and pulled it down, pressing his fingers against her swollen vulva, rubbing, kneading. "Please," she cried. "Oh God, please."

"You want my fingers in your pussy?"

Pussy. The word increased her excitement. The power of the words. She wanted to say them. She wanted to be forced to say them. She wanted. "Yes," she said, her breathing ragged and harsh. "I want your fingers inside me." Saying them felt so forbidden, so dirty, so good. She took a breath. "I want your fingers in my pussy."

Eric moaned, then plunged two fingers deep into her cunt, sawing in and out, fucking her with his hand. "Yes, baby, take it," he cried.

"Eric," she said, looking at his face, "fuck me." She saw it all, including the effect her voice was having on him.

He unrolled a condom onto his stiff erection and climbed over her. She grabbed his cock and rubbed it over her clit. The power to give pleasure, to excite, to drive him as crazy as he was driving her. It was intoxicating. She wanted to touch him, to drive him a little crazy too.

She placed her palms against his lightly furred chest and stroked his skin. As he moved, she caressed the skin over his contracting muscles. She wanted to touch his soft belly, and she did, sliding her hand lower and lower until she heard his harsh intake of breath.

"You'll kill me doing that," he groaned.

"But it will be worth dying for," she said, his passion making her bolder. She found his hard cock and did what she imagined would feel good. She laid his shaft in her palm and stroked the length of him.

"Oh, Jessica," he moaned and she revelled in the giving, exploring his excitement. She grew bolder, finding his sac and cupping his heavy testicles. She squeezed his cock and watched his face contort with pleasure. She wanted and needed and took. She placed the tip of his cock against the opening of her cunt, slid her hands to his buttocks, and pulled him into her.

The power of it was as enlightening as it was exciting. She moved with, then against him. They varied their rhythm, first fast, then slow and languid. He pulled out, then drove into her. He slid to the opening of her sheath, then slid in, inch by teasing inch. He was quiet inside of her, then pounded hard and fast.

Finally, she felt him tense and he reached between their bodies and rubbed her clit. "Yes," she screamed, "now, do that, yes. Do that." They came almost simultaneously, but the orgasm was only the culmination of the pleasure, not the pleasure alone. It wouldn't have mattered if she hadn't come, she realized with amazement. There were so many climaxes before her orgasm.

"It's so wonderful," she said later, running her hand up his side. "I never realized until now."

"Well," Eric said, panting, "I'm afraid I've created a monster."

Jessica propped herself on her elbow. "You have, you know. You certainly have."

SEVEN

———————◆▷◁◆———————

"Tell me about Gary," Jessica asked Steph the following Tuesday morning over breakfast.

"Gary Powell is quite a story," Steph said. "When he was in his early twenties he invented some kind of computer chip. I have no clue what it did, but it did it faster than anything else. So he started a manufacturing company and made a bundle. I mean a real bundle." She sipped her coffee. "About three years ago, someone offered him a couple of gazillion dollars for the firm, lock, stock, and patents."

"Obviously he took it."

"It was more than that somehow. He took the money and dropped out. Of everything. He was, and still is, mind you, single and very interesting. Although he's not especially good looking, he's always been sexy as hell. Now he's that and rich as Croesis as well. For a while mothers would invite him over to meet their eligible daughters, run into him accidentally at parties, whatever they could do to lure him into the family. Him and all that money."

"And . . . ?" Jessica said.

"Nothing. He owns a huge estate in Scarsdale. It's on about fifty acres with tennis courts, three pools, a ten-car garage. The landscaping is gorgeous, and you know how I feel about flowers.

"The house has to be seen to be believed. He gutted an old inn, and had the entire thing rebuilt. Actually, now that I think about it, Eric designed the inside. It has a dozen guest bedroom suites, three entertainment rooms, a main kitchen and two auxiliary ones for people who stay over and want to make breakfast or what-have-you."

Jessica let out a long, low whistle.

"And the house has twenty-two bathrooms."

"Does he still work at the company?"

"That's the amazing thing. When they bought him out, they offered him a seven-figure salary to stay on as CEO, but he turned them down flat. He took his money and he decided to enjoy it. He travels, spends time in the city, dines at the best restaurants, sees shows and goes to concerts, sometimes with a woman on his arm, sometimes by himself." Steph laid her hand on Jessica's arm. "Get this. He even learned to ride and keeps a stable of thorough-breds. He flies his own plane and goes to Boston for lunch. But he gets his jollies throwing parties."

"How do you mean?"

"He throws lavish parties and spends money like it's water. One party was a masked costume ball. He prepaid for everyone to rent costumes from one of the biggest Broadway distributors. We all went down and took our pick. Lord, that was some party."

"I'm impressed. Does anyone else give parties like that?"

"We all agreed early on not to play can-you-top-this. We all have the type of party we want to and leave the conspicuous consumption to Gary.

"Once he rented a yacht for an evening and we went out into the lower harbor and partied. Another time he flew us all to a private Caribbean Island for a weekend. He'd had the whole place set up with tents, food, wine, even a dance floor. Warm breezes, good champagne, and free love. For another weekend, he took over one of those hedonism resorts, the ones with the champagne-glass-shaped hot tubs in every room."

"You're kidding."

"He's a hedonist, with the money to indulge himself. The costume party was the one during which Brian and I first discovered one of our favorite pastimes."

"Don't tell me you discovered sex. I remember you and Brian in the backseat of a certain Pontiac."

"Not sex but a new and particularly exciting way to enjoy it."

"So tell me everything."

Steph raised an eyebrow. "I think you're ready to hear the next installment in my sexual education. I remember it so clearly, even though it was two years and many parties ago."

"We have to dress as our favorite sexual fantasy," Steph said.

"For what?" Brian said absently.

"For Gary's party a week from Saturday. It's a costume thing and we have to dress as our favorite fantasy." She turned the invitation over and there were the names and addresses of one costume shop in Manhattan and one in White Plains.

Brian looked up from the current issue of *Time* magazine. "My favorite sexual fantasy? In costume? I don't think so." They sat at the dinner table over dishes of fresh fruit and cups of coffee.

Brian's tone seemed harder than usual. Steph looked up at him. "Why not?" she asked, curious.

"I don't have many sexual fantasies but the ones I have are mine and I don't share. And certainly not in dumb costumes." He looked back down at his magazine.

"We've never talked much about sexual fantasies. I assume you have a few."

"Enough," he growled.

Ignoring his harumphing, Steph pushed a bit harder. "Come

on, tell me. Chasing Heather Locklear around Melrose Place maybe? Or making love in the bathroom of a 747? Tell me. Please?"

"No."

Stephanie sensed that he was protesting too hard and might enjoy talking about his desires. She poured two glasses of brandy, walked to Brian's chair, pulled the magazine from his hands, and plunked herself in his lap. She handed a glass to Brian and said, "Come on."

"This is dumb," he said, sipping the drink Steph had handed him. "If you want me to tell you a fantasy, you have to tell me one of yours. And not one of those lightweight backrub or bubble-bath fantasies either. I assume you have a few, don't you?" he said, mimicking her question. When she was silent for a moment, he continued, "See. It's not easy to just tell someone that secret."

"I thought we didn't have secrets," Steph said, standing up.

"We don't," Brian said seriously. "Not real secrets. It's just that fantasies are personal. It's risky to tell someone that you want to, oh let's say make love in the pool."

"We've done that," Steph said.

"Don't pick nits with me. You know what I mean."

"Actually, I do." Steph was thoughtful. She did have some fantasies that she'd never shared with another soul. She was sure that if she said them out loud, everyone would know she was really perverted. Several vivid pictures flashed through her mind and her eyes glazed.

Several moments went by, then Steph snapped back to the present. She looked at Brian and found him staring at her. "You were a million miles away," he said. "Fantasies?" Steph's cheeks turned pink. "Holy cow," Brian said. "You're blushing."

Steph giggled and covered her face with her hands.

Brian picked up the two brandy glasses and said, "Follow me."

Steph followed him up to the bedroom. He placed the glasses on his bedside table, then placed one hand on each of his wife's shoulders and pushed her over backward onto their bed. He turned out all the lights, then stretched out beside her. "You know, I must admit that I'm so excited by this fantasy idea that my cock is almost painfully hard."

Steph propped herself up on one elbow, reached over and started to unzip Brian's jeans. He placed his hand on hers and removed it from his crotch. "Not yet." He hesitated. "This is really tricky," he said with a sigh, "but part of me wants to share a fantasy I've had for a long time. If I tell you one of mine, will you tell me one of yours?"

"Phew. This got serious in a hurry." She dropped onto her back.

"It's not serious, just intense."

"Why now, after all these years?"

"You started this, you know. And now we're playing with other people and, without realizing it, I've played out some fantasies with them. But part of me wants to play out a fantasy with you." Steph could hear his voice brighten. "Of course," he continued, "part of me is scared as hell."

"Scared I'll think you're weird?"

"Exactly."

"Scared to say it out loud? Because I'll think you're perverted?" When he remained silent, she added in a small voice, "Me too."

Brian rolled onto his side and kissed his wife softly on the lips. "Nothing you could tell me could make me think you were weird, at least any weirder than I already know you are."

"And nothing you could tell me would ever, ever make me think less of you. I promise," Steph said.

Brian took her hand and rolled onto his back in the dark. There was a long silence while each considered the new ground they were treading on. "Why don't I tell you a story," Brian said finally. "Let's see how far I get."

"Okay," Steph said.

"Once there was a young man. He was in his late twenties and he was the janitor at an all-girls high school. It was one of those schools where the girls all wear uniforms. You know the ones." Brian dropped her hand and lay not touching his wife.

"Sure," Steph said softly, trying to encourage what she knew was a difficult revelation. "Maybe the uniforms were blue-and-green plaid skirts and crisply starched white blouses."

"Yeah," Brian said. "Just like that. And this janitor, maybe his name's John, he likes to listen to the girls giggle. Most of the time they forget he's even around and they talk about their dates and boys and things like that."

Steph thought about taking Brian's hand, but didn't. She didn't want to do anything that might interrupt.

"John's particular favorite was a girl named Missy. She was all blond and blue-eyed, with a great body, only partly concealed by the dumpy clothes she was forced to wear. He would slowly sweep the floor and watch her as she talked about her dates. He'd watch her mouth and her hands and her hips and her large breasts. More and more, he became fixated on her breasts. He had to see them."

When Brian lapsed into silence, Steph encouraged, "Go on."

"Anyway, although he never wanted to really hurt anyone, over the months he decided that he had to see her, have her all to himself. So one afternoon he drove along the route he knew she took home every afternoon. He saw her up ahead, her cute tush swaying as she walked. He pulled his car to a stop beside her."

Brian took a deep breath. " 'Hi, Missy,' he said to her. 'Need a lift?' 'Oh hi, John,' she said back. 'Sure, if you don't mind. I just live a few blocks from here.' So she comes around to the passenger side of the car and opens the door."

Brian was silent for a long time. Steph took his hand in the dark. "This is really difficult for you. You don't have to tell me any more."

"I know I don't," Brian said. "And a lot of me wants to stop, but part of me wants to tell the story. God, telling it makes me horny."

"Want to get naked?" Steph asked.

"You know, it's funny but it's easier to do this with clothes on and in the dark."

Steph rolled against Brian's side and pillowed her head on his shoulder. "Okay. Missy's climbing into John's car so he can drive her home. Except I don't think he's going to drive her home. Is he?"

"No. He lives in a remote part of town, in a house where they won't be disturbed. That's where he's going to go."

"When does she catch on that they're not going to her house? What does she do?"

"Well," Brian said, slipping back into the story, "he's planned this all very well. He's got the car's seat belt rigged so it's really tight and doesn't release. Missy throws her books and stuff into the back and sits down in the passenger seat. John reaches over and pulls the seat belt over her, trapping her hands at her sides. He snaps it into the holder and speeds away.

"It takes a minute before Missy realizes that she's in trouble."

Steph slipped into the fantasy. " 'Let me go,' Missy says, squirming, unable to get loose. 'What are you doing? Where are we going?' What does John answer?"

"John is silent. He's enjoying her struggles. He likes to watch the way her breasts are separated by the seat belt and how they move as she wriggles. 'I'll scream,' Missy says. 'Don't bother,' John says. 'With the windows closed and the heater on, no one will hear you.'

"So eventually they arrive at John's house. Missy is thinking that she'll get loose when he tries to take her into his house, but he's thought all that through very well. He gets out, comes around to her side and, before she can yell, he's tied her hands behind her and put a scarf into her mouth so she can't scream."

Steph wanted to give Brian the option of a cooperative scenario. "Maybe she's only pretending to struggle. Maybe she has enjoyed watching him watch her all along."

Steph could feel Brian thinking about her option. "Oh yes," he said, "maybe that's right. She's a little tease and enjoys making the boys sweat before she lets them have her."

"Maybe," Steph said, "but she'll never let John know that."

"He wants her to fight, but it's comforting to know it's all an act."

"You know, I always wanted someone to kidnap me," Steph whispered. "And ravish me while I fought as hard as I could, knowing that I couldn't win." It had become so much easier to share her fantasy, too. It was the sharing that made it all right.

"Really?" Brian said.

Steph took Brian's hand and pressed it against her crotch. Even through the denim of her jeans, he could feel the wet heat.

"I never suspected," Brian said.

"Will you continue the story?"

"Sure," Brian said, his voice stronger. "John carried Missy into the house, placed her on the bed, spread her legs, and tied her ankles to the bedframe. He tied her arms to the headboard, wide apart."

Steph spread her legs and arms on the bedspread. "Turn on the light," she whispered.

Brian flipped the switch and looked at his wife, spread-eagled on the soft rose bedspread.

"Like this?" she whispered.

Brian drew a ragged breath. "Just like that, except she was tied."

"Was she?" Steph said softly. "How?"

"Shit, baby," Brian said, trembling. "Are you serious?"

"Tie me down, then tell me more of the story." God, she wanted this. It had been a fantasy of hers for as long as she could remember.

Brian pulled several stockings from Steph's dresser and awkwardly tied her wrists and ankles to the head- and footboards of the bed. Then, for a long time, Brian stared down at his wife. What had started as a small, risky story had turned into something far more intoxicating. Although she was still fully dressed, Steph looked so vulnerable. "Are you okay? Is this all right with you?" he asked hoarsely.

Steph wanted even more. "Am I allowed to speak?"

Brian looked as if she had ignited him. She had asked his permission to speak. "Tell me," he said.

"I am much more than okay. I'm so turned on I could come

just listening to your story. Tell me more. Show me what John did in that remote house."

Brian swallowed hard. His voice was trembling. "John had Missy tied to the bed, but she still had her uniform on. He was prepared for that, though. He had a big pair of scissors and he slowly cut off all her clothes."

"Did he do it very slowly? Did he watch her face as she slowly revealed her body? Did she tremble as his fingers touched her bare skin?"

"Oh yes," Brian said. "He mostly liked looking at the white cotton underwear she had to wear under her uniform."

"I'm not wearing anything like that," Steph said, "but there's a pair of scissors in the hall closet." When Brian continued to stare at her she nodded. "Do it," she whispered.

He hurried to the closet and returned with the scissors.

"What did he cut off first?" Steph asked.

"He started with her socks." Brian worked around the stocking-ties and cut Steph's socks off.

"What do you see?" Steph asked as Brian gazed at her ankles.

"Those ties around your legs are the most erotic things I've ever seen." He looked into her eyes. "Next he cut her pants."

"I've got other jeans," Steph said. "And these are old anyway."

Brian smiled and started at the cuff of her right pant leg. He cut up to her belly, then repeated the process with the other pant leg. Then he connected the openings by cutting across just above her pubis. He looked at her tiny black-lace panties, then touched the crotch. "You're soaked," he said, incredulous.

"What did John do next?" Steph asked.

Brian unbuckled Steph's belt, cut up the front of her pants and pulled them open. With less hesitation, he cut up the front of her black sweatshirt, then down the arms until she lay in the tatters of her clothing, wearing only her bra and panties.

"Does he like what he sees?"

"John likes what he sees. Missy struggles, knowing what John has in mind. As she moves against the ropes that are holding her body wide open for him, he watches her breasts and her pussy, knowing they are his for the taking."

Steph pulled against the stocking holding her limbs. She writhed, her breathing uneven, her nipples pressing against the lace of her bra. When Brian reached underneath to unhook her bra, she said, "Cut it. Cut it off of me."

Brian cut the thin strip of fabric that connected the two cups, then the straps above them. He feasted his eyes on his wife's luscious body.

"God, baby," she said, "you're making me crazy. What next?"

A slow smile lit up Brian's face. "John did things very slowly. He liked to stretch out every part." Brian reached down and rubbed the nylon-covered flesh between Steph's legs. He found her swollen clit and rubbed and stroked until her hips were bucking beneath his hand. "He also had a few surprises for Missy. He had prepared for a long time for this moment."

Brian went into the bathroom, rummaged in the closet for a moment, then found an old plastic toothbrush holder. He washed it, then brought the phallus-shaped instrument back into the bedroom. He and Steph had never played with toys, but this was his fantasy and he would know it if he went too far. From the look on Steph's face, he suspected that she was hot enough for almost anything.

He stood next to the bed, brandishing the bright red phallus. " 'I'm going to fuck you with this, Missy,' John said. 'And you can't prevent it.' John pulled her panties aside and rubbed his toy all over Missy's pussy." Brian took the scissors and cut the sides of Steph's panties and pulled the fabric free. The he rubbed the red plastic through the soaked folds of her cunt. "Then John slipped the toy inside."

Steph felt the cold plastic invade her body. She was beyond any coherent thought. "God, Brian, make me come."

Brian rubbed her clit with one hand and fucked her pussy with the plastic cock with the other. "Missy fought the orgasm," he said, "but John kept fucking her. Missy didn't want to come but

John had complete control of her body." Brian bent low over Steph's bush. He knew just what his wife liked. "When he ate her, she couldn't hold it back." He slid the plastic in and out of Steph's pussy while his mouth sucked her clit.

Steph screamed, unable to control what was happening to her. She climaxed in a blaze of heat and clenching muscles. Usually her orgasms were sharp and short, but this one went on and on and Brian wasn't letting her body calm. She felt him rub and suck until finally she shrieked, tightened all her muscles, came again, then became limp.

Brian quickly untied Steph's wrists and ankles, then stripped off his clothes and stretched out beside her.

Steph's hand found his hard cock and her fingers wrapped around it. "You're so hard," she purred, "and so big. I'll bet Missy would be impressed." She squeezed. "But she couldn't use her hands if she was still tied up, could she?" She got onto her knees and, still trembling from her violent climax, clasped her hands behind her back and lowered her mouth toward Brian's cock. "All he could do would be to hold her hair, bend her head back, and force his cock into her mouth." Steph pursed her lips around Brian's cock and sucked it deep into her wet mouth. Up and down she bobbed, sliding her tongue and cheeks over his slick erection.

"Shit, baby, I'm going to come."

"Do it," Steph said.

"But. . . ."

He had never come in her mouth before but now she wanted it all. "Do it," she said, fucking his cock with her mouth. In only moments, he spurted deep into her throat. She had always been afraid it would make her gag, but, although it tasted strange, it didn't bother her at all. She swallowed some and let the rest of the thick fluid flow down her husband's penis. Then she lay her head on his stomach and wrapped her arms around his waist.

They gazed at each other silently, then burst out laughing. "That was not to be believed," Brian said.

"I'll bet people in the next county heard me scream."

"Was that really a fantasy of yours?" he asked quietly.

"Yes," Steph admitted. "I've always wanted to be ravished."

"Why?"

"I don't know. I guess I like someone else to be in control. You can put layers of psychological gobbledygook on it, but I just like it. Wow, did I like it."

"Me, too, baby. Me too."

Steph finished telling Jessica the story. "I guess that's quite an admission, friend to friend. But I do love to be play-raped. Brian and I do that often now."

Jessica was silent for a long time.

"Are you shocked?" Steph asked, suddenly afraid she'd said too much.

Jessica grinned and patted Steph's hand. "Not at all. I'm sorry for my silence. I'm just thinking about my own fantasies." She chuckled. "Rob would be mortified to hear me say this, but I would lie in bed after we'd made love, frustrated and angry. I'd wish that he would do things to me, things that at the time I thought were dirty and weird. Let me tell you that I never even masturbated while we were married, but it would have helped at those moments. But I'd fall asleep remembering a scene in a movie I saw once. I was snapping past the Playboy channel late one night. I didn't even have the courage to watch the damn thing, although I was curious. But as I snapped past, a woman had a man on a leash and was ordering him to do things to her."

"Like what?" Steph asked.

"You know, the funny thing is that I was never sure what. Now, however, I've got a few ideas." She shook her head to clear her thoughts. "Did you go to that party?"

"Believe it or not, we found a schoolgirl uniform in my size, just like the one in Brian's story. And we got a pair of coveralls for him, and a mop and bucket." She smiled dreamily at the memory. "We came home from the costume shop and, although he couldn't cut the clothes, we did the next best thing. He tied and untied me until he stripped me naked, then we fucked and fucked. . . ." Steph squirmed in her seat.

Both women took deep breaths. "I wasn't sure about going to this party before but now I'm really looking forward to it," Jessica said. "Does it have a theme?"

"That's right. I got the invitation last evening, but I forgot to open it." Steph fetched the small square envelope and ripped it open. "Storytellers," she read, "have existed for thousands of years. In days of old they told tales of bravery, sacrifice, beauty, and devotion. More recently they tell of submarines and crime. The kind of story I like best tells of love and desire. So, for Saturday night, if you like, write an erotic story for us to share. Make it as hot as you like, as hot as I'd like. Submit it anonymously or sign it. Read it yourself, or I'll read it. I've already written one about an alien couple making love to an earth person, but of course you can pick your own subject. Have fun writing and I'll see you Saturday."

"What an interesting idea for a party," Jessica said.

"I love the idea of a story about making love with an alien. Are you going to write one?"

"I might just," Jessica said. Ideas were whirling in her head. "But I've never written anything like that. I've never even read anything like that, except for Hollywood novels."

"Come upstairs with me a minute." Steph and Jessica went to the master bedroom where Steph opened her closet and pointed to several large stacks of books and magazines. "My collection."

Jessica stared. There were copies of x-rated magazines, books of erotica, books of sexual advice, even books devoted to sexual games and fantasies. Steph pulled several out of the pile and handed them to Jessica. Then she added a few magazines to the stack. "Read."

"Wow."

"But I'm warning you that this stuff," she patted the magazines, "gets you very excited. Do you have a date with Cam tomorrow night?"

"He called last evening. He's picking me up about three tomorrow and we're driving to Connecticut."

Steph smirked. "You'll be eager to see him, I'm sure. And, when you're ready to try writing a story, Brian's laptop computer's in the den."

"Can I take it upstairs?"

"Sure. Plug it in in your room. I'll use the one downstairs."

Jessica giggled. "I'm going to do a lot of reading, then we both can write something deliciously outrageous?"

"I think we must."

It was late that night and Jessica lay in the dark on her bed. A wide shaft of moonlight colored the room in a soft blue. Steph's story had fascinated her, opening new realms for her fertile imagination, as had the books she'd read all afternoon.

So much was possible. She could do anything, be anyone. It was as if someone had opened an entire area of her mind and thousands of pictures poured out. Pandora's box was open.

She looked at her body, glowing in the moonlight. She played Steph's story through in her mind for the dozenth time. It had become as familiar as if she had lived it. She was tied to the bed, helpless, not responsible for anything but taking pleasure. In the fantasy, however, she was also Brian, having someone under her control. She closed her eyes and thought about several stories she had read. Pieces moved, separated and reformed. Pictures, images, positions. I am JessicaLynn, she thought, in control of myself and my sexual destiny. She thought about her ideal partner in this new world.

He was tall, in his mid twenties, with sandy hair and deep blue eyes. He had a gorgeous body, honed by hours of daily heavy manual labor. His muscles were well developed and, because he worked without a shirt, his skin was heavily tanned, smooth, and hairless. When he lifted heavy two-by-fours his muscles rippled and sweat trickled down his chest and disappeared in the waistband of his jeans.

He worked for her, constructing an addition to a house she was selling. His crew had left for the day, but he remained to finish a small piece of work. His name was Walt.

As Jessica lay on the bed a soft breeze wafted across her naked skin and she smiled. Yes, she thought, his name is Walt.

"Ms. Hanley," Walt called from just outside the kitchen door, "I'm done for today."

JessicaLynn was dressed in a pair of short-shorts and a tank top that left little to the imagination. She had been aware of Walt's stares but she had been waiting for just the right moment to take advantage of the situation.

"How about a cold drink?" JessicaLynn asked.

"That would be great," he said. "Thanks." He walked into the kitchen and sat down at the table as JessicaLynn put a glass of iced tea in front of him. "It's really shaping up," he said, his gaze moving from her nipples to his hands.

"Yes," JessicaLynn said. "It's coming along nicely. You do excellent work."

"Thanks," he said, finding his eyes more and more drawn to her breasts.

"You look very warm. I'm sorry the air conditioning isn't working properly yet." She walked around behind him, leaned over his shoulder and took his frosty glass from his hand. "This might help." She wiped her finger through the beads of condensation on his glass, then down Walt's spine. "Better?"

His only answer was a quick intake of air.

JessicaLynn placed the cold glass against his overheated back and, when he jumped, placed the flat of her tongue against the cold spot. "Sorry," she whispered, "I didn't realize it would be so cold."

He turned in his chair and looked up at her, the obvious question in his eyes.

"Yes," she said, "but my way." She paused, watching passion darken his eyes. "You can leave at any time. But, for as long as you stay, you will belong to me. And it will be the most fantastic time of your life."

"That's all right with me," Walt said softly.

"In which case, you will obey the following rules. You will call me Mistress and speak only when you are spoken to. Do you agree?"

"Yes."

"Yes?"

"Yes, Mistress."

"You will do as you are told without hesitation. If anything is distasteful you may say, 'Only if you wish it' and I will reconsider. Do you understand?"

"Yes, Mistress."

"And you will not be restrained in any way. At any time you may leave. If you do, however, you may not return to me for this, just to work on the house. You will do what you do willingly. Do you understand?"

"Yes, Mistress."

JessicaLynn cupped her right breast through her tank top, extending it to Walt. "Suck," she said. When he reached out to wrap his arms around her waist, she added, "No hands."

Walt leaned forward and took the fabric-covered nipple in his mouth. He sucked and licked until the material was slick with his saliva. JessicaLynn backed away. "Enough. I'm going to change now, and you will sit here." She watched his fists clench and unclench. She reached down and pressed her palm against the fly of his jeans. "And that is mine. You may not touch it without my permission and I do not give my permission. Do you understand?"

"Yes, Mistress," he said.

JessicaLynn pulled the tank top off over her head, exposing her naked body to Walt's eager gaze. "You will be able to do wonderful things that will excite both of us, but only if you behave."

"I will, Mistress."

"You know," JessicaLynn said as she headed toward the kitchen door, "I like that eager look in your eyes. I like knowing how much you want me. You'll do anything to have me, won't you?"

Walt sighed. "Oh yes, Mistress. I'll do whatever you want."

JessicaLynn smiled. "Of course you will." She walked out and upstairs. While she changed clothes, she thought about Walt, sitting in the kitchen, waiting for her hungrily.

As Jessica lay on the bed in her moonlit room, creating the scene in her mind, she slid her hands over her ribs and up to her full breasts. He's so hungry, she thought.

When JessicaLynn arrived back in the kitchen she was wearing a tight black-leather teddy with metal studs and openings and covered with chains and hooks in various places. Her breasts were uncovered, as was her pussy. Her matching high-heeled leather boots came to just below her knees and she wore narrow, butter-soft black leather straps around her wrists and a wider one around her neck. She had several matching straps in her hand. She walked to within a foot of Walt and watched his eyes.

He stared, his gaze moving slowly from her out-thrust nipples to the tangle of red hair that peeked out through the open crotch. He looked at her face, now made up with heavy eye shadow and liner and deep crimson lipstick, then lowered his gaze to the floor.

"Do you want this?" JessicaLynn asked.

"Oh yes, Mistress," he said.

She reached out and ran her hand over his smooth, rock-hard chest. "Nice," she purred. She fastened a leather collar around Walt's neck and one around each wrist. "You're not restrained in the usual sense," she said. "But these straps mark you as my possession. Strip."

Clumsily, his hands shaking, he pulled off his work boots, socks, jeans, and shorts. His cock was fully erect, rising from a thatch of sandy hair.

JessicaLynn handed him a leather jockstrap. "Put this on."

Walt stared at the tiny garment, then down at his enormous cock. "But. . . ."

JessicaLynn raised one eyebrow.

"Yes, Mistress," Walt said, pulling the garment on and stuffing his cock into it as best he could.

"Now," she said, "you like sucking my tits, don't you?"

141

"Oh yes, Mistress."

JessicaLynn placed two kitchen chairs about two feet apart. "I want you to kneel, one knee on each chair."

Walt scrambled to obey. With his knees widely separated, the awkward position left his jockstrap-covered cock and balls exposed.

"Clasp your hands behind your back." Walt did.

JessicaLynn moved so her erect nipple touched Walt's cheek. When he turned to take it into his mouth, she backed up. "No," she said. "Move only when you are told to." He turned back and she rubbed her nipple over his cheek, his chin. She watched as he licked his lips, but made no other movement. She heard his thick, heavy breathing, saw his thighs begin to shake with the exertion of his strained position. Finally, she brushed her nipple against his lips and he opened his mouth slightly. "That's fine," she said. "Open your mouth but don't move unless I tell you to."

He did and JessicaLynn rubbed her erect nipple over his teeth and tongue. "Such a good boy," she said. "You may lick it."

She felt his tongue lave her flesh, gently caressing. "Suck," she said, needing him, wanting him.

He was like a man first starved, then given a feast. He sucked and licked, pleasuring first one breast, then the other. The erotic sensations were so intense, JessicaLynn felt as if she could come just from the feeling of his mouth. But that wouldn't do at all.

Jessica opened her eyes and looked down at her moon-bathed body, naked and so hot. Her hands played with her nipples, pinching them and making them hard and tight. She felt the heat in her belly and slid her hand down, tangling her fingers in her red bush. She found her flesh warm and moist as she had several times in the past few days. She knew now where to touch to give herself the most pleasure. She touched those magic places.

"Enough," JessicaLynn snapped. She grabbed Walt's crotch and squeezed his cock. "You're very good at that. It pleases me."

"I'm so glad, Mistress. I like giving you pleasure."

JessicaLynn smiled. "Are your legs tired?" She ran her hand

down one steel-hard thigh, straining from the difficulty of holding himself up for so long with his knees separated.

Walt hesitated, then said, "Not if it does not please you, Mistress."

JessicaLynn patted his pouch, then said, "Come inside."

Walt took a moment to stretch his aching thigh muscles, then followed JessicaLynn into the living room. His feet sank into the thick carpeting and he watched her stretch out full length on the black leather couch, one foot on the back and one foot on the floor. She snapped her fingers and pointed so he knelt at her side at the level of her knees.

She handed Walt a comb. "I like my bush looking nice," she said. "Comb it nicely."

He used the comb so the teeth just touched her skin, caressing her with the plastic.

"And I like my thighs to be very soft." She handed him a bottle of baby lotion. As she watched intently, he filled a hollow in his palm. When he took some on his fingers, she added, "It must be warmed first."

He held the lotion in his cupped hand until it was body temperature, then rubbed it into her thighs with long, powerful strokes. He rubbed the lotion into every inch of her skin, raising her legs so he could stroke the backs as well.

"Is it all to your pleasure, Mistress?" Walt asked.

JessicaLynn reached down, ran a finger through her dripping cunt, then extended it for Walt to lick. "Do I taste good?" she asked.

He sucked her finger. "Oh yes, Mistress."

"Would you like to lick my pussy now?"

"May I please?"

JessicaLynn nodded and Walt lay the flat of his tongue against her clit, pressing gently. She placed her hands on his muscular shoulders and felt the play of his muscles beneath his skin as he caressed her with his mouth. "Yes," she said, "right there. Lick it and suck it good."

Eyes glazed in the moonlight, Jessica's hand slid through her folds, rubbing her clit. She inserted one finger of her other hand into her waiting cunt, filling herself, driving herself higher. In her fantasy, she came, yet in her bedroom she wanted more, and she now knew what it was.

As spasms rippled through JessicaLynn's cunt, Walt filled it with his fingers, pumping, rubbing, spreading. He licked, sucked, rubbed, and caressed until her body was drained of every ounce of her climax. She lay, panting, while Walt watched her. "That was very good," she purred. "But there's more. You watched me come, now I get to watch your pleasure too."

Walt looked a bit startled.

"Haven't you ever touched yourself with someone watching you?"

Walt paused a moment, then said, "No, Mistress."

JessicaLynn stared at his swollen crotch. "But you're so excited, you want to come very badly, don't you."

Walt groaned. "Oh yes, Mistress."

"Well then, you'll have to do it yourself." She pointed to the leather jockstrap he wore. "Take that thing off."

She smiled as she watched his hesitancy. She loved his embarrassment. "There are no shackles on you. You know where the door is. But, if you want to stay, take that off."

While his eyes remained staring at the floor, he wriggled out of the leather garment. He stood, trembling, his engorged cock jutting from his body.

"Pull that glass table over here," JessicaLynn said, indicating a chrome and glass coffee table in the corner of the room. Walt pulled the table near the sofa. "Now kneel," JessicaLynn said. When he knelt on the soft carpeting, his cock was just above the level of the table.

JessicaLynn reached out, placed her hand on top of his cock and pressed it down against the cold glass. "Feel good?"

"Yes, and no, Mistress. I like your hand on me, but the glass is very cold."

"You take the good with the bad," JessicaLynn said. She stroked his cock, keeping it pressed against the table. She could feel him twitch, almost ready to come. She pulled her hand back. "But I said I wanted to watch you. Touch it yourself."

Hesitantly, Walt touched his cock with one hand. "Wrap your fingers around it, rub it with long strokes." She grabbed the lotion. "No wait, hold out your hand." She filled his palm with lotion. "Now do it."

JessicaLynn watched his face as he drifted deeper into his own sensation. She could see as his pleasure took precedence over his embarrassment. "Use both hands," she said.

His other hand joined and they rubbed and squeezed. "Oh," he moaned. He was lost. Spurts of thick come erupted from his cock, splashing onto the table.

"That's a good boy," JessicaLynn purred. "A very good boy."

In her room, Jessica couldn't hold back anymore. The vision of a man masturbating while she watched drove her over the edge. She gave in to the spasms that filled her body, feeling the rhythms that filled her. She sighed audibly, long and low as her body continued to climax. She touched the spot that extended the climax and trembled, panting, the picture of Walt coming filling her mind.

When she was calm again, she thought about her fantasy. She wondered whether it was best to keep this idea in her mind. No, she decided. If she had the opportunity, she would act this one out. But with whom?

EIGHT

―――――•◦✦◦•―――――

"I guess I've always found sex to be a bit of a letdown for me," Cam said as he and Jessica walked, hand in hand, along the water. They had driven to a small strip of beach in Fairfield, Connecticut, after a sumptuous dinner at a local seafood restaurant. They had removed their shoes and walked across sand still warm from the heat of the day, to the water's edge. Cam had rolled up his pant-legs and now walked calf-deep in salty foam, with Jessica on his left, only ankle-deep.

"A letdown?" Jessica said. Jessica had been puzzled by the fact that, although this was their third date and Cam talked about how sexy she was and how much he wanted her, he hadn't made a serious pass at her.

"I've dated lots of women, don't get me wrong, and I've been to bed with many of them. But it hasn't been, well, you know, skyrockets, the earth moving, that sort of thing. From what you've told me, you seem to have found that in the past few weeks, and I'm envious."

146

"I guess I thought that you men had it easy. You're always ready, willing, and able and you can do what you want in bed."

"Not so. I spend most of my time worrying about whether I'm making my partner happy."

"Haven't you ever had anyone ask for what they want? Wouldn't that make it easier for you?"

"Sure it would," Cam said, standing still and gazing out over the ocean, watching the sky darken. "But not many women are willing to do that. Or at least I haven't found any."

"Take a big risk with me," Jessica said, holding Cam's hand tightly. "Describe to me your perfect sexual evening."

"Phew," Cam said. "That's really difficult."

"I know it is, but it may just get you what you want. Is the risk of telling me worth that reward?"

Cam took a deep breath and let it out very slowly. "I don't think I can."

"Okay," Jessica said, holding Cam's hand tightly. "Let me try to help. . . ."

Interrupting, Cam started walking. "This is going too far," he said. "Let's just walk and enjoy the evening."

"Stop," Jessica said. "Stand right there." Jessica felt the tightening of Cam's hand as he stopped in his tracks. "That's better," she continued. "Now, I really want to know what you're thinking because I think there's something very wonderful here. Do you trust me?" Cam nodded. Jessica leaned over and kissed Cam on the cheek. "I'm going to say a few things and, if what I say excites you, squeeze my hand. Okay?"

"This is really silly," he said.

"Scary is more like it," Jessica said, noticing that Cam's erection was now clearly visible under the fly of his navy trousers. "Will you trust me?" Cam remained silent, so Jessica continued. "You said you would enjoy making love to someone who told you exactly what to do to give them pleasure. What if a woman was very clear and forceful about what she wanted? What if she told you how to give her pleasure?" She felt Cam's hand tremble.

147

"What if she went further? What if she ordered you to do things?"

Releasing her hand, Cam turned his back to Jessica and stared out to sea.

Jessica stood behind him and reached around his waist. Since he wasn't much taller than she was, she moved her mouth close to his ear. She deliberately switched from 'she' to 'I.' "What if I told you to take both of my hands in yours?"

Slowly, Cam's hand covered hers, his fingers interlocking with hers. Jessica's breathing quickened. This was her fantasy, and, it seemed, his too. She was going to make the decisions. She had read so much about it but had never actually experienced anything like this. Should she go slowly? Should she jump right in? In for a penny . . . she thought.

"Cam, unzip your pants." When he hesitated, she whispered, "Do it."

"But. . . ."

"No talking," she snapped. "Do as you're told."

Jessica could feel Cam's body tremble and he moved his hands slowly to his fly. Ever so slowly, Cam pulled his zipper down. Jessica reached for his cock, which peeked through the opening in his clothes. "Touch it," she said, moving to his side so she could see his hands. "You know you want to, Cam." With a groan, he moved one hand toward his erection, then dropped his hand and again turned his back.

"It would give me great pleasure to see your fingers wrapped around your cock," Jessica said, placing her hands on his shoulders and turning him to face her. "Do it to please me."

Cam looked into her eyes and Jessica watched the battle raging within him. Then Cam's shoulders dropped and his facial muscles relaxed as he gave in to what was happening. He took his cock in his hand and held it. "Oh yes," Jessica said. "You're so beautiful and so excited. Nothing has ever felt like this before, has it?"

"No," he whispered.

Jessica took his free hand in hers. She had to ask him for confirmation one last time. "You don't have to tell me anything with words, but tell me with a squeeze of your hand. Is this what you wanted?"

Jessica felt Cam's hand squeeze hers.

"This is a fantasy of mine, Cam," Jessica said, clearly able to see how excited Cam was. "You're going to be mine for tonight. But I don't want you so hot that you're in pain. Do you know what would please me? I want to see you come. Right here, right now."

Cam looked stricken. "I can't."

"Oh yes, you can," Jessica said. "You know you're so close now that if you slid your cock into my pussy you would come immediately. Close your eyes if you need to and think about pleasing my demanding pussy." She touched Cam's hand, and the hard cock within. "Tightly," Jessica said. "Hold it and think about my pussy. Later tonight, you'll know how wet it gets, how it feels, how it tastes." She felt his free hand twitch. "Tasting me. Is that what you want? Then I'll order you to lick and suck me until my juices are flowing into your mouth."

She watched Cam's eyes close and his hand begin to stroke his cock. "Maybe I'll sit in a chair and order you to your knees in front of me. . . ." Cam's cock erupted, spraying thick fluid into the ocean water. "It's so beautiful to watch you come."

The two were silent for a few minutes as Jessica pulled a tissue from her pocket and handed it to Cam. When he had cleaned himself off, he mumbled, "I don't know what to say."

"Don't say anything. But watching you has made me so horny that I want you right now," Jessica said. "Is there a nice motel nearby?"

They drove to a small motel in town and Cam registered for them. He drove around back and used the key to open the door to room 203. It was a standard room, with a double bed, several chairs, a table and a long dresser. Jessica walked inside. "Close the door," she demanded, "then I want to see all of you. Take off your clothes."

Clumsily, Cam stripped off his slacks, shirt, and shorts.

149

"Now stand there while I look at you." Jessica walked around Cam's naked body, slapping his hands when he started to cover his limp penis. "Keep your hands at your sides," she said. She ran her hands over his shoulders and back, soft, with an extra layer of fat under the skin. She took a handful of his buttocks in each of her hands and dug her fingers into the soft flesh, pulling the cheeks slightly apart. She smiled as she felt him quiver. There were so many things she wanted to try, but one step at a time. She walked around and stood, facing him. Because he had climaxed only a half hour before, his cock was still soft.

"There are so many things I want you to do to pleasure me," she said. "But I need to be sure of one thing. If I do anything, or ask you to do anything that doesn't make you feel good, tell me. Say 'Please no,' and we'll stop. Promise me."

"I promise," Cam whispered.

"Unbutton my blouse." Slowly and awkwardly, Cam pushed each silver button on Jessica's gray silk blouse through its button-hole. "Now unhook my bra." He worked at the center-front clasp until the fastening parted. "Do you want to see them? Touch them? Lick them?" God, she wanted him, but she was enjoying extending her pleasure by making both of them wait.

"Oh yes," Cam said, his eyes glazed.

"I like gentle fingers and soft lips," Jessica said as Cam parted the sides of her bra, exposing her breasts. Softly, reverently, he swirled the pads of his fingers over her skin. He traced the line between tanned skin and creamy white flesh.

Jessica cupped her right breast and held it up. "Suck."

His lips touched the tip of her nipple and shots of electricity stabbed through her body. She pulled back and dropped into a chair. She pointed to the floor and Cam knelt beside her chair. "Yes," she purred, "suck my tits."

Hungrily, Cam's mouth pleasured her breast, kissing, sucking, tasting. She wanted more, and suddenly realized she didn't have to wait until he decided what to do. She could ask for anything she wanted. "Pinch this one," she said, guiding his hand to her other breast. "Harder. Make me feel it."

"But I'll hurt you," Cam said.

"That's not your decision. You do as I ask."

"Oh yes," he sighed.

He pinched her nipple, driving heat through her. "Enough," she said, standing. "Undress me."

She stood, stepped out of her shoes and Cam quickly removed her blouse, slacks, and underwear. When she stood in the middle of the motel room, gloriously naked, she watched Cam's hungry eyes as he looked at her. "Do you like what you see?"

"Yes," he groaned. "And I like what you're doing."

"That's good," she said. "Very good." They were both learning, she realized, each trying to find the ideal place for this fantasy to go. "Is there anything particular you want to add to this?"

"Yes," he said.

"Tell me."

"I want to be able to see it all," he said. The closet doors in the vanity area were mirrored and, slipping out of his submissive role for a moment, he opened first one then another. Soon he had a three-sided, floor-to-ceiling, mirrored area in which his naked body was reflected over and over. He pulled a chair over, repositioned it a few times, then nodded. "If it pleases you," he said softly.

"Oh it does," Jessica said, as she seated herself in the chair. She could see her cunt for the first time between her widely spread legs. Watching in the three mirrors, she slid her fingers through her springy hair, then pointed to the floor between her feet. Cam sat. "Very nice," she said. "We can both watch everything." As Cam stared at Jessica's wet, swollen pussy lips, she asked, "What do you see?"

"I see that your body likes what's happening."

"It does," Jessica purred. "It wants you to touch and watch as you do it."

Cam's fingers slid up the insides of her thighs, and Jessica saw them reflected over and over in the mirrors. She slid her hips forward and pushed Cam's head against one leg to improve her view. She guided Cam's fingers to just the right spots. "Rub here, very slowly. Yes. Faster now. Oh yes." She revelled in being able to tell Cam exactly what she liked.

"I want your mouth," she said, suddenly. "Lick just where your fingers have been. Lick with the flat of your tongue. Yes. Like that. Now suck my clit into your mouth and flick your tongue over it." She was soaring. She closed her eyes, then opened them so she could see Cam's moving head reflected in the three mirrors. Would she let him bring her off this way, with his mouth? Was that what he wanted? But this wasn't for him. It was for Jessica-Lynn. "Put two fingers inside me," she said. "Fuck me with your hand. Hard. Now."

He did and, only a moment later, Jessica came, her fists tangled in Cam's hair. "Don't stop," she yelled. "More." As her orgasm continued she felt Cam's fingers continue their rhythmic fucking while his mouth worked its magic. She spasmed for what felt like hours, then, as her orgasm ebbed, she told Cam to stop.

He laid his head against her belly and said, "I've never felt a woman climax like that," he said. "I could feel the sensation on my hand." He looked up at her and grinned. "It was truly remarkable."

"It certainly was," Jessica said. She looked down at Cam's cock, surprised that he wasn't erect.

Cam's laughter warmed her. "I got a great deal of joy from your orgasm," he said, looking at his limp penis, "but I'm not as quick to recover as I once was and I came less than an hour ago. I'm not ready to make love so soon again."

"I've learned a lot recently and the most important thing is that we *have* been making love. For hours."

"Yes," Cam said. "We have, haven't we."

They stretched out on the bed, pulled the quilt over themselves, talked and napped. Later, they touched and stroked each other, free now to share what gave each of them pleasure. When Cam's hard cock finally slid into Jessica's waiting body, it was a completion to an evening of loving.

Hours later, as Cam's car pulled into the Carltons' driveway, Cam said, "I hope we can see each other soon again."

"Me too. How's your schedule?"

They made plans for the following week and Cam promised to consider new ways that he would like to make love. "Think about something totally outrageous," Jessica suggested. "Then, if it turns me on, we can do it. If not, we'll think of something else."

Cam smiled and kissed her. "With you, this all seems so possible."

"It's all possible," Jessica said, climbing out of the car. "Everything's possible and most things are probable between us."

All day Friday, Jessica worked on an erotic story for Gary's party. She wrote, edited, printed, but wouldn't let anyone read it. When it was as good as she thought it could get, she printed it, without her name on it. "Did you write a story?" she asked Steph Saturday morning over coffee in the plant room.

"Brian and I coauthored one about an alien and a human. We only wrote a few paragraphs at a time. I think we fucked more yesterday than we have in ages."

"At least you had someone to work out your frustrations on."

"You can borrow Brian any time, you know."

"You say that, but it feels weird."

"Eventually, you and Brian will find the right time and the right place. If and when it feels right, you'll know it's fine with me."

"I guess," Jessica said, patting her friend's hand.

"So we each have a story for tonight," Steph said. "Do I get to read yours?"

"Not a chance. I've mentally chickened out several times already, and almost threw it away twice. But I've now decided that Gary can read it at the party tonight. Probably."

Steph laughed. "Brian and I agreed that we'd allow Gary to read ours too. But, even though it's fiction, it's so personal, somehow."

"Yeah. I know what you mean. What are you wearing?" Jessica asked.

The two women discussed the party, then, when Brian returned from a tennis game, the three friends spent the day anticipating the evening to come.

"And you must be Jessica," the tall, almost emaciated-looking man said as he took her hand. "I've heard a lot about you." His eyes held Jessica's.

She inhaled deeply. "And I've heard a lot about you, too." Gary had deeply set eyes and hard, angular features. He's almost homely, Jessica thought, fleetingly, enjoying the heat that his gaze engendered.

"Hello, Gary," Steph said from behind Jessica. "We're here too. Remember us?"

Gary's laugh was rich and deep. "I do remember you," he said, dropping Jessica's hand, grabbing Steph by the waist, lifting her up, then sliding her down the length of his body. He placed a deep kiss on her open mouth, then set her down. He reached for Brian's hand and clasped it warmly.

"Jessica," a voice from the living room called, "it's so nice to see you again."

Jessica remembered Marcy from Steph's party. "It's good to see you too," she said, walking into the enormous living room, comfortably decorated in shades of soft blue, toast, and ecru and filled with comfortable chairs and sofas. Plants softened the otherwise masculine aura and a heavy tweed carpet, overlaid with small patterned area rugs, covered the floor.

"Great news, guys," Marcy said to the three newcomers. "Steven James Albright, Junior weighed in at eight pounds fourteen ounces."

"Fantastic," Steph said. "When did Nan have the baby?"

"Late this afternoon," Marcy announced. "Steve is already saying how considerate his wife was. She woke him about six this morning and the baby was born at five. Eleven hours of labor with no lost sleep and no midnight rides to the hospital."

The room filled and, when everyone had a drink in hand, Marcy said, "To Steven James Albright, Junior." The dozen or so people touched glasses and drank. It was an interesting group. Besides Marcy and Chuck and Pete and Gloria whom she knew from Steph's party, there were three other couples, all between thirty-five and fifty. Jessica considered her previous notion of what swingers would look like. This slightly conservative group wasn't it.

The doorbell rang yet again. "Sorry we're late," a female voice said. "The baby-sitter was late."

Steph leaned over and whispered to Jessica. "Hank and Lara. You remember I told you about them." When Jessica didn't immediately connect, Steph said, "The Boggle game? My first outside activity?"

"Ah yes," Jessica said, looking at the balding man who entered the room, followed by his laughing wife. "I do remember." Steph quickly introduced Jessica to the newest arrivals.

Finally Eric arrived, looking particularly attractive in a black sport shirt and white slacks. Heat flowed through Jessica's body at the sight of the familiar grin. God, he's sexy, she thought. Eric, as if reading her mind, winked.

"Steph," Jessica said softly, "doesn't Gary have a date?"

"Sometimes he does and sometimes not," Steph explained. "Sometimes he does a threesome with another couple. And, of course, couples form, dissolve, and reform during one of these evenings. I can guarantee that I won't spend the evening with Brian, and Gary won't end up alone. It's whatever anyone wants."

Jessica gazed at Eric, who was talking with another couple, then wondered where Gary would end up. "Are there any people here who don't play?" she asked.

"Not tonight," Steph answered, looking around, "although Pete and Gloria won't swap, at least not yet. But they get really excited nonetheless, and take a bedroom and make love all night."

"Anyone who wrote stories," Gary said, "put them on the mantel within the next half hour, with or without a name. Then we'll have my dramatic reading. I've written a fantastic piece of pornography, by the way. Maybe I can even get it published."

"Modesty was never your strong suit, Gary, my love," Marcy said.

"How can you be modest when you're as terrific as I am?" Gary answered.

For the next half hour, the party was not unlike many that Jessica had attended with Rob. People talked about everything from politics to the weather. They ate crab puffs, shrimp in pastry, miniature bacon and spinach quiche, and lamb riblets. Eric made her close her eyes and fed her a roasted green chili stuffed with goat cheese. Some drank champagne, others a soft, Chilean merlot, and still others fruit and rum. A few of the guests drank soft drinks. Jessica slipped away from Eric for a moment, took her story from her purse, and put it on the mantel, with several others.

At about nine o'clock, Gary got everyone's attention. "Okay, reading time. Everyone cuddle up with someone, or some ones, and I'll turn out most of the lights."

People pulled pillows into the middle of the floor, others stretched out on sofas, or sat one atop another in chairs. Gary turned out most of the lights, leaving only a small spotlight shining on the chair in which he sat. Eric had pulled several pillows together and he and Jessica lay side by side, holding hands.

Gary cleared his throat. "Okay, I thought I'd read mine first, just to loosen things up." In a low-pitched, mellifluous voice, he began to read.

THE ALIENS

Louise lay in bed, unable to sleep. She kept thinking about the strange incident at the pool today. The couple who had come over and sat beside her as she dangled her legs in the water were two of the most attractive people that she had ever seen. They had asked her questions about herself that were so personal that she would not have answered them if asked by anyone else. But somehow, after talking with them for only a few minutes, she had felt completely comfortable with the intimacy of their questions. Although she had never met them before, she had felt their warmth, their caring, and their seemingly genuine interest in her. When they got up to leave, Louise had felt an almost overwhelming urge to go with them. Now, lying in bed, she was creating the most wonderful fantasies about them as she stroked herself beneath her nightgown.

As she slid her fingers between her legs, Louise became aware of a glow outside her bedroom window. As it grew brighter and brighter, she became frightened and jumped out of bed to see what was happening. Suddenly she was engulfed in a glowing light that rendered her powerless, unable to move. She felt hands pull her nightgown over her head and lift her into strong, muscular arms. Although she was still afraid, she also realized that the hands and arms that held her were gentle. She somehow felt certain that they would not hurt her and she felt most of the fear flow from her.

Louise opened her eyes to find herself lying on her back on a table in a brightly lit room with bare walls. Her wrists and ankles were bound to the corners of the table by a material that was both the softest she had ever felt and totally unyielding. Strangely, although she should have been uncomfortable, the table was the most restful thing she had ever been on. It molded itself perfectly to her body, firm, yet softer than down.

Suddenly Louise became aware of the couple from the pool, standing, looking down at her. They were wearing long robes of a transparent, shimmering material that seemed to flow over their bodies like a glowing liquid. It was also obvious that they wore nothing underneath.

"Where am I?" Louise asked.

"You wouldn't understand," the man replied, in a voice so warm and soothing that Louise found herself relaxing despite her fear and the strangeness of her surroundings.

"We're not going to hurt you," the woman said in a low, throaty voice. "I am called T'Mar and this is P'Lan. We're from a place that's very far away, but we have learned from long contact with the people of your planet that we're a lot like you. We have been sent here to study the ways our two races are the same and explore the ways we differ. Our particular field of study is sexuality."

"We have been observing your people's mating rituals," P'Lan said. "In many ways, it's similar to our ways of lovemaking. But we prefer small groups rather than pairs. And we have certain sexual abilities that your people don't seem to have. The experiment that we are about to do is designed to find out whether our abilities have sufficient stimulative effects to permit mating between your people and ours."

Louise realized that she was going to be the subject of a sexual experiment and she was helpless to do anything about it. But, she realized that she felt more excited than frightened.

"I'm going to touch your breast," T'Mar said. "You will feel a sensation, but it will not hurt. Just relax."

The woman slowly brought her hand toward Louise's body. Instinctively, Louise tried to move away, but she could not. The woman kept her hand open so that the palm of her hand touched Louise's nipple. Louise's body jolted against her restraints as a sensation instantly made it contract and turn hard. The sensation in her nipple was echoed by an instant feeling of wetness between her legs. As T'Mar placed her other palm on Louise's other nipple, then cupped both of her hands over Louise's breasts, Louise felt an incredible pleasure and heat spread through her. An electric tingling combined with an irresistible need overwhelmed her, and her body bucked and strained against the restraints. She could feel wetness flow between her legs.

T'Mar removed her hands from Louise's body and, as Louise relaxed, smiled down at her. "Now you know what the restraints are for," she said. "They're not to keep you from escaping. Just to prevent you from hurting yourself when we stimulate you."

Louise's head was spinning. All fear was now gone. All she wanted now was to be touched again by this wonderful creature.

Suddenly Louise realized that P'Lan had been watching her while she was being touched by T'Mar. He had seen her naked body writhe and had heard her moan with pleasure. Through his flowing robe, she could see that his erection was not unlike those of the men she had made love with in the past, although thicker and longer. She felt her face turn hot as he gazed into her eyes and smiled knowingly. His face said that he knew she ached to experience his touch. Without realizing what she was doing, Louise spread her knees slightly.

P'Lan tried to explain the wondrous sensations Louise had just experienced. "In your world, there are creatures that use electric currents for defense or for capturing prey. On our world, our bodies are able to generate electric currents also, but we use it only for sexual stimulation—as part of our mating ritual." His eyes conveyed a loving warmth as he continued. "We are going to stimulate you in various ways. If you look around, you will see that you are surrounded by machines that will record your body's reactions to our probing. The only difficult part for you is that you will not be allowed to climax until we have completed our experiment. Now, we want you to just relax."

Relax? Louise's body tensed in anticipation of what she was going to feel. She watched the woman move toward the head of the table and the man toward her legs. Suddenly she felt a warm glow and soothing vibration as the woman began to stroke her temples and forehead. Just as she began to calm, she was jolted against the restraints as the electricity from P'Lan's fingers touched her inner thighs. The calming warmth of the hands on her head only intensified the sexual intensity of the burning pleasure as the man's fingers stroked the bare backs of her knees and the entire length of her naked inner thighs, stopping only when he reached the crease. She gave herself up to the pleasure and whimpered as she felt his hand move over her mound and caress her.

159

T'Mar bent forward and Louise could see her breasts through the shimmering robe. She slid her hands over Louise's breasts until her robe touched Louise's face. Suddenly Louise realized that the robe was not a solid material. It was warm and flowed across and around T'Mar and over Louise's face like water. As the robe flowed over her nose and mouth, Louise could feel the woman's nipple touching her mouth. The electricity sent a burning pleasure over her lips. Instinctively, she opened her mouth and began to suck the woman's pillow-soft flesh. She felt a warm, electrically charged fluid enter her mouth and felt the hot pleasure spread down her throat just as the man's fingers began to stroke the insides of her labia and her clitoris. Desperately she sucked the woman's tit and felt the electricity of the woman's hands caressing her body. She cried out as the man inserted fingers deep into her cunt and she helplessly strained against the restraints, begging T'Mar to let her come. "Just a little longer," the woman crooned. "It will be over soon."

Finally P'Lan looked at the woman and said, "I think we have almost all the data we need. We'll just do the anal stimulation study and then we can give her relief. But you had better hold her. The restraints may not be sufficient."

As Louise began to tremble, T'Mar came alongside the table and stretched out across Louise, belly against belly, breast against breast, leg against leg, pinning her entire body to the table. Louise felt bathed by the warm liquid flow of the woman's robe over her skin, and T'Mar gently spoke into Louise's ear. "Because of the intensity of the erotic stimulation, this part will be difficult to bear but we will soon be finished."

Louise's entire body tingled where the woman pressed against her, and the woman's nipples burned as they pressed against Louise's breasts. Suddenly she felt P'Lan's finger slide between her legs and under her until it touched her anus. With no hesitation, he plunged into her ass and the burning need that filled the entire lower part of her body made her shriek and press upward frantically against the woman who was holding her down. With the man's finger still in her ass, Louise felt the woman slide her hand down between Louise's legs and plunge her fingers into Louise's cunt. For a few seconds there was no electricity, just the sensation of both her ass and her cunt being filled. Then T'Mar crooned in her ear. "Are you ready, Louise? Do you want to come?"

"Please, please," was all Louise could whimper.

The woman looked at the man and in a low, gentle voice said, "Now."

Suddenly Louise shrieked and strained as the electric current from the invading fingers melded into a flame of molten heat and she felt the sensation of her throbbing clitoris spread to every limb, every vein of her body. She felt her cunt contract against T'Mar's fingers and her sphincter contract around P'Lan's hand as wave after wave of orgasm wrenched her body. Moments later she was enveloped in a warm glowing light. And then there was darkness.

Since that day Louise searches the sky every night. She loves to masturbate under the stars, pretending that she is being made love to by aliens. Most people think she's crazy. . . .

Eric's hand had been teasing Jessica's nipple while Gary read the story and now she was squirming, anxious to wrap her legs around his waist and drive his cock into her hungry cunt.

"I do love that story," Gary said. "It makes me so hot to read it." He looked around at the assemblage of hungry bodies. "Don't leave yet. I have other stories and no one's allowed to satisfy hungers with anything except strawberries until I'm done."

Jessica had a flash of Eric rubbing a strawberry on her hot, swollen tissues, then pushing it inside and sucking it out.

Gary's laugh was a deep, rich, highly erotic sound, and, as if reading her mind, said, "And you can't do that either. At least not until I'm done."

"You, dear sir," someone said, "make the Marquis de Sade look like a wimp."

Gary laughed again and Jessica wondered how that laugh would feel rumbling against her nipples as she held him. "Good," he said.

"That's exactly what I had in mind." He picked up a second set of pages. "This one was written by Steph and Brian and, at first glance, it looks like another alien story."

Jessica looked across the room and saw Steph sitting on the floor with Marcy and Chuck, then found Brian stretched out near a woman named Angela.

Gary cleared his throat. "This one is called 'Assimilation.' "

"What have you got?" I asked, looking through the observation glass at the humanoid who had been brought in from sector seven. His back was facing the glass as he sat on the bench in the middle of the sterile room. I could see that he didn't look like any of the inhabitants we'd encountered from the planets in this part of the galaxy. All I had been told was that the alien had walked into sector seven almost one solar day ago and had come to our facility willingly. The report said he seemed to be waiting ever since. Waiting for what? We had no idea. I knew that the research team had been monitoring him since his arrival here, trying to determine his level of intelligence.

"Hi Libby," said Dirk, our chief scientist. "We're not sure what he is. He appears to be a humanoid, but he hasn't responded to any language we've used. He's six feet tall, weighs about two-hundred pounds, and by his build, we're assuming most of that is muscle. His skin looks leathery and he seems to have no hair anywhere on his body." He continued reciting the notes off his clipboard as we walked around the corner to view him from another angle.

"We've been referring to him as male," Dirk continued, "but as you will notice, he has more than one phallus." From the angle at which I was observing, I couldn't make out what Dirk was referring to.

"Has anyone gone in?" I asked, looking at the alien's face from the side. It was smooth and round, giving him an almost human look, except that he had no eyebrows and his eyes were widely spaced, giving him a curious expression.

"No," said Dirk. "We were waiting for you." I was in charge of the research lab and authorized all first-contacts with aliens.

"I'm going in," I said, taking off my clothes.

"Are you crazy?" yelled Dirk. "He could snap you in half in a minute."

"You can use the force shield if I run into problems," I said, pulling off my jumpsuit.

"Do you really need to take off your clothes?" he asked as I handed him my jumpsuit. "It's a little disconcerting."

"Thanks, Dirk, but you know how this works. Tell them I'm going in." I was used to being naked in front of the research team. Throughout our space travels we had found that most civilizations did not wear any type of clothing and it had become a standard practice to take off ours when we interacted with any non-humans.

Dirk looked at me as he pressed a button on the neck of his jumpsuit and spoke into the tiny mike. "Libby is going in to observe. Be ready with the force shield in case she has problems."

I opened the door slowly and the alien turned to look at me. His eyes were peaceful and I saw no tension in his body. I let the door close behind me and entered the room. He was only a few feet away from me when I stopped.

"Hello," I said, smiling at him. "Can you understand me?"

He stood up slowly and turned to face me. My eyes immediately dropped to his groin and I stared at the unique combination of sexual organs. He did not appear to have any testicles, but instead had one penis in the front and a longer one hanging behind it.

He held his hands palm outward in front of him, extending them to me. Looking down at my hands, he nodded for me to raise them. He was only a foot away from me and I swallowed hard as I held my hands toward his.

"Be careful Libby," I heard Dirk say through the intercom.

Our fingers touched and I could suddenly hear his thoughts and feel his emotions. "I am many people, called by many names," he said with his mind. I looked in his eyes, and my thoughts told him my name was Libby.

"Where am I?" he asked telepathically. I told him our galactic location. He explained that he had found our outpost after his ship had been hit by a meteorite. He was a scientist, exploring the galaxy, studying and learning. Then, ever so slowly, his eyes lowered to my breasts and I could feel his sexual need increase.

"Are you okay Libby?" I heard Dirk ask.

"Yes," I said back. "He's communicating telepathically through his fingers."

I could hear his thoughts as he asked me if he could touch my body. I nodded yes and he dropped one of his hands and slid it down my chest until it stopped at my breast. The nipples I had noticed on his chest slowly inverted and started making a sucking sound as he moved his hand from one of my nipples to the other.

I looked down and saw the front penis had extended itself. His hand slid down my stomach and touched the hair around my pubis. When his finger slid between my legs and touched my clit, then rubbed my soaked vagina, I shuddered.

He brought his hand back up and touched his wet fingers against mine. The intensity of his sexual hunger flashed through my body as he stared into my eyes. I felt myself being pulled toward him and I took two steps nearer.

"Are you sure you're all right?" said Dirk over the speaker.

"Yes," I said, keeping my eyes on the alien.

We were standing face to face and he slowly lowered our hands to our sides, keeping our fingers touching at all times. He leaned toward me and, as my nipples touched his inverted breasts, like tiny mouths, they drew them in. I couldn't believe the sensation of the leatherlike suckers on my breasts.

Over the sound of my pounding heart I heard him tell me not to be afraid. He wanted to join with me. The magnetic pull was so strong that I was soon spreading my legs as he pushed his knobby penis inside. I let out a gasp as I felt it slide deeper, moving in and out even though he was standing completely still.

Little knobs around the penis-shaft pulsated against my vaginal walls as it pushed in and out. Soon tiny lips appeared above his penis, locked onto my clitoris, and started sucking.

"Libby!" I heard Dick yell. "What's happening?"

"Oh God!" I said, trying to keep my knees from buckling. "I'm getting fantastically fucked!"

"Do you want us to stop him?" yelled Dirk.

"No!" I yelled. The sensations were magnificent and I most certainly didn't want them to stop. I felt something touch my buttocks and I suddenly realized that his secondary penis had extended itself up to my anus. He heard the panic in my mind and somehow made me relax with his thoughts. His rear penis felt wet and oily as it touched my rear opening, then slowly inserted itself into the hole. It pulsed against the thin wall in unison with the one in my vagina. I wasn't sure how much longer I could stand there. My knees were buckling.

His eyes were intense as he stared at me, but no other visible signs indicated what was going on. His breathing was normal even though I was visibly panting. I tried to move my hands away, but he gripped them and held them tightly against my buttocks, holding me still against him.

His penises were moving in and out seemingly with a life of their own and the lips around my nipples and my clitoris were increasing the pressure of their sucking. I could feel an orgasm building inside of me but I heard him tell me to wait. Then, as he pressed his forehead against mine, a jolt of pure pleasure shot through me that set off a chain reaction. I came. I tried to scream but no noise escaped my lips. I suddenly understood that, despite his physical immobility, he was sharing my orgasm as we stood frozen against each other.

The climax pulsing through my body wouldn't stop and I wondered how long it could go on. "Much longer," I felt him say. Instead of deflating, his penises became harder and pumped in and out faster than before. The sucking became more intense against my clitoris and my nipples, and I felt my legs give out.

His arms held me securely as he braced my body against his. Our foreheads still touching, wave after wave of orgasm continued until I thought I could take no more.

"It's time," I heard him say in my mind.

"I don't know what you mean."

"It's time to become one," he said.

"One?"

"Follow the orgasm." His pumping became harder, faster, increasing the sensations. I could hear Dirk yelling at me, but now I couldn't respond. I was drawn further and further back into his mind with each wave of the orgasm until I saw myself standing next to him. I was somehow inside his mind. It was warm, soft, and unbelievably peaceful as I flowed within him. I watched my body go limp in his arms.

Dirk and two others came running in and pulled the body that had been me out of the room. Then Dirk ran back in, his face filled with rage, and pointed a laser gun at me.

"Wait Dirk!" I said holding up my hand. "It's me." I could hear my voice coming out of the alien's body.

"What do you mean it's you, Libby? What happened?"

"We joined, Dirk," I said. "I'm now a part of him." I now understood everything, and it was wonderful. I watched Dirk drop to the bench and stare at the alien, at me, at the one that was us.

"This is why he travels the galaxy. Every time he mates," I explained, "he incorporates the mind and spirit of the person into him, me, us. I have become part of some complex entity. In addition, when he joins, he takes a body part he needs to grow. He chose my voice because he didn't have one." I/we reached over to pat Dirk's hand and he jumped up off of the bench and bolted toward the door.

"I'm sorry Libby," Dirk said. "I have to consider this for a while."

"I understand, Dirk," I said. "I need some time to adjust as well. But don't be angry or afraid. It's the most miraculous feeling I've ever had."

NINE

❖━━◆◆◆◆◆━━❖

After Gary had read several more stories, he said, "I have one more." Jessica knew it had to be hers. "It's called 'Educating Paul' and," Gary grinned, "it doesn't seem to have anything to do with aliens." Feeling the now-familiar tightness she placed her hand on Eric's thigh as Gary began to read.

It was a bright sunny day and, since Paul's parents were away for the weekend, he was all alone in the house. Although he was a reasonably attractive seventeen-year-old boy, he was painfully shy. Girls thought that he was snobby and aloof and generally avoided him. On his rare dates, he was clumsy in his sexual approaches, and usually did not get very far. He was still a virgin.

As he usually did when his parents were away, Paul had taken advantage of the rare period of privacy by pulling out his collection of erotic pictures and masturbating. It was a treat to be able to spread out his collection of magazines and pictures without having to hide or worry about being *caught*. As he gazed at the pictures of beautiful naked women, he tried to imagine what it must feel like to be touched by one, to feel a girl's tongue against his tongue, to suck a girl's nipple and to feel his hard cock slide deep into her cunt. His cock was rock-hard as he lost himself in his fantasies.

Suddenly he heard the doorbell. Shit, he muttered to himself. He remembered his mother telling him, "I've asked the Jacksons next door to check on you while we're gone." But he had seen the Jacksons drive away about an hour ago. When the bell chimed again he decided to ignore it. Whoever it was would think no one was home and leave him alone. Then he heard the front door open and a woman's voice call, "I know you're home Paul. I saw you through the window."

Paul immediately recognized the voice. It belonged to Terry, the Jacksons' twenty-one-year-old daughter. She had been away at college all year, but she must have come home for the summer. Terry had flaming red hair, long legs, and was gorgeous. Although she was the subject of many of Paul's fantasies, Paul had never had the nerve to talk to her.

"My folks asked me to check up on you," Terry called, as Paul heard her close the front door behind her.

Quickly, Paul shoved his magazines and pictures under his pillow and started to throw on his clothing. Paul wondered what she had seen through the window.

"I'll bet you're in your room," Terry called.

Paul met her at the doorway to his room. They faced each other, Paul's clothing in disarray, his face flushed and Terry dressed in a sundress that displayed the tops of her ample breasts. Her skirt came to mid-thigh and her legs were bare.

Terry smiled at him and looked at the rumpled bed. "Well, it's a good thing I came up to check on you," she said, teasingly. "What have you been doing?"

"Nothing," Paul mumbled, not knowing what to say.

Terry brushed past him, her breasts grazing his arm, and walked over to the bed. Paul's arm felt as though 1000 volts of electricity had gone through it at the point of contact. Sunlight streamed through the window onto Paul's pillow and the corner of the magazine that protruded from beneath it.

Terry slowly reached over and pulled out first one magazine, then the others, along with pictures that Paul had hidden under the pillow. She sat down on the bed and smiled as she slowly leafed through everything. Paul stood and watched, unable to move. "I guess now I *know* what you've been doing," she said with a grin. "But looking at pictures isn't nearly as exciting as looking at the real thing. Come over here," she ordered.

Now trembling as much from excitement as embarrassment, Paul walked over to Terry and looked down at her as she sat on the edge of the bed. Her skirt had ridden up almost to her hips and the sight of her bare thighs and her nipples poking against the thin material of her sundress was making Paul's cock so hard that it was forming an obvious lump in the front of his pants.

"Come closer, Paul," Terry said, her voice low and throaty as she looked directly at the crotch of Paul's pants. She spread her knees apart. "I want you standing right between my knees."

As Paul stood between her legs, Terry calmly and efficiently undid his belt and pulled down his pants and underpants. Then she carefully began to fondle his swollen cock and balls. "What a big cock," she said, stroking the length of its shaft with her right hand while cupping and gently squeezing his balls with her left. Looking up at him she said, "I saw you looking at my tits. I'll bet you're thinking about what it would be like to suck them. Aren't you?"

Paul felt his face get red and the trembling of his body increase.

"And, I saw you looking at my legs. I'll bet you want to touch them. Have you ever put your hand between a girl's legs, Paul?"

Paul's throat was so tight he could not reply.

"Well, I think it's time you learned a few things. Such a big, beautiful erection shouldn't be wasted." Her fingers danced over his skin from his anus, across his balls to the tip of his cock.

Suddenly she removed her hand. "It will be all over too quickly if I keep doing this," she said. Terry reached out and took Paul's right hand and gently pressed it against the front of her dress.

The feel of her nipple and the softness of her breast burned the palm of Paul's hand. He found himself gently squeezing her breast.

"That's very good," Terry said. She removed his hand and slipped the straps of the sundress over her shoulders, lowered the top, then put Paul's hand back on her naked breast. She guided his hands as they roamed across the softness of her bare tits.

"I want you to kneel between my legs now," Terry said. As Paul kneeled, Terry cupped her right hand under her right breast and sliding her left hand around the back of Paul's neck, pulled his face toward her tit. "It will taste so good, Paul," she crooned as Paul opened his mouth.

As Paul sucked, he felt Terry stroke the back of his neck. Her breathing quickened and he heard small sighs and felt her nipple harden in his mouth as he sucked and licked. After a little while, Terry pulled his head away and gave him the other tit. As he sucked and gently bit her nipples, Paul began to stroke Terry's legs and the inside of her thighs. He felt her spread her legs wider, inviting him to explore.

"Don't be afraid, Paul," she encouraged. "It feels wonderful there." As he sucked her tits, she gently took his right hand and slowly guided it deeper into the cleft between her legs. She wore nothing under the dress and soon Paul felt the hot, soft wetness of her mound. He heard Terry sigh as she guided his middle finger along the center of the heat and moisture. He felt the lips separate and then his finger was stroking the slippery insides of her labia.

Terry held Paul's head tightly against her breast, and demanded, "Suck it good, baby, suck it good." She was groaning and her hips were pressing against his hand. With her hand, she guided his finger to her swollen clitoris. "Can you feel that?" she asked him.

"Yes," Paul replied breathlessly, releasing her nipple from his mouth.

"Well, I want you to lick right there. Flick your tongue across it."

Paul hesitated.

"Now do it like a good boy," she ordered, pressing Paul's head down toward her lap, and spreading her legs even wider. "That's such a good boy."

Paul inhaled Terry's wonderful musky aroma as he buried his head between her legs. She tasted delicious when he ran his tongue along the length of her crack then began to suck on the knob of her clitoris. As he licked Terry's cunt and clitoris, she whimpered with pleasure. His balls and cock were aching for Terry to touch him again and he knew that now the slightest touch would make him come. He had never been so excited.

Suddenly Terry's naked thighs clamped hard against the sides of Paul's head and her hand pressed his face hard against her cunt. She cried out as her hips began to press rhythmically against his mouth. After a short while she relaxed, then placed her hands on the side of Paul's face and guided his face away from her.

"Did I do something wrong?" he asked, puzzled, looking at Terry sitting on the edge of the bed, bare-breasted with her dress bunched up around her hips.

"Definitely not," she smiled. "You gave me a wonderful orgasm. And now it's time for your reward. Take off the rest of your clothes."

Paul stepped out of his pants and underpants, still bunched around his ankles, then pulled off his shirt while Terry pulled off her dress and, completely naked, stretched out on the bed with her legs spread. She held out her arms. "Come here, baby. It's time to fuck me."

As Paul positioned himself between her legs, Terry gave his cock one long stroke, then guided it to her pussy. For the first time, Paul felt his cock slide deep into the ripeness of a woman's cunt. Looking down at her face, he saw her smile as he slowly withdrew then again pressed his cock into her until his naked hips were grinding against hers. Suddenly he was out of control. He pounded

171

his cock as far into her as he could, over and over, until, with a shriek, clutching her naked body, he felt himself spurt deep inside her.

Terry and Paul spent a lot of time together that summer. Sometimes Terry would be the *teacher* but, since Paul learned quickly, sometimes, he would do the *teaching* and Terry would pretend to be a virgin. Paul was sad the day Terry returned to college, but, over the years, he found many other girls he could teach and be taught by.

"And that, ladies and gentlemen," Gary said, "is the last of our wonderful stories. There are drinks and food for any who want them, and you know your way around the house."

"Good stories."

"That last one was your story, wasn't it?" Eric asked softly, his mouth close to Jessica's ear.

"How did you know?"

"I could tell by the tenseness of your hand on my thigh and generally in your body." His hot breath on her neck made her quiver. "Which person were you when you wrote it," Eric continued, "the student or the teacher?"

"Sometimes I was one, sometimes the other. I was feeling what each of them felt at the time."

"And right now, which are you? Or are you something else entirely?"

Jessica propped her chin on her palm. She was excited and curious about all the things she had yet to experience. "Actually, I'm open for almost anything. The more I read and the more I experience, the more interested I become. There were a lot of things in the stories that Gary read that I've never done."

"That's what I had hoped you'd say." Eric walked over to Gary, whispered something in his ear, then returned. "Gary has a special room downstairs. I'd like to show it to you."

"Special?"

"He and I designed it when we redid the house. It's full of toys and equipment to play with." Eric took a deep breath. "I've got another question. How do you feel about Gary?"

"He's very nice, why?"

"Look at him," Eric said, directing her gaze to the tall, angular man still draped over his chair. "Think about his hands on you, my mouth sucking you while he does enticing things to your body. Does that sound exciting?"

Jessica looked at Gary, who was talking to another couple. She watched his long hands move as he talked and thought about them on her skin. She thought about two men making love to her at once and her knees shook and her hands trembled. She felt herself swell and moisten. "Yes," she said hoarsely.

"I'd like to invite Gary to join us. Would that be all right?"

"Yes," she sighed. "Is it all right with you?"

"Gary and I go way back and we, shall we say, understand each other. I'd like to share your pleasure with him."

Jessica nodded and watched as Eric approached Gary again. As they spoke, Gary turned to look at Jessica and his gaze travelled all over Jessica's body. A smile spread over his face, then he winked. Jessica couldn't help but return his grin. She trusted Eric completely and, without having exchanged more than a few sentences with him, she found she trusted Gary as well.

Gary mouthed 'Are you sure?' and Jessica nodded. Gary winked again, then said something to Eric, who returned to her.

"Gary will be along in a little while. He has a few host duties to attend to. Let me show you the downstairs."

Shaking with excitement, Jessica followed Eric down a flight of carpeted stairs into a large entertainment room. There were both a pool table and a ping pong table, several pinball machines, two television sets, and an octagonal card table with eight chairs. In addition, there were several comfortable seating areas and a fully stocked bar. Surprisingly, the room was empty.

Answering her question before she asked it, Eric said, "Most of the guests prefer the comfort of the bedrooms upstairs. The room

I told you about is used only on special occasions, or with special people."

"Oh," was all Jessica could say.

They crossed the large open room and Eric used a key to unlock a door, almost totally hidden by cleverly designed panelling. "Remember that if anything makes you uncomfortable you have to say so." Eric opened the door and flipped on the lights.

Jessica stared. Two opposing walls were upholstered in white leather and the other two walls and the ceiling were mirrored. Eric turned the dimmer switch so the recessed lights gave the room a soft glow. In the center of the room were several benches of differing heights and shapes and a few chairs. The floor was covered with a thick white carpet. Eric crossed the room and pulled a small handle in one of the leather walls. A closet door opened. "Would you like to pick something to wear?" he asked her.

Jessica looked into the closet. On one side hung stretch-lace cat suits, teddies, stockings, garterbelts, and bras in every color. On the other were leather outfits, collars, masks, hoods and, on the back of one door, whips and paddles of every description. Jessica was awed.

"You aren't into the whip stuff, are you?"

Jessica looked saddened. She momentarily thought about saying what she thought Eric wanted to hear, but then remembered her promise. "I don't think so. Are you?"

"When the moment is right I enjoy giving pain. But only when it's pleasure for my partner."

Jessica swallowed. "I don't know."

"Then the answer is no. It must be pleasure for you yourself, not pleasure because it excites me."

Jessica smiled weakly. "I know. But if something gives you. . . ."

"It won't please me unless you enjoy it. Enough said. Now, pick something fun to wear. And think about who you want to be for a few hours. Do you want to be the one in control?"

Eric turned his back and Jessica rifled through the clothes. She selected a navy-blue teddy with matching stockings. As she pulled off her clothes she thought about what she wanted for the evening. "Shouldn't this be a mutual decision?"

"It will be. I need only one thing from you and that's who do you want to be?"

As Jessica pulled the left stocking on, she said, "I don't know."

"Okay. Let's do this. Let's pretend it's one hour from now. Tell me about how you feel. Are you excited?"

Jessica pulled on the second stocking, sliding her fingers up her leg, feeling the springy nylon hugging her legs. Still having a difficult time sorting out her feelings, she said, "Oh yes."

"Are you watching me as I try to get free of my bonds, or are you tightly bound?"

Almost unable to pull on the teddy, she took a deep breath and said, "I'm bound." She adjusted her clothes, stepped into her shoes and walked up behind Eric's back. She rested her head against his shoulder and said what was in her mind. "I want to be crying for help, knowing no one will help me."

Eric turned and took her in his arms. He pressed his pelvis against her and Jessica could feel his excitement. "Can you feel what that idea does to me?"

Jessica giggled. "It's hard to miss."

"Okay. We need safe words. Rather than 'cease and desist' which I'm always afraid someone will forget, let's use 'red' and 'yellow.' Red if you want me to stop *for any reason*. I mean any reason. Yellow for 'I need a moment to catch my breath,' or 'My foot's asleep.' Is that okay?"

" 'Red' and 'yellow'. I think I can remember that. Are we really going to do this?" Jessica was incredibly excited.

Eric kissed her deeply. "Oh yes. We certainly are." He stepped back. "Mmmm. I love you in that outfit." He ruffled her hair, which fell loosely at her shoulders. "Now," he said, "we have to talk about the rest of the evening. First, do you trust me?"

"Absolutely."

"Let me tell you about Gary. He's a dominant. That means that he enjoys being in complete control of his sexual experiences. He likes to give the orders and have them obeyed without question. Do you think you could enjoy letting someone else control everything?"

Jessica thought about the story that Steph had told her about being tied to the bed and having Brian 'have his way with her.' "I think I could really get into that. I've sorted a lot out."

"Good. Tell me."

"Well," Jessica said, trying to put her feelings into words, "I've fantasized about being in complete control and it makes me a bit uncomfortable. It bothers me that I might not be giving my partner complete pleasure. I don't much like that responsibility. When I tried it, it was satisfying, but. . . ."

"And giving up complete control? Does that excite you?"

"The idea does, but I don't know about in reality."

Eric wrapped his arms around Jessica's waist and pulled her toward him. He slid his fingers into her hair, cradled her head, and pressed his lips against hers. After a long, hot kiss, he said, "I love your honesty. I would have worried if you had said anything else. Do you remember what I told you about the words 'red' and 'yellow?'"

"Yes."

"And do I have your promise that you'll speak up if anything disturbs you. Anything at all?"

"Yes." Jessica shivered. She assumed that Gary was going to join them, somehow giving orders about what they were going to do, all three of them. God, she was excited at the prospect. "And Gary's going to join us?"

Eric's smile was warm and caring. "Yes. And thanks. I've been looking forward to this ever since we first got together. I'm going to tell him that we're waiting. Would you like something to eat? Some wine, maybe?"

Jessica took a deep breath. "A glass of wine would be nice."

"I'll only be a minute."

While Eric was gone, Jessica prowled the room. There seemed

to be several doors of varying sizes concealed in the leather paneling. She touched one of the three benches, and found the white leather covering to be butter-soft and supple, with lots of foam padding beneath.

Every time she looked up, it was almost impossible not to look at herself, reflected on both walls, then rereflected again and again. She ran her fingers through her hair, fluffing it out, giving it a wild, almost animal appearance. When the door behind her opened, she jumped. Eric walked back into the room, a drink in each hand. Jessica took a glass from Eric and took several swallows. She heard the door open again and turned.

"Jessica," Gary said, looking at the teddy and stockings she wore, "you look enchanting."

Jessica stared. Gary's angular, slightly mussed appearance had been radically altered. He now wore a pair of skin-tight, black leather pants that disappeared into a pair of thigh-high, black leather boots. His slender upper body was covered by a matching black leather vest, and his hands were covered with leather gauntlets. All he needed, Jessica thought, was a sword and a scarf around his head and he would be the stereotypical pirate. Ichabod Crane had been replaced by Jean LaFitte.

"Eric says that he's told you about my sexual preferences."

"He has."

"And you're willing to be mine for the rest of the evening. With or without Eric?"

Jessica looked at Eric, whose smile reassured her. "Yes," she said.

"Wonderful. Eric has told you the safe words. Now the rest of the rules. First, you will do whatever I ask without question. If what I ask, or what I do, makes you uncomfortable you will use a safe word. If I can be sure of that, I can do anything I want."

"I understand," Jessica whispered.

"I like to be addressed as 'sir' at all times."

Jessica looked at Gary's boots and said, "Yes, sir."

Gary grabbed a handful of Jessica's red hair and used it to pull her head backwards. He captured her mouth, driving his tongue into the dark, moist depth, tasting, probing, inflaming. He let her go and stood up while Jessica caught her breath.

"Eric," Gary said, "she's magnificent. We shall have a delightful evening. Now, fix her clothes."

"Yes, sir," Eric said. He went to the closet and got a pair of scissors from a drawer. He cut the cups from the teddy, just above the underwires, and then cut across the crotch both front and back, and removed the small panel of fabric. "Gloves, sir?" Eric asked.

"Yes," Gary said.

Jessica watched as Eric opened another drawer and pulled out a pair of long, fingerless gloves. He handed them to Jessica. As she pulled them on, she noticed one side of a zipper ran up the inside of each. When she had the gloves on, Eric pulled her arms behind her and somehow zipped the two gloves together. Now Jessica's arms were imprisoned, held behind her, forcing her breasts forward. She felt a moment of panic.

"Test them, Jessica," Gary said. "Try to pull your arms out. Get used to the fact that you belong to me now. Be afraid of the helpless feeling, then let it go. Release yourself to me and to all the new pleasures you will feel this evening." He walked up to her, cupped her chin and looked into her eyes. "If you can't let go of the fear, tell me and we'll stop now." He continued to gaze into her eyes. "You will feel no more fear, just intense, tightening pleasure."

Jessica felt the fear ebb. She wasn't afraid. As the panic faded, it was replaced with a flood of heat through her body. She looked into Gary's eyes and smiled. "No fear at all," she whispered.

"Oh God, Eric," Gary said, "she's perfect. Eric tells me you're not turned on by pain."

"I don't think so, but I've never thought about pain as pleasure before."

Gary took one of Jessica's nipples between his thumb and index finger and twisted, hard.

Jessica gasped.

"Good or bad?" Gary asked as he released the pressure.

Jessica looked down at the hard, deep brown point that extended from her breast. The pain had been erotic and had made her very wet.

Gary pulled off one of his gauntlets and slid one finger between her legs. He laughed when she trembled at his touch. "You're soaking, Jessica. I may try a little light pain and I think you'll enjoy it. If you don't, you know I'll stop any time."

Jessica smiled as her trust in the two men increased. She could completely let go. It was a level of freedom different from any she had experienced before.

"Eric, release her hands for a moment," Gary said, and Eric unzipped the glove-connection.

"Offer your tits to me, Jessica," Gary said.

Jessica slid her hands up the sides of the satiny fabric of the teddy until she cupped one breast in each hand. "It's JessicaLynn, sir," she said.

"JessicaLynn it is. And what a tasty morsel you are." He leaned over and drew her erect nipple into his mouth. He motioned to Eric who suckled at her other breast.

The intensity of the sensations was almost too much for Jessica-Lynn. "Oh my God," she whispered.

When the two men stood up, Gary said, "You spoke without my permission, JessicaLynn. I understand that this is all new to you, but independent actions are not allowed."

JessicaLynn looked at the floor. It was hard not to smile, but in her most serious voice, she said, "I'm sorry sir."

Gary took one nipple in each hand and twisted. "I'm sure you are."

The feeling that started in her nipples and stabbed through her belly wasn't pain. It was molten fire, irresistible and unquenchable.

"Eric," Gary said, "refasten her arms." Eric did. "And let's begin with the chair."

Joan Elizabeth Lloyd

Eric reattached the gloves behind her back, then opened a panel and pressed a button. A strange-looking chair attached to a sliding platform glided into the room. "Sit down, my dear," Gary said.

The chair had wide, leather-covered arms and legs and virtually no seat. There was a ledge around the border of the seat-space and, when JessicaLynn sat on it, it supported her weight but left her cunt exposed. It was an excitingly vulnerable position. Quickly Eric attached her lower legs and her thighs just above the knee to the chair with wide elastic bands. Then, with her arms behind her still encased in the gloves she felt Eric pull a wide elastic band from behind the chair around her ribs and fasten it in the front with velcro. It encased most of her upper body, but left her breasts exposed and available.

"My god, you're a succulent piece," Gary said. "What size would you estimate, Eric?" Gary asked.

What size for what?

"The queen or the rook, I'd guess," Eric said, handing a large box to his friend.

Gary opened the case and showed the contents to JessicaLynn. "I bought this on a trip overseas a few years ago. These are hand-carved phalluses. Notice that there are eight smaller ones, then two of each of three larger sizes, one each of the large and the largest, here." He pointed and JessicaLynn suddenly smiled. "You've guessed," Gary continued. "It's a chess set made up of dildos."

"Amazing," JessicaLynn said, then added, "I'm sorry for speaking, sir."

"You do show the proper respect, and I like that so I'll excuse it one last time." He lifted one of the larger phalluses and showed JessicaLynn a notch around the base. From a drawer in the base of the box, he withdrew a holder with a large ring attached then fitted the phallus into the holder. The holder created a small flange around the base of the phallus, with a ring attached. "You see? Isn't this clever? This is the rook." He held it in front of her face.

180

"Now I want your mouth to experience what your delicious little pussy will feel in a few minutes. Open."

JessicaLynn opened her mouth and sucked the cool smooth wooden cock into her mouth. Gary moved it in a fucking motion as she sucked. As she started to close her eyes, Gary said, "You will look at me at all times. You may look me in the eye or you may watch in the ceiling."

Jessica's gaze strayed to the ceiling. She saw herself, bound, half naked, as Gary fucked her mouth with the dark dildo. She saw Eric stroking Gary's shoulder with one hand and her breast with the other.

Gary looked up. "Oh yes. That's quite a sight, isn't it." He held Jessica's head and forced her eyes to lock with his. "But, when you're being fucked by me or by Eric, I want you to look into my eyes."

JessicaLynn looked deeply into Gary's eyes and saw his excitement. Out of the corner of her eye she could also see Eric, standing, fully clothed, at Gary's side, obviously enjoying the tableau as Gary pistoned the dildo into and out of her mouth.

"Yes, that's fine," Gary said, pulling the large phallus from JessicaLynn's mouth. He tipped the chair back slightly on its rear legs and, to her surprise, it remained at that rakish angle, her head resting against its raised back. "Yes, this chair does some wonderful things. I had it built to my specifications." He caressed JessicaLynn's wet pussy, then slipped the large dildo into her.

She was full. She arched her back, trying to pull the smooth, cool wooden dildo farther into her body. She squeezed her vaginal muscles, hugging the penis inside of her.

"Too small," Gary said, removing the dildo from her body.

She felt bereft and yearned to be filled again as Gary removed the queen from the phallic chess set. He connected the holder, then handed it to Eric. "You do the honors," he said.

Eric slowly inserted the larger dildo into JessicaLynn's body, stretching her almost to the point of pain, but not quite. She groaned and it took a tap under her chin from Eric to remind her to look Gary in the eyes.

Gary pulled a slender strap from the elastic cincher at the small of JessicaLynn's back, ran the end through the ring on the end of the dildo-holder, then fastened it to the elastic in the front. The large wooden phallus was now imprisoned deep in her body, filling her, stretching her, but unmoving.

JessicaLynn didn't want the dildo to remain quietly in her body. She wanted it moving, fucking her. She moved her hips, trying to move the dildo, trying to satisfy the growing craving.

"No, my dear," Gary said, "that won't help. That's part of the fun of this. Like that woman in my story, you will climb higher and higher and get no satisfaction until I decide it's time." He smiled and stroked her thigh. "Oh I love to see a woman's pleasure pushed to its limits." He turned to Eric. "Strip," he said. "Then give yourself to me and don't move."

JessicaLynn watched as Eric quickly removed his clothes. His erection stuck straight out from his body like the branch of a great tree. Gary cradled Eric's cock in his hands, then ran his fingers up and down the length of it. Despite Gary's order for her to watch only his eyes, JessicaLynn stared at the soft look of pleasure on Eric's face, then at his huge erection. She wanted that cock for herself, to hold and stroke it. She was envious of Gary's freedom to use his hands to give pleasure.

Gary looked at her. "You want this, don't you?"

"Yes, sir."

She watched Eric's head fall back, his arms hanging limply at his sides. "I can deny you your pleasure," Gary said to her. "I can give him satisfaction this way." He caressed and petted Eric's cock. "But you've been so good, I'll let you. Suck him."

Quickly, Gary tipped the chair farther back until JessicaLynn's mouth was level with Eric's cock. "Eric, don't move your hands." Eric moved so his cock brushed JessicaLynn's lips. Gary held it and stroked her mouth, cheeks, and chin with the wet tip. "Open." JessicaLynn opened her mouth and Gary pushed Eric's cock inside.

She felt so complete. With Gary's hand on the back of her head, JessicaLynn caressed Eric's cock with her tongue. She trapped it between her tongue and the roof of her mouth and moved her head slightly so it rubbed the rough surfaces. She couldn't get enough. When she again started to close her eyes to savor the sensations, Gary tapped her cheek and she gazed into his eyes as Eric, unable to hold back any longer, erupted, groaning and ejecting semen deep into her mouth.

As Eric continued to pump his hips against JessicaLynn's mouth, Gary tapped on the end of the dildo, causing heat to ripple through her body. When he reached under the slender strap and touched her puckered anus, JessicaLynn almost came. But she knew that Gary wouldn't let her. Not yet.

When Eric's cock was finally small and soft, he withdrew. Gary filled a bowl with warm water and used a soft cloth to wash his friend's body as JessicaLynn watched. When everyone was calmed, Gary said, "I think we need the pawn, too."

JessicaLynn had no doubt what he had in mind. She was frightened for a moment as she stared into Gary's eyes. She took a deep breath, then let it out slowly. It was all right.

"Good," Gary said, knowing what she had been thinking. He opened the chess box again and pulled out one of the smallest dildos and fit it into another holder. With deliberate slowness he took out a jar of lubricant and slathered it over the dark wood. "You know where this is going, don't you, JessicaLynn?"

JessicaLynn swallowed, then said, "Yes sir."

"Have you ever had your lovely ass fucked before?"

"No sir."

Gary grinned. "Wonderful. That's an added pleasure for me." Gary unfastened the crotch-strap and wiggled the end of the dildo, still buried deep in her cunt. He said, "Eric, hold this and move it just a bit. I want her right at the edge."

Eric held the ring on the end of the dildo and rotated it slowly in JessicaLynn's pussy. "Ohhh," she moaned.

"Let's let her come when I do this." Eric nodded. "That way

she'll always associate having her ass fucked with a good, hard climax." Gary rubbed the slippery dildo against her anus, then slowly pushed the tip inside.

JessicaLynn felt her body tighten. "No," she said. "Don't."

"You know the words," Eric said.

"Red or yellow," Gary said.

"Oh please don't."

Both men laughed. "She knows how to increase our pleasure, doesn't she?"

Whether it was increasing their pleasure or not, it seemed important for her to protest, although she wanted to be filled more than she could have imagined. "No more, please."

Gary pushed gently and suddenly JessicaLynn's body opened to the new invasion. She felt the dildo slide into her ass while Eric withdrew the one from her pussy, then pushed it in again. The pleasure was too much. "Yes," she screamed. "Do it, do it, do it."

Gary nodded. "Watch me as you come, JessicaLynn," he said as Eric fucked her cunt with the large wooden phallus. "Look up."

She climaxed violently, watching her body writhe in the mirror on the ceiling. Heat and light blazed through her. Eyes on the ceiling, she felt the two penises continue to fuck her. Over and over she came, her pleasure almost too much to take.

When she was finally calm, Gary put the dildos aside and kissed her deeply. "I like to come in someone's hand," he said. He unfastened the cincher and freed JessicaLynn's arms. "I want both of you to touch me."

He unfastened his leather pants and his cock sprang free. Gary moved close to the chair and JessicaLynn took his cock in one hand. Eric wrapped his hand around hers, fingers intertwined, all touching Gary's penis. "Watch our hands," Eric said to Gary.

Eric spread a gob of lubricant on their hands, then the ten fingers formed an elongated tube. Eric placed one hand in the small of Gary's back and pushed his cock into the slippery passage. As the two hands massaged Gary's cock, he grabbed each by a shoulder, bucked his hips and came, spurting thick fluid on the arm of the chair. "Yes," he growled.

Later, having showered and redressed, Gary guided Eric and JessicaLynn to the front door. "That was quite an experience," she said.

"I hope you enjoyed the evening, JessicaLynn," Gary said.

"I did," Jessica said. "Tremendously. And out here, I'm still Jessica."

Gary kissed her deeply. "I understand," he said. "And I'll tell Brian and Steph that Eric drove you home."

"They're still here?"

"I think so," Gary said, pointing to their Lexus in the driveway.

Jessica grinned. "I hope they are having as wonderful an evening as I did."

"I'm sure they are," Gary said.

Eric helped Jessica into the car and started toward the Carltons' house. "Are you sure that wasn't too bizarre for you?"

"If you had asked me yesterday, I would have said that it would be. But it was all terrific."

They drove up the driveway and Eric helped Jessica out of the car. "I'll call you," he said as she found her key in her purse.

"I'll look forward to that." Jessica unlocked the door and walked inside.

TEN

———◆———

Jessica slept until after eleven the following morning, then showered and dressed in a pair of white cotton slacks and an olive-
green camp shirt. She wandered downstairs, both eager and a bit
reluctant to share her experiences with Steph.

"Good morning," Steph said as Jessica carried a cup of coffee
and a toasted English muffin into the plant room. "Did you enjoy
the party? I lost track of you after the stories but Gary said that
Eric had driven you home."

"I had an incredible evening," Jessica said, settling into a lounge
chair. "And you?"

"Let's just say it was incredibly satisfying."

"Where's Brian?" Jessica asked.

"He had a tennis date at noon so he just left."

"Oh," Jessica said, nibbling at her muffin. "This is almost as
awkward as going to the party in the first place. Part of me wants
to tell you everything, and hear about your evening, and part of
me is. . . ."

Steph's head snapped around. "Not ashamed?"

"Absolutely not. Not ashamed at all. Just a bit embarrassed. I did things last evening that I didn't know existed a month ago. Hedonistic and more damn fun than I've ever had. Are you ashamed of anything you did?"

"Not in the least," Steph said. "But, it was unusual."

"I'd love to hear about your evening," Jessica said, "but only if you want to tell."

"Tell me about yours first."

"Well, let me begin with the fact that JessicaLynn was in her glory." Jessica spent almost half an hour telling Steph about her adventures in Gary's special room. Except for an occasional 'You're kidding' Steph was silent.

When Jessica was done, Steph said, "Oh Lord, that sounds so terrific. I'm shaking just thinking about it."

"I'm excited just talking about it. It was the most intense orgasm I've ever had."

"What about you and Eric? Is this getting serious?"

"I hope not. I care about him a lot. I love the time we spend together, in and out of bed. I enjoy Cam too, and Gary is a wonderful lover and I'm hoping he'll call and we can continue some of the adventures we began last night. I'm not ready to even consider something exclusive and I don't think Eric is either."

"You amaze me, Jessica," Steph said. "I never would have expected this from you. You were so serious, so married."

"I always thought so too," Jessica said. "But that was the Jessie inside of me. Now that I've grown and become Jessica, I realize that there are so many wonderful things to try. Do you want to tell me about your evening? You don't have to, you know."

"I know that, silly. But I'd like to tell you. It's a bit offbeat. It seems that we both had a new experience."

"You mean that you did something last night that you've never done before? From all you've told me, I didn't think there was anything left."

"Oh, there are things I've never done and some I never want to do. But last night I got to try one of those secret things that tickles your mind but you never believe will actually happen."

"So tell all," Jessica said, refilling her coffee cup, then Steph's.

"Well," Steph began, "during the storytelling, I was sitting with Marcy and Chuck. You remember that I told you that Brian and I spent an adventurous weekend with them in the Adirondacks last winter. Well, halfway through that story about the teenaged boy, he whispered in my ear, 'What are you doing after the show?'"

"What did you have in mind, Chuck?" Steph answered.

"Marcy and I have been talking about you."

"And . . . ?"

"Later," he said, turning back to Gary.

Later. The word echoed in Steph's mind. She and Chuck had been together a few times as part of a foursome with Brian and Marcy, and she had always found him to be a talented and intuitive lover. He always seemed to know what she wanted, sometimes before she knew herself. And he had no hesitation about doing the unusual.

After Gary finished the final story, Steph, Marcy, and Chuck talked. She noticed Eric and Jessica walk to the stairs toward the downstairs playroom. Steph felt Chuck's hand on the back of her neck, but decided to wait until he was ready to explain about the rest of the evening.

Finally, he said, "When we spent that weekend together last winter, I got some feelings about you." Steph remained silent. "My relationship with Marcy has changed since that weekend." Chuck reached over and lifted Marcy's hand from her lap. He held it so that Steph could see the heavy gold bracelet she wore. "Marcy belongs to me, now, body and soul." He fingered the tiny gold charm on the bracelet. Steph looked more closely at the tiny gold object and saw that it was a tiny pair of handcuffs. "She does what I want, when I want, and she loves it."

"May I?" Marcy asked.

"Of course," Chuck said.

"It's wonderful. At work I have two secretaries, three private phone lines, and a stack of incoming information that I have to digest each morning." Marcy was vice president of a medium-sized, international bank. "I make decisions that involve tens of millions of dollars every day. But when I get home Chuck tells me exactly what he wants me to do to please him."

Steph was surprised. Marcy had always been a no-nonsense type in her early fifties with salt-and-pepper hair cut in a short business-like style. Ever organized and efficient, she had been the one to orchestrate their reservations and transportation for their week-end away.

Chuck picked up the story. "Remember that evening when the four of us made love on the floor in front of the fire?"

"How could I forget?" Steph said, memories of naked bodies flashing through her mind. She pictured a particularly exciting moment when she held Brian's cock in one hand and Chuck's in the other.

"At one point, I ordered Marcy to jerk me off, and she did. When we got home, we talked and discovered this mutual need, hers to serve, mine to give the orders." He ran his fingers through the wings of silver hair above his temples. "It changed everything."

"We've been together several times since," Steph said. "You never shared this before."

"I know," Chuck said, "but we had to get completely comfort-able with it ourselves."

"Are you two happy?" Steph asked.

The smile that lit Marcy's face was dazzling. "I've never been happier. It's the perfect life for us right now. The kids are long gone and we can play to our hearts' content in the house."

"You're the first person we've told about this," Chuck said.

"I'm honored," Steph said, getting genuine pleasure out of the fact that these two people chose to share their discovery with her. "I have the feeling that there's more to this revelation than just information."

"We want you to join us this evening," Chuck said. "Just the three of us." He paused, then said, "I told you before that I had a feeling about you." Again he ran his fingers through his hair. "I think you might enjoy following my orders for an hour or so." He grasped Steph's wrist in one hand and his wife's in the other. He tightened his grip. "I brought a few toys for us to play with, if you're willing."

Steph's heart was pounding. She looked down at the hand encircling her wrist, then at Marcy.

"I would enjoy it too," Marcy said.

With a smile, Chuck said, "I can feel your pulse and your heart is racing. The idea excites you, just as it excites Marcy and me. Play with us. Say yes."

"Yes," Steph said.

Marcy got a small paisley tote bag from the hall closet and the three of them climbed the stairs. They found a bedroom with a red ribbon beside the door, tied it around the doorknob to indicate that the room was occupied, then went in and locked themselves inside. "This is a fantasy come true," Chuck said as he set the bag on the desk in the corner. The room was masculine, with navy, red, and white bedding, a red rug, and white wallpaper with a thin navy stripe. Chuck switched the radio to a music station and stretched out on the bed. He interlaced his fingers behind his head, sighed and said, "Okay, ladies, I would like to see a bit more of you both. Take off your clothes for me, slowly and sensually."

Steph realized that her decision to wear a sleeveless black sundress that zipped up the back hadn't been a wise one. In order to unfasten it, she would have to twist her arms into an awkward, very unsensual position. Chuck read her mind as he often seemed to do. "Marcy, help Steph undress."

Marcy's red silk blouse hung open, revealing a shiny red waist cincher. She walked around behind Steph, found the tab on the zipper and stroked Steph's back as she pulled the zipper down.

Steph had never been caressed by a woman before. She liked the smooth soft feeling of Marcy's fingers. She felt Marcy slide the dress from her shoulders and guide it down over her hips. She stepped out of it and Marcy draped it over a chair.

"Turn around, Steph," Chuck said.

Steph turned to face him, knowing that her choice of undergarments had been much better than her choice of dress. She wore a black-lace demi-bra through which her dark brown nipples showed prominently. Her black-lace bikini pants matched it, as did her thigh-high lace stockings.

"I had almost forgotten how beautiful your body is. Now you, Marcy," Chuck said, not moving from his regal position on the bed.

Marcy removed her blouse, then opened the full-length zipper on her black skirt. It parted and she put both garments aside.

"It's latex," Steph said, gazing at the tight red waist cincher that raised Marcy's full breasts and squeezed her body tightly. The garment went from halfway down her breasts to just above her black bush. Long garters down the front and sides held up her red stockings.

"Yes," Chuck said, "it is. And it's very tight. Sometimes, when we go out, I make Marcy wear it. She feels it all the time and it reminds her of me. Show her the chain," he added.

Marcy reached into her pussy-hair and showed Steph a thin gold chain that attached to the cincher front and back, stretching tightly between her pussy lips. "Every time she walks," Chuck said, "a special gold loop rubs her clit. It keeps her wet for me at all times. Move your hips for me, Marcy."

Marcy swiveled her hips hula style and Steph could see her knees tremble as the loop rubbed her clitoris. "Not too much," Chuck said and Marcy became still.

"Stand face to face," Chuck said and the two women did as he said. Because they were of similar height, they stood eye to eye, breast to breast. "Closer," he said and they moved so their nipples touched, Marcy's bare, Steph's barely covered by the lace of her bra. "Oh yes," Chuck said, "I've dreamt of this."

Steph looked into Marcy's eyes, soft and kind and almost loving. "I've dreamt of this too," she heard Marcy croon. She felt Marcy reach out and touch her hair, caress her cheek, run her fingertips over her eyebrows and lips. Marcy's hand slipped behind Steph's neck, drawing her close. She pressed her soft, warm lips against her friend's.

Her lips are so much softer than a man's, Steph thought, her breath sweet, her touch ever so gentle, like a butterfly caress. She sighed, then sank into the kiss, matching lip for lip, tongue for tongue. Steph's hands held Marcy's face as their lips changed position to draw forth every nuance of sensation. Steph felt Marcy's hands slowly make their way down her upper arms to rest on the sides of her breasts. Featherlight fingers teased the lace, then slipped inside to flick the erect nipples beneath.

"Have you ever been with a woman before?" Chuck asked softly, not wanting to break the spell of the moment.

"Not until now," Steph said.

"Nor has Marcy," Chuck said. "But we've talked about it and I know that Marcy has fantasized about being with you."

That remark gave Steph a strange, warm feeling deep in her belly. She smiled, and Marcy returned her grin. The women separated.

"Marcy," Chuck continued. "Pull off Steph's panties, then get the vibrator from the case." As Marcy complied, Chuck said, "I know each of you has masturbated with a vibrator before, and I've watched Marcy make herself come. Now I want to watch you pleasure each other. Steph," he said, taking her wrist, "lie here." He positioned her on the bed, arms over her head, legs widely spread, then lay beside her, his body in the opposite direction, his head close to her pussy, his fully dressed lower body level with her head.

Steph was liquid inside, filled with heat and longing. She made small purring sounds to assure both Chuck and Marcy that she was anxious to continue.

"I can smell your juices," Chuck said, sliding one finger through her bush. He brought the finger to his lips and licked. "And I always did like the way you tasted." Steph felt the bed move as Marcy joined them. "Marcy, think about what gets you hot, then do it to Steph."

Steph heard a click, then the hum of the vibrator. Suddenly a bolt of heat speared through her as the cool plastic tip of the vibrator touched her inner lips. Like an expert, Marcy slid the humming machine around Steph's cunt, touching all the sensitive places, driving Steph closer and closer to orgasm. When Marcy rested the vibrator against Steph's clit Steph cried, "You're going to make me come!"

"Finish her with your mouth," Chuck said, taking the vibrator.

Steph felt Marcy's warm lips draw her clit into her mouth. The sucking and a finger, she didn't know whose, penetrating her slit drove her over the edge. Sharp contractions of pleasure knifed through her, making her scream as she came.

Chuck pulled his clothes off and lay on his back, motioning to Marcy who mounted him, filling herself with his cock. Chuck took Steph's hand and placed her fingers on Marcy's clit. "Hold still," he told Marcy. Then to Steph he said, "She likes to be rubbed right here," he said, holding Steph's fingers against his wife's sopping pussy. Steph rubbed, feeling Marcy's clit swell under her touch.

"It's hard to hold still," Marcy groaned.

"Another moment," Chuck said, releasing Steph's hand. "Do it," he told her. "Make her come the way she made you come."

Steph probed, inserting her fingers between Chuck's pelvis and Marcy's. She could feel Chuck's cock as it filled Marcy's body. She rubbed, watching Marcy's face, sharing her increasing excitement. She explored, reaching every part of Marcy's cunt she could. Hearing Marcy's sharp intake of breath Steph knew she had found the spot. She rubbed and stroked until Marcy moaned and her body became rigid.

Steph was surprised that she could actually feel the tiny muscle movements of Marcy's climax.

"I love to feel you come when I'm inside you," Chuck said. "Now for me," he moaned. As Marcy rode Chuck's cock, Steph reached between Chuck's thighs and tickled his balls. As she sensed his approaching orgasm, she rubbed the band of flesh between his balls and his anus. He roared, arching his back and holding Marcy's bucking hips tightly against him.

"Jesus," Jessica said as Steph finished her story. "It must have been sensational. I'm a wreck just hearing about it."

"It was remarkable," Steph said. "I never suspected that making love with a woman would feel so different."

"I don't know how I'd feel. I don't have many hang-ups left, but that one. . . ."

"If you are exposed to the possibility sometime you'll decide then. I didn't think I could do it before last evening either."

"Will you do it again?"

"Same answer. If and when the time comes, I'll decide."

"It was quite an evening for both of us," Jessica said.

"It certainly was."

The weeks sped by. Jessica spent time with Eric and Cam, learning about them and about herself, growing and changing. One morning in August, Jessica joined Steph for one of their frequent mornings in the plant room.

"Steph," Jessica said, "I'm going back home for a few days."

"Just a few days, I hope," Steph said, her face showing her unhappiness.

"Just a few days for now, but I can't stay here forever, you know."

"Sure you can, if you want to. You can get your own place and I'm sure there are dozens of real estate agencies that would be glad to have someone with your talent."

Jessica hugged her friend. "I'm sure that's true. I could make a life here. That's part of the reason I'm going back, Steph. I don't know where I belong anymore or what I want do to or be for the rest of my life. I've seen and experienced so many things and it's all confusing the hell out of me right now."

Steph looked bemused. "I can imagine that," she said.

"Actually, I talked to my friend Viv, you know, the woman in my office. There are several people seriously interested in buying my house and she thinks that my presence might just push one to make an offer. She also thinks I might get close to my asking price."

"That would be great, babe," Steph said. "One less thing to think about."

"And Viv also said that Rob has been asking for me. He and bimbette split."

Steph looked incredulous. "You're not thinking of seeing the louse when you go back?"

"Actually, I am. I loved him for a lot of years, and I think seeing him might help me sort out my feelings for Eric and Cam and who and what I am."

"You're a big girl now, Jessica, but just be careful. You've changed a lot over the past month. You're not the same woman who loved Rob for all those years."

"I know that, but I have to do this, Steph."

Three days later, Jessica disembarked at O'Hare Airport from an early morning flight and rented a car to drive to Ottawa. The air was hot and steamy, but it smelled like home, the breeze filled with the odors of farm and fields. Despite the heat that dampened her underarms and caused a tiny trickle of sweat to run down between her breasts, Jessica rolled down the windows of her rented Ford and a grin spread across her face as she approached her home.

She wanted her house to stay perfect-looking so Jessica had made a reservation at a local motel. Since it was barely noon, however, she decided to stop at the office. Ferncrest Realty occupied a small house on a side street in Ottawa. Jessica pulled her rented car into the small lot in front of the building, got out and straightened her tailored white blouse and navy linen pants.

"Jessie," three women squealed as she walked through the front door into the cool, cozy sales area. "You look sensational," one said. "I love your hair," a second said. "Oh Jessie," Viv said, standing quietly behind her desk, "we missed you."

After the three women hugged Jessica they filled her in on the details of the past weeks. "Well," Jessica said when they finished, "things seem to have gone very well. You can't even tell I was gone."

"We knew," Kathy, a short, round, and bosomy agent said. Kathy had a knack for knowing exactly what a potential buyer was looking for. Once or twice a month she could be heard on the phone saying, "I have three houses to show you, but after the first, you won't want to see the others. I've found one that's perfect for you." Usually it was and Kathy made a good living for herself and her ailing husband.

"We missed you a lot," Marie, the second woman, said. She was tall and appeared slightly anorexic but she had a charm that made her beautiful. Viv would giggle as she relayed all calls for 'the lovely tall, skinny woman with the great smile' directly to Marie. "Are you back to stay?"

"I think I still need some time," Jessica said. "But you are doing so well without me that maybe I'll just stay gone."

"You're not serious," Viv said. Warm with her friends, but shy with strangers, Viv was Jessica's best friend in Ottawa. She had tried selling early on, but had found that her strength was in organization and paperwork. She kept everything running smoothly and each time she took a vacation, the office took weeks to recover.

Several phones rang simultaneously, and Marie and Kathy directed their attention to their customers. Jessica crossed the office and dropped into the comfortable chair beside Viv's desk. "I don't know what I'm going to do in the long run," Jessica said with a sigh. "The liberated life has been fantastic. Hot, heavy and very exciting, in all ways." Jessica spent the next half hour telling Viv some of the details of her weeks in Harrison. Viv's eyes widened at her descriptions of Cam and Eric, and widened still further as Jessica shared some of the details of her adventures.

"It must seem really boring here," Viv said, sadly. "We're so low-key we look forward to the next issue of *Cosmo*."

"How would you know anything about the sexual adventures of the average Ottawa citizen?" Jessica said. "You and that husband of yours have been monogamous forever."

"True. And I like it that way." She looked abashed. "I didn't mean that the way it sounded."

"Of course you didn't," Jessica said, sitting forward in her chair. "Anyway, let's order pizza and talk about my house."

Over slices of pizza the four women discussed the people interested in buying Jessica's house. "I hope you don't mind, but knowing you were coming in today, I arranged to meet the MacDonalds at the house at three. They're so nice that I really wanted you all to meet."

"Great," Jessica said. "Let me drive over and return this rental car, pick up my car, and I'll meet you there."

At quarter of three she drove up the driveway of the house that she and Rob had shared for nine years. It had been just this time of year when she and Rob had finally moved out of their tiny apartment, having saved enough for a down payment. As she crunched across the dry lawn she remembered how they had danced around the empty living room the day they closed, knowing that their few pieces of furniture wouldn't make a dent in the lavish space. They had made love right then, in the middle of the bare bedroom floor, she remembered. Marie pulled up with the MacDonalds's car right behind.

For the next hour, Jessica wandered through the rooms with their carefully chosen furnishings, showing the MacDonalds all the advantages of the house. "I love your furniture," Mrs. MacDonald said wistfully, "although it will be a long time before we can afford anything this nice." The couple was in their late twenties and Mrs. MacDonald was quite obviously pregnant. "The only thing I would change is that your husband's den would make a great nursery "

197

"That's the perfect place for it," Jessica said, smiling at the young woman. Jessica liked the young couple more and more as they toured the outside. She and Carol MacDonald shared a love of azaleas and they spent five minutes discussing fertilizers and acidifiers before Mike MacDonald dragged them back to the driveway.

As they walked, behind the young people's backs, Marie winked at Jessica and gave her the thumbs-up sign.

"Darling," Mike said, "let's think about it and we can call tomorrow."

"That will be fine," Marie said.

"And listen," Jessica said on the spur of the moment, "I was planning to sell all the furniture but I think that, if you decide to make an offer, we can come to some understanding about the contents too." She suddenly liked the thought of the charming couple eating breakfast at her table or storing their clothes in the matching dressers in the bedroom. And a baby. . . .

Carol MacDonald wrapped her arms around Jessica's neck, bumping her pregnant belly against Jessica's flat one.

"You'll really like it here," Jessica said as Carol climbed into the couple's seven-year-old Nissan. "It's a good house."

The MacDonalds left, followed immediately by Marie, leaving Jessica to wander the grounds, glad she had hired a yard service to keep things tended. As she arrived back at her car, she saw a familiar black Honda Del Sol speed up the driveway. Her heart pounded as Rob got out, stood and stared. "Jessie, my god, you look wonderful. What have you done with yourself?"

Jessica fluffed her shorter hair and straightened her back. "Hello, Rob. How have you been?" He hadn't changed a bit, she realized. He looked exactly the same as he had when she had last seen him, his sandy brown hair carefully blown dry, his short beard and moustache neatly trimmed. He was wearing his uniform: gray slacks, a light gray shirt, tiny-print paisley tie, and a navy blazer with gold buttons.

"I've been the same, but you . . . You look stupendous." He enveloped her in his arms and hugged her close. Jessica stood stiffly, not yielding to the familiar embrace. Funny, she said to herself, the things you notice. He still smells of Old Spice.

"I know," Rob said, backing away. "I've been a louse. The whole thing with Suzanne."

Suzanne. Jessica had forgotten her name. She tuned back in to Rob.

"That's all over. I guess it was some kind of midlife thing. I don't know what could have made me do something so dumb."

"I don't know either," Jessica said dryly.

"I've missed you something fierce, Jessie," he said, "and I'd like to see you now that you're back."

"First of all, I'm not back. I'm just here showing two wonderful young people the house. They remind me of us years ago, except she's pregnant." When Rob remained silent, Jessica continued, "And by the way. How did you know I would be here?"

"I've been driving past here several times a day. Viv let it slip that you'd be coming back to show the house and I wanted to see you." He hugged her again.

He smelled so comfortable that this time Jessica hugged him back automatically.

"Oh Jessie," he said. "It's so good to have you back."

"I use the name Jessica sometimes, now," Jessica said.

"Jessica? Nah. You're not the Jessica type. You're my Jessie." He looked at his watch. "Look. I've got a patient at five, but he's the last for the day. Meet me at The Grotto for dinner." When Jessica hesitated, he smiled his most charming smile. "Please? We've got a lot of catching up to do."

The Grotto. Their place. She hadn't been there since about a week before the infamous bimbette-in-the-dental-chair incident. "Okay, just for dinner."

Rob leaned forward and pressed a quick kiss on Jessica's lips. Without thinking she kissed him back. "I'll see you about six," he said, sprinting toward his car.

Puzzled by her reaction to her ex-husband, Jessica drove to the motel, registered and found her room. As she hung up the few clothes she had brought she wondered. Have I been wrong about him all this time? Have I been wrong about myself? She pictured Eric and the erotic room, then Cam and his deliciously subservient attitude. Was this all her own mid-life crisis? Was it something she had had to prove to herself? Something that wasn't real?

She showered, dressed in a conservative white summer dress and paisley shawl and met Rob at the Grotto. Hector, the owner of the family-style Spanish/Italian restaurant, greeted them like long-lost relatives and indicated a quiet table in the back. "I'll get you a bottle of Rioja on the house. I'm so happy to see you Dr. Hanley, Mrs. Hanley. It's so good to see you two together again." He hustled away.

"Together again?" Jessica whispered to Rob.

"I called when I got back to the office and reserved our special table. I guess he just assumed."

"A powerful assumption," Jessica muttered as Rob possessively took her elbow as they made their way between the tightly packed tables.

They sat and, when Hector returned, Rob ordered for both of them without looking at the menu. "We'll both have the gazpacho, we'll share an order of the roasted peppers with anchovies and, for the main course, we'll have linguini with your lemon and dill pesto."

"Hector," Jessica said, "didn't you used to make a garbanzo bean salad with an herb dressing?"

"Of course, Mrs. Hanley. Shall I bring you some?"

"Please," Jessica said. She hadn't had that salad for many years.

"Jessie, you know that gives me gas."

"Then don't have any," Jessica said, glaring. "I'd like some."

"Well, oh yes. Of course. Then you should have some," Rob said and Hector disappeared. "Now," he continued, leaning across the table and taking Jessica's hands in his. "Tell me about your little vacation in New York."

Jessica pulled her hands back, then told Rob a severely expurgated version of her last few weeks.

Looking surprised, Rob said, "You seem to have enjoyed yourself with Steph and Brian. It's good for you to get some of that, you know, carrying on, out of your system. One needs that sort of thing. It should help you to understand my Suzanne silliness."

"Silliness?" She swallowed the rest of her comments as Hector brought the wine and the gazpacho.

"Tell me about the shows you saw," Rob said as they ate their soup.

She told him about *Phantom* and he smiled enviously. "I wish I had been there," he said wistfully. "Maybe next time."

Jessica almost choked on her soup. Next time? "How's your practice going?" she asked, changing the subject yet again.

"Oh it's about the same." He brightened. "Actually I've gotten at least a dozen new patients. . . ."

Jessica sat back and looked more closely at Rob as he chattered on. He was wearing a different shirt. The one earlier had been pale gray while this one was pale blue, carefully ironed, with a different small-patterned tie that was so like all his others. She tuned out his conversation and just looked at him. It was as though there were two images, superimposed. One was the Rob of high school, young, charming, and a bit daring, with dreams of their life together. He was arrogant but enthusiastic. Then, as Jessica forced that image aside, there was an older Rob. Still sure of himself and arrogant, but with a hard edge that robbed his face of any of its previous boyish charm.

She brought herself back to the present when Hector arrived with their peppers. "These aren't totally skin-free," Rob said, covering his annoyance with a smile. "Your kitchen staff is slipping."

"I'm so sorry doctor," Hector said. "I'll replace them immediately for you."

"Don't bother, Hector," Jessica said. "They're just fine. If there's a bit of peel on one, I'll take it."

"Jessie," Rob said, "I'm paying good money for this and it should be perfect."

Jessica patted his hand, a placating gesture that was surprisingly familiar. "It's fine Rob."

Hector placed the plate of garbanzo salad beside Jessica's water glass. "I'm sure you'll enjoy this too, Mrs. Hanley."

Rob looked dubious, but said nothing.

During the rest of the meal, they talked about trivialities. Rob handed his credit card to Hector and signed the receipt. As they were leaving, Rob again took Jessica's arm. "I'm so glad you've missed me as much as I've missed you."

"Did I say that?" she asked.

"You don't have to say it. I know you've been lonely. I can see it in your eyes. And I understand why you went to New York. You thought it was all over between us."

"Is that why?" Jessica found she was gritting her teeth.

"Of course, Jessie. What we had was good and," he draped his arm across her shoulders, "we could have it again."

Jessica thought about how she had once longed to hear those words. She almost laughed. He was such an ass. How long had he been like this? Was this the Rob she had been married to?

"I know you've been as hungry for me as I've been for you." He hugged her to his side and smothered her breast with the hand that had been loosely on her shoulder until a moment ago. He kneaded her flesh, then grasped her hand and pressed it against the crotch of his slacks. "See what you do to me? Let's go back to the office and I'll remind you of how good it used to be."

What an idiot, she thought. I can't believe him. She was so astonished that she didn't move for a moment, during which he continued to knead her breast with one hand and use her hand to stroke his erection with the other. "Remember?" he whispered in her ear.

She remembered. She remembered all the evenings he had insisted she have a shot of bourbon to get her relaxed enough for his lovemaking. She remembered him sucking on her nipples, then spitting on his palm to make his cock wet enough to penetrate her not-yet-excited body. She remembered his lectures about how she should read a few books about how to be better in bed. She remembered it all.

Slowly, a smile crept across her face and she nodded imperceptibly. Then she squeezed his cock. "I remember," she said. "Let's go back to your office. That's a wonderful idea." She walked to her car. "I'll follow you there."

On the short ride to Rob's dental office Jessica turned the radio up loud and sang along to several old Beatles songs. As she pulled into the parking space next to Rob's car, she smothered the urge to laugh. She had all her plans made.

Holding hands, they went up to the second floor in the elevator and Rob used his key to open the glass door to the plush outer office. His face was flushed, his breathing rapid as he flicked on the lights. He quickly loosened his tie and unbuttoned his shirt.

"Let's go in the back," Jessica said, noticing that he never had changed the fabric on the chairs in the waiting room. They seemed even shabbier to her now. She glanced at the glass door to the hallway, then at Rob. "It's too public here."

"Of course, Jessie. Whatever you want. Oh babe, you turn me on."

They walked back toward the operatory where she had stumbled upon him humping bimbette all those months ago. "You know, Rob," she said, "I've changed a lot since we were together."

Rob was panting, pulling his shirttails out of his slacks. "I'm sure you have."

"I like to take charge of lovemaking now."

Rob flipped on the light in the operatory, threw his shirt on the counter, and turned to Jessica. "You do?"

She realized that she had accidentally alluded to her other lovers, but he didn't pick up on the slip. If he wanted, he could believe for another minute or two that she was pining for him. "I like to do all kinds of wonderful things." She reached underneath the waistband of his slacks and grabbed his cock. "I've learned all kinds of new ways to have fun." She squeezed and Rob groaned. "Let me show you." As Rob stood in the middle of the room, stupefied, Jessica unzipped his pants and pulled them off, along with his shorts, shoes, and socks. Kneeling, she took his cock in her mouth and sucked, looked up through her eyelashes at his wide eyes.

"Oh, Jessie. Oh God, Jessie." His fists clenched and unclenched at his sides.

"It's Jessica," she said, pulling off his shirt. "How about playing with me?" She pushed him, now totally naked, into the dental chair. "You just watch." She turned her back and slowly unzipped the back of her dress. "It unzips just like this, all the way down." Her voice was low and throaty. She turned and lowered the front of the dress until it fell at her feet. Her gaze never left his eyes as he stared at her breasts, half exposed in her white lace and satin bra. She pinched her nipples, making them hard and pointed.

"Jessie," Rob moaned, "you're making me crazy."

She lowered first one shoulder strap, then the other, lifting her breasts out of their cups, then, finally, unfastening the clasp and dropping the tiny garment on the floor.

"Do you want to touch? You always did love my tits." She walked over to the side of the chair. When he reached out to grab her tits, she held his hands. "No, no. My way, Rob." She took his hands and pressed the palms against her erect nipples and watched his head fall back against the headrest of the chair.

"You've got the greatest tits. And you feel so good," he groaned.

"Do you want a taste?" She placed his hands in his lap and moved closer to the side of the chair.

"You know I do. I want to suck you as much as you want me to," Rob said.

"You have no idea," Jessica said, rubbing one erect nipple across his cheek. When he reached for her, she said, "I said my way. You're very grabby. Maybe we should do something about that." She opened a drawer in one of the rolling cabinets and pulled out a roll of adhesive tape. She placed Rob's right forearm on the arm of the dental chair and taped it down tightly.

"This isn't like you, Jessie."

"I know, but it's like Jessica. And it makes you excited, doesn't it?" His cock was enormous, bobbing in his lap as he moved.

"Oh yes," he said.

She taped his other wrist, then wrapped tape around the chair, then around his thighs and ankles. "That's much better." Jessica massaged her breasts while Rob watched, pulling at the nipples until they stood out from her white flesh, firm and tight. Then she slid her hands under the front of her lacy panties and buried her fingers in her wet pussy. She was hot, but not for the reasons Rob was thinking. She loved this. He was hers. He was all hers. And she could do what she now realized was what she had wanted ever since getting off the plane that morning.

She rubbed her pussy until she could hold back no longer. Watching Rob's eyes on her hands and seeing his cock twitch, she came, shuddering, standing in the middle of his operatory. "Good," she purred. "Very good."

"I don't believe this." He struggled, but couldn't move. His cock stood up in his lap, a tribute to Jessica's power.

"I've changed a lot in the past few months," Jessica said, slowly putting her clothes back on. "And this evening has been a revelation." She zipped her dress, slipped back into her shoes and picked up her handbag. "You, my darling ex-husband, are a jerk. You're worse than that, because you had me convinced that I was the one who was sexually incomplete. You had me convinced I was frigid. Remember all those 'discussions' we had? Remember how you threw that word at me? *Frigid*." She stared at his lap. "Your cock doesn't think so." She went into the receptionist's area and returned with several sheets of paper from the copy machine. "I was hoping that your receptionist still smoked so she'd have these." She brandished a pack of matches.

Rob struggled to get his hands free of the tape that held them against the arms of the dental chair but neither his arms nor his legs would move.

"I was going to leave you here until morning, but you might get sick or something and I wouldn't want anything to happen to you, Robby baby." She twisted the paper tightly into a torch, then struck a match and lit it.

"What are you going to do, Jessie?" Rob asked.

"You never will understand that it's Jessica. JessicaLynn. And by the way, are you still doing the dental work for that fireman's organization?" When he didn't answer, she nodded. "I thought so. Try explaining this." She waved the smoking torch under the smoke detector. As the alarm started, she said, "It should be only a few seconds until the sprinklers go off and then about two minutes later the fire department will arrive." She grinned. "Bye-bye, Robby, baby."

As she crossed the reception area, water started to gush from the sprinklers. She shook her head like a wet puppy and laughed as she walked down the single flight of stairs. She sat in the car for a few minutes, and watched as two fire engines pulled up. Still laughing, she drove back to her motel and booked a flight back to New York for the following day.

At nine-thirty the next morning, on her way to the airport, Jessica stopped by her office. "The MacDonalds made an offer," Marie told her as she walked through the door. "Only five thousand below your asking price, but I don't know how much higher they can go. I think they're pushing their ability to get a mortgage now, with the new baby and all."

"You know," Jessica said, thinking about Eric's reaction to the house he had built, "I've made a nice profit on that house and I like that couple so much. Take their offer and offer them most of the contents for another five thousand."

"Five thousand? You're nuts. You spent twenty times that on the furniture."

"I know. But they liked it and I want them to have it. I just want the right of first refusal if they sell any of the contents."

Marie shook her head. "If you're sure, Jessie."

"I am."

"Jessie," Viv called. "Telephone."

"I didn't even hear it ring." When she went to pick up the

extension on Marie's desk, Viv said, "Pick it up in your office, why don't you."

With a quizzical look at her friend, Jessica walked into her office and lifted the receiver. "Jessica Hanley."

"Jessie," a gravelly male voice said, "it's Steve. Steve Polk."

"Steve, how are you?" She pictured the tall, bespectacled man in his early forties with whom she'd had dinner several times the previous spring.

"I'm fine. I've missed our dinners together. How has New York been for you? Replenishing?"

"Very. A good way to put it. How did you know I'd be here this morning? I'm leaving at noon."

"I asked Viv to call me. I really have missed you. It's too bad you're leaving. I was going to invite you to lunch today."

He sounded so disappointed that Jessica smiled. "Listen. I was going to rent a car and drop it at O'Hare but, if you can get away, how about driving me to the airport. We can talk on the way." A successful local contractor, he might be able to take some time off.

"Great. I'll pick you up in fifteen minutes."

"Meet me in front of the municipal lot next to Hertz at . . ." She looked at her watch. "Make it ten o'clock."

She hung up and walked back to Viv's desk. She leaned over and placed both palms on her friend's blotter. "Have you and Steve been conspiring?"

Viv grinned. "Maybe just a little. I wanted you to remember that Ottawa does have a thing or two to recommend it."

Jessica leaned over and kissed Viv's cheek. "Thanks babe. You're right. I need to figure out a balance to all this."

"Oh, and by the way. Did you have anything to do with the craziness at Rob's office last evening? The fire department responded. Then they had the cops and lord knows who else."

Jessica winked. "Did he get into trouble?"

"Nah. The fire chief wasn't happy about the false alarm, but he want upstairs, and then, I understand, he came back down laughing."

Viv came around her desk and the two women hugged. Then Jessica bade farewell to Marie and told both women to say goodbye to Kathy, who was out showing houses to a young man who had just been hired by a large local computing firm.

Jessica drove to the municipal lot and put her car in a special section for long-term parking. When she exited the lot, Steve was waiting for her. They embraced, then he took the suitcase from her. "I missed you more than I thought I would."

They had been friends for about six months and things had never gone any further. Suddenly, her arms around Steve's muscular body, Jessica began to wonder what he would be like in bed. Down girl, she told herself.

On the way to the airport, they talked and Jessica remembered why she had liked him so much. He was comfortable, never pushing her, seemingly content to wait until she felt ready to move things to a more personal level.

"How long will you be gone this time?" Steve asked.

"I don't really know. I'm going to coast for the rest of the summer, then make some decisions around Labor Day."

He concentrated on the view out the front window of his car. "I'm worried that you won't come back."

"You're the second person who's said that to me."

"We're not New York here," he said, speeding East on I80, "but I just want to be sure you remember that there are things here for you, too." He placed a hand on her knee. "All kinds of things when you're ready for them."

Jessica felt her heat rise. There was certainly no doubt that he was propositioning her. How long had he been suggesting this? She had no idea, since she wouldn't have been aware of his offer two months previously. She patted his hand. "I understand, Steve. I really do."

An hour later, as she took her suitcase from Steve in the parking lot, she said, "I'll stay in touch. And keep the fires warm for me for a while, will you?"

Steve leaned over and kissed her gently. "For you, certainly."

She walked toward the terminal with a happy spring in her step.

*   *   *

"How was your trip back home?" Eric asked the following evening. He and Jessica were sitting on the flagstone deck sipping Timmy's extra-spicy Bloody Marys.

Jessica started to laugh. Over the next half hour, she told Eric the story of her encounter with Rob. "You're a pisser, woman," Eric said. "I admire your style."

"Thanks. You know what the last straw was? He kept calling me Jessie. He refused to understand that I'm a different person now, and that it went much further than a name. But the name was a symbol of everything, somehow."

"Well, Jessica, you're too much."

"Thanks, Eric," Jessica said. "But, despite Rob, I am seriously thinking about moving back to Illinois after Labor Day."

Eric was silent for a few moments, then he said, "I'd like you to stay here."

"Part of me would like that too. But this is an interlude, a piece of another world. I feel like I belong in Ottawa. Anyway, I can't sponge off of Steph and Brian forever."

"You could move in here." Surprised that the words had slipped out of his mouth, Eric suddenly realized that he meant it. The thought that this wonderful woman would disappear from his life made him miserable. "No commitment. No exclusivity, unless that's what you want." He moved on quickly. "You could have the same sort of setup here you had at the Carltons'."

Jessica grinned and squeezed Eric's hand. "Thanks for the offer, Eric, but the more I think about it, the more I realize that Ottawa feels like where I belong. This is an island, a refuge, but not a life, at least not for me."

"Don't go back to being Jessie."

Jessica leaned forward and kissed Eric warmly. "I'm not going back to being Jessie. I'm taking Jessica back with me."

"Shit, Jessica." Eric looked deeply unhappy. "What about us? I love you, Jessica. Very much."

"Whoa, Eric. I thought this was a non-exclusive, just-for-kicks thing between us. I love you in a very special way, but not the way I think you mean. The airplane is a terrific invention. I hope you'll visit me and I'll be here once or twice before the first of the year." Jessica winked. "Gary invited me to his party the first Saturday in October. I wouldn't miss that for anything."

Eric leaned forward and grasped Jessica's hand. "You're not getting my message. I love you."

Jessica pulled back, raised an eyebrow querulously, and smiled.

After a moment, Eric's shoulders relaxed and he smiled. "Okay, Jessica." He chuckled. "You're right. I guess I got a bit carried away but the thought of your leaving makes me sad."

"It makes me sad too, Eric. But I have a real life to lead and this just isn't it. Still, I also want you to be part of whatever comes after. Visit me. I'm just a quick plane flight away."

"And we have the rest of the summer."

Jessica's conversation with Cam was similar, and they also agreed to spend time together both in Harrison and in Ottawa.

"Jessica," Steph said one morning the following week. "I need to explain something to you and it's important that you understand."

"Okay. Shoot."

"I am going to be away next Friday night."

"And . . . ?"

"With a man you've never met."

"Oh."

"This is really weird, but I wanted you to understand something."

"Hey, Steph, it's okay. If you want to spend a weekend with some guy who lights all your bulbs, go ahead. This is Jessica, not the Jessie who arrived here a few weeks ago." Sometimes the changes that had occurred in such a short time amazed her.

"It's not just that." Steph shifted in her seat and stared at her hands.

"I'm totally puzzled." Jessica put her hand on her friend's shoul-

210

der. "We've shared fantasies, told our innermost secrets. What is making you uncomfortable?"

"Brian."

"I'm still confused."

Steph sat up straight and looked Jessica in the eye. "If you and he want to fool around while I'm away, I want you to know it's really okay with me." She let out a deep breath. "This is silly, you know." She took Jessica's hand. "I know that you turn Brian on. I also know that you are attracted to him but that you wouldn't do anything, even knowing our odd lifestyle. I want you to understand, deep down, that it is really all right with me. The thought of you two together, knowing you both as I do, is very delicious. I think you'd have a great time."

"You're right. This is weird. My best friend is giving me permission to go to bed with her husband."

Steph laughed. "Only in America."

"Have you discussed this with Brian?"

"I wanted to tell you first. If the situation arises, say yes or say no. But do it because it's what you and Brian want. Not for any reason that has anything to do with me. That's all I'm trying to say."

"And you know what I'm going to say? Let's go buy some new lingerie, for your weekend and for my whatever."

Later that afternoon, the two women arrived back at the Carlton house with their purchases. They carried their shopping bags up to Jessica's room and dumped the contents of the bags on the bed. "I love that little green thing you bought," Steph said, stretching out on the bed.

Jessica rummaged through the boxes, then held up a deep green lace bodysuit with a triangular cutout just above the breasts. "I got matching thigh-high stockings too, you know. And I have just the shoes."

"Try it all on, Steph said. "Let's see how it all goes together."

Jessica pulled the shoes out of her closet then, boxes in hand, went into the bathroom. She changed into the outfit, pulled on the stockings and slipped into a pair of four-inch-heeled black opera pumps. Then she looked at herself in the mirror over the sink. She grabbed a comb and teased her titian hair into a wild tangle around her face, then added dark green eye shadow, liner, and heavy black mascara. She applied a thick coat of deep coral lipstick, then opened the bathroom door.

"Holy shit," Steph said. "Brian would love you in that."

"You're serious, aren't you."

"I love Brian with all my heart and I love knowing he's having fun. That's all there is to it."

"You have no doubts about him."

"I set him free and he always comes back. He's his own person and I'm mine."

"Thanks, Steph," Jessica said, hugging her friend.

When Brian arrived home from work Friday evening, Jessica had prepared dinner. "I haven't cooked in so long that I wasn't sure I still could. I thought this would be nice." She had grilled a thick steak, made hash-brown potatoes, biscuits, and apple, celery and walnut salad and, while they ate, the two friends talked. As they pigged out on rum raisin ice cream, Brain asked about her plans.

"I'm leaving the day after Labor Day."

"I'll miss you like crazy, JJ. I've really enjoyed having you here."

"Me too," Jessica said, licking her spoon.

Brian took her hand. "You know Steph's away."

"Yes."

Brian kissed her fingers. "I want you."

"I know you do, Brian," Jessica said, gently disentangling her fingers from his. "And in some ways I want you too. But you're my friend. I'm very afraid that if we do end up in bed together part of our friendship will never be the same."

Brian looked crestfallen.

"And I understand what Steph said, and I know about your

212

adventures at the party and all, but it just doesn't feel right to me. Not right, as in right and wrong, but right as in comfortable."

Brian sighed. "I'm disappointed."

"I'm sorry you are and in a way I am too." She picked up the ice cream bowls and put them into the dishwasher. "Let's go to the video store, rent a couple of old westerns, and make a bowl of popcorn."

As the credits rolled on the second John Wayne film, Brian looked at Jessica. "This has been a wonderful evening, JJ."

"For me too," Jessica said with a sigh.

"Steph never did get into old westerns."

"If your next remark is going to be 'My wife just doesn't understand me,' it won't float."

Brian's amusement was obvious. "You know, I must confess something. Part of me still wants to make long, leisurely love to you, but part of me has been making passes at you for so long it sort of got to be a habit."

"Well, don't break that habit," Jessica said, kissing him firmly on the lips. "One of these days I may just change my mind." They went to bed that night in their own rooms.

Jessica's remaining time in New York raced by. She spent evenings with Eric and Cam, and had a fantastic overnight with Gary in the special room. She especially enjoyed Steph and Brian's company, doing everything from crossing New York Harbor on the Staten Island Ferry to nude swimming in the Carltons' pool.

On the day after Labor Day, Steph and Brian drove Jessica to Newark Airport. The three friends hugged and finalized plans for Jessica to fly out for Gary's party in October. As her row number was called to board, Jessica kissed Steph. "We'll see you October sixth, right here. I'll miss you till then."

"Me too," Jessica said, turning to hug Brian.

"Maybe that weekend, JJ," Brian whispered, then nipped her earlobe.

"Maybe," Jessica said, grabbing her suitcase and almost running to the gate. She walked the length of the runway, boarded the 707, found her seat and stowed her small suitcase, glad she had packed several boxes and mailed them to herself at her office so she wouldn't have to check baggage. She was sad to leave Steph and Brian, but exhilarated to be returning to Ottawa.

She had called Viv and in response to Jessica's request, Viv had lined up several condos for her to visit, any one of which, according to Viv, would be perfect for her in her new life. She had appointments to see three of them the following morning. And she had a date with Steve over the weekend.

She realized she'd miss Eric and Cam. It wouldn't be as easy to see them and she had no real idea where she would find an outlet for her creative sexual energy, but if she had to, she'd suppress her libido until her next trip to New York. She snapped her seat belt, opened the new suspense novel she had bought the preceding day, and began to read.

"Terrible book," a deep voice said.

"Excuse me?"

"That's a terrible book. I read the first fifty pages and realized that if the hero just called the newspapers and told a bunch of reporters everything he knew, the whole plot would fall apart."

"Really?"

"Sorry, but I hate to see people waste their time."

Jessica closed the book. The man sitting next to her was pleasant looking, with toast-brown hair and deep blue eyes. "Well, that's that. I guess we'll have to talk. My name's Jessica. Jessica Hanley."

The man extended a large hand and engulfed hers in his warm grasp. "My name's David Scharff. And I was hoping you'd say that. You see, I hate flying."

Jessica noticed that his palms were damp. "I'm sorry. That must make this difficult for you."

"More than you know. I have to fly at least once a month on business."

Over the next hour, she found out that David lived in Joliet, a city between Chicago and Ottawa, was recently divorced, and worked as a salesman for a computer software company. When she mentioned Gary's name, the man's face lit up. "You actually met the elusive Mr. Powell? I'm impressed. He's a legend in the business. When he sold his company for all that money he dropped out of sight. Where is he now?"

"He lives north of New York City. He's a nice man with interesting hobbies and the money to enjoy them," Jessica said, smiling to herself.

As they fastened their seat belts for landing, David said, "Landing is the worst part for me. May I hold your hand? It helps."

"Sure," Jessica said. As she grasped David's hand and squeezed it tightly, she thought she felt a slight tremble that went beyond his nervousness about the flight. She slid her hand up and placed her palm over his wrist where it lay on the armrest. She pressed it down firmly and held it there, her fingers on his racing pulse.

David turned, gazed intently at her, then looked down at her hand. "Why are you doing that?" he asked, his voice a bit ragged.

"I thought it might help." She smiled as he adjusted his position to loosen his slacks. Amazing, she thought.

"It does."

Jessica leaned over and pressed her breast against his arm. Close to his ear, she said softly, "I'm sure it does. Tell me the truth. Are your pants getting a little tight?" When he remained silent, she said, softly, but strongly, "I asked you a question."

"Yes," he whispered, his voice now really trembling.

"Do you have to be home at any specific time?"

"No," he said.

Jessica looked at her watch, not releasing David's wrist. "It's almost five. Would you like to buy me dinner?"

David looked at her and smiled. "Very much." More softly but clearly audibly, he added, "Ma'am."

Jessica grinned as the wheels of the plane touched down. "You can call me JessicaLynn."

Dear Reader,

I hope you've enjoyed *The Pleasures of JessicaLynn*. I think there's a little Jessie, a bit of Jessica and a drop of JessicaLynn in all of us and I had a great deal of fun exploring all three.

If you liked my friends in Harrison, drop me a note and tell me which of Jessica's adventures you particularly enjoyed and what you would like to read about in my next book.

I look forward to hearing from you,

Joan Elizabeth Lloyd
PO Box 221
Yorktown Heights, NY 10598